THE LONER

Detective Jason Smith Book – 27

For Emma-Jane:

You are a true inspiration

to all of us.

Copyright © 2024 Stewart Giles

CHAPTER ONE

"You don't talk much, do you?"

Melissa Grange looked at the man she'd met only three hours earlier. She guessed his age to be somewhere close to thirty. Perhaps a little bit younger – she'd never been particularly adept in that department, and there was something different about him. He wasn't at all like the men she usually found herself attracted to.

His eyes were a peculiar shade of green. If she were to get the chance to know him a while longer, she would realise that they changed colour when his mood dictated it. Sadly, she was never going to see them change with the change in his mood. Melissa Grange had less than five minutes to live. Her heart would stop beating before the wine on the coffee table had had the opportunity to breathe.

"Strong, silent type, are you?"

She looked into his eyes, and he stared right back.

"I like that," she added. "Eye contact. Sebastian. I don't think I've ever met a Sebastian before. What do your friends call you? Seb?"

"Sebastian."

Even his voice was different. There was something in his tone that suggested he didn't use his voice much.

"What do you do, Sebastian?" Melissa asked.

"This and that."

"Where are you from?"

"All over."

"You're a strange one, Sebastian. Shall I pour the wine?"

"I don't drink."

"Don't drink," she repeated. "Don't talk. What do you do?"

"I'm going to show you."

"Easy tiger," Melissa said with a chuckle. "Let's drink some wine and get to know each other a bit more first."

"I don't want to get to know you."

"But..."

That was as far as she got. She noticed a flash of movement, and then she experienced an excruciating pain in her neck. But the scream her brain was telling her to let loose didn't come.

"You talk too much."

Sebastian yanked the knife free, and a jet of blood followed it.

"I've destroyed your vocal cords," he said. "Now you can stop talking and listen. You asked me what I do, and now you know. This is what I do. This is what I'm destined to do."

Melissa's eyes were bulging dangerously in their sockets. She was struggling to breathe, and each painful breath was accompanied by a bubbling of blood.

"I'm going to stop your heart soon."

The knife was held in front of her face.

"You should be careful who you trust, Melissa. You should be wary of who you let inside."

He grabbed a handful of hair and yanked her head back. There was a loud crack as her trachea snapped in two and this was followed by a hiss like the air being let out of a car tyre. Melissa put her hands to her neck and looked into Sebastian's eyes. They were closed, and he was breathing calmly.

He let her go – she gasped a few times then she was still. Sebastian found the bathroom and cleaned the blade of the knife in the sink. A glance in the mirror told him he had spots of blood on his cheek, so he washed these off too. He went back to the living room and took in the scene for a moment. Melissa Grange was staring, unblinking at the ceiling.

"So humble," Sebastian said in a voice that sounded alien to him. "So pure, so mortified, so patient."

He placed the tip of the knife in the centre of Melissa's forehead and pressed down. He made an incision an inch across then he ran the blade across his forearm, drawing his own blood.

"With such compassionate love for thy crucified Jesus that thou couldst obtain from Him whatsoever thou askest."

He pulled a pair of latex gloves from his pocket, put them on, then he picked up the wine and emptied the entire bottle onto the sofa.

He walked down the three flights of steps to the entrance of the apartment block and held the door open for a man on his way in. Later, when questioned by the detectives investigating the murder of Melissa Grange, Howard Moore would remember one thing in particular about the man he saw that day. He would recall the colour of his eyes, and he would describe them as being intense and blue.

CHAPTER TWO

"Things are about to change."
Superintendent Jeremy Smyth had already spoken these words three times, but he repeated them again for good measure. The men and women forced to listen to him needed to understand the severity of the situation. It was Friday afternoon and some of them were counting down the minutes until they were allowed to leave the large conference room and go home.

Detective Sergeant Jason Smith was one of them. Smith was planning on heading home and grabbing a quick shower before treating his wife to a meal out, but time seemed to have slowed down. It had a tendency to do that where Superintendent Smyth was concerned.

"We need to prepare ourselves," the public-school buffoon carried on. "For drastic changes. Lockdown is imminent, and we need to be aware of the implications of that. I've taken the liberty of outlining some guidelines, and I've put those guidelines in an email all of you will have received. Read it and learn from it. Let the words in that email be imprinted on your brains. Read them when you wake in the morning. Read them before you go to bed at night."

"Dickhead," DS Bridge whispered.
Smith laughed. DS Whitton did too.
"What was that?" Superintendent Smyth asked.
"I said hear, hear, sir," Bridge said. "I couldn't agree with you more."
"Very good. Lockdown is going to bring with it some challenges for us. The movements of the people of York are going to be restricted and as such criminal elements will, in all likelihood, take advantage of it. There will be more opportunity to commit crime with fewer people on the streets. We need to be vigilant. We need to prepare ourselves for an increase in looting. We need to be ready for a sudden influx of house burglaries."

Smith debated whether to remind the Superintendent that statistically speaking, the majority of burglaries occurred when the occupants were not home but he decided he couldn't be bothered. *Statistically speaking* were Superintendent Smyth's two favourite words and Smith knew from experience that he could drone on for hours on the subject.

"In all likelihood we will see a sudden increase in panic buying." Old Smyth hadn't quite finished yet. "And that can lead to frustration and the possibility of violence. What we can expect in the upcoming months is something none of the people of this city have ever had to deal with before, and as such the behaviour of these people will be unpredictable. We need to be prepared for this."

Prepared for the unpredictable? Smith pondered.

He'd never heard such guff in his life before. It was ridiculous, even by Superintendent Smyth's standards.

"The duties of every single one of you are about to change. You will be expected to uphold the new regulations as set out in the government mandates. Curfews will be in place, and it is your job to ensure these curfews are adhered to. We cannot afford to be complacent. Are there any questions?"

A hand went up in the front row. It was PC Jim Black.

"Yes," Superintendent Smyth urged.

"Are these new regulations definitely going to be put in place?" PC Black asked.

"Without a shadow of a doubt. It's happening and it's happening soon. We've already seen measures put in place elsewhere around the world, and similar changes will be enforced here in York. Anything else?"

Smith was relieved when there were no more questions. The emergency briefing had already dragged on for over two hours and he wasn't sure how much more he would be able to bear. He got to his feet.

"I'm not finished yet," Superintendent Smyth informed him.

Smith reluctantly sat back down.

"I'm sure all of you are aware of the new additions to the station," Superintendent Smyth said. "Hand sanitizers have been installed in all of the areas open to the general public. More of these will be installed in the restrooms around the station. You are to use them. Proper sanitizing is essential to keep this virus at bay. Face masks will also be compulsory. This is not up for debate. Are there any more questions before I wrap things up?"

PC Black raised his hand again and there was a collective sigh in the large conference room.

"When can we expect these new measures to be implemented?" he asked.

"As early as next week," Superintendent Smyth replied. "This is the new normal and you need to get used to it. That will be all."

"What a prick," Bridge said in the canteen afterwards. "Does he realise how ridiculous he sounded?"

"What else did you expect?" Smith said.

He took a sip of his coffee and sighed deeply. It was really good coffee, and it was just what the doctor ordered after having to listen to Superintendent Smyth rattle on for two hours.

"This thing is serious," Whitton said. "It's already hit Italy and Spain with a vengeance, and it's only a matter of time before it causes chaos here."

"I'll take my chances," Smith said.

"It's serious, Jason."

"I reckon I've come up against worse enemies than a virus before. When it's your time – it's your time. There's nothing you can do about it."

"Very deep," Bridge said. "Do you fancy a pint?"

"I do," Smith confirmed. "But not with you. No offence."

"Suit yourself. I'll check in with the lovely Billie Jones then. See what the sexiest forensics officer on the force has planned for tonight."

"I'm in the mood for a steak and ale pie," Smith said. "And a few pints of Theakston."
"You're getting really boring in your old age," Whitton told him.
"And you're stuck with me, my dear. Hog's Head it is then."

CHAPTER THREE

"Mel, it's Brian."

He'd knocked three times with no response.

"Mel," he shouted once more. "You left your phone at the wine bar."

Nothing.

"I'm not here to disturb you. I know you have company, but I also know how you can't live without your phone. I don't want to leave it outside the door."

He waited a moment before placing a hand on the door handle. He turned it and the door opened slightly.

"I'll just leave it inside the door," he said and pushed it open wider.

The smell was what he registered first. It wasn't a particularly unpleasant odour – it was a combination of something metallic and the sweet tang of perfume, but there was something else in there too. There was a hint of sourness. It reminded Brian of the smell of the wine bar when he first opened up in the morning. The funk of the night before tended to linger long, especially after a late night.

"I'm going to leave the phone in the living room," Brian said. "Are you in here, Mel?"

He walked the few steps of the small hallway and stopped outside the living room door. He didn't know why he stopped – something inside him told him that something wasn't right. His brain was sending signals to his legs without him knowing. The smell was stronger here. He pushed open the door and took in the room.

He wasn't initially sure exactly what he was looking at. The rational side of his brain was finding it hard to process it. Melissa Grange was on her back next to the leather sofa. There was a red, sticky film on the white leather. The carpet beneath it was also stained red.

Melissa was dead, of that there was little doubt. Her head was bent back unnaturally as though something in her neck had given way. There was a deep wound in her throat and blood had covered the top of her blouse. Her eyes were open, but a milky film had already started to form on the irises. There was a deep laceration on her forehead.

Brian Welburn had seen death before. Three tours in Afghanistan and a lengthy spell in Iraq meant he was no stranger to it, but it was something you were never really prepared for. He could feel that his breathing had quickened. His heart was pumping much faster in his chest and his face felt flushed.

He put Melissa's phone on the sideboard, took out his own mobile and called the police. The man he spoke to informed him that someone would be there soon. He was told not to touch anything, and he was also told to wait at the scene.

* * *

Smith was struggling to get into a pair of jeans and he couldn't understand why. He was sure they'd fitted just fine a few weeks ago.
"You've put on a few pounds recently," Whitton told him.
"Rubbish," Smith said. "They must have shrunk in the wash. Jeans do that."
"OK," Whitton said. "Whatever you say."
"I haven't put on weight."

He admitted defeat and found another pair of jeans. These ones weren't so tight.
"I can almost taste that steak and ale pie," he said. "It's been a while."
"It's been just over a week," Whitton reminded him. "That's probably why you've got a bit chubby – too many of Marge's pies."
"I'll pretend I didn't hear that."
Smith breathed in and managed to get the top button of the jeans fastened.
"I'm going to have a quick beer and a smoke before we head off."

Lucy was talking to someone on her mobile phone when Smith went downstairs. The sixteen-year-old didn't even acknowledge her adoptive father when he walked into the kitchen. Smith assumed she was talking to Darren Lewis. The father of Lucy's unborn baby was a constant part of Lucy's life now. She couldn't hide the fact that she was pregnant anymore. She was halfway there and her belly was a dead giveaway. Smith wasn't looking forward to the day when there would be another little human in the house. Everything was going to change.

He got a beer out of the fridge and took it with him outside to the back garden. Theakston and Fred followed him out. The chunky Bull Terrier and the grotesque Pug headed straight to the bottom of the garden to do what they needed to do. Smith lit a cigarette and sat down on the bench. He thought about Superintendent Smyth's speech, and he wasn't quite sure what to make of it. He'd seen snippets of news reports from around the world and there was no denying the fact that this thing was very real, but Smith was yet to make up his mind about how much it was going to affect the people in his life. He decided to wait and see. There wasn't much point in dwelling on something that hadn't happened yet.

The sound of laughter next door interrupted his thoughts. The laughter was very familiar – it was the unique giggle of Smith and Whitton's seven-year-old daughter Laura. She was having a sleepover with her friend Fran. Smith hadn't always seen eye to eye with their next-door-neighbour but he had to admit that Sheila Rogers' close proximity was very convenient when they needed someone to look after Laura for a while.

Smith lit a cigarette and took a sip of beer. The giggling next door carried on and Smith smiled.

Lucy came outside. "Darren's asked if I can go round to his."

"Me and your mum are going out," Smith said. "Do you need a lift?"

"Darren said he'll come and pick me up. He can borrow his brother's car."

"He's sixteen, Lucy," Smith reminded her. "He's not allowed to drive."

"He's been driving for years."

"That's not the point. In case you've forgotten your parents are police detectives."

"He's a really good driver," Lucy said. "It's a five-minute drive. He's never been stopped by the police before."

"I give up. Will you be staying over?"

"If that's OK."

"I reckon it's a bit late to give you *the talk* now anyway," Smith decided. "How are you feeling?"

"I feel him kick all the time now."

"Him?" Smith repeated.

"Darren thinks it's definitely a boy, and he's going to play for Liverpool."

"Not York?"

"Come on, Dad. Who wants their kid to play for York City?"

"Fair enough," Smith said. "I've never seen the point of football anyway."

He stubbed out his cigarette and stood up. "I suppose we'd better be off. My stomach is growling. When will you be back?"

"Tomorrow morning," Lucy said.

"We've got the weekend off anyway. Laura is having a blast next door, so there's no need for you to rush back for our sake."

"I've got an assignment I need to get finished," Lucy said. "For English, and I want it to be perfect."

"You're weird, Lucy Smith," Smith told her. "Studious and rebellious at the same time."

"It's a good combination. And I wonder where I get it from."

"Point taken. I've fed the dogs. See you tomorrow then."

Smith's stomach was now grumbling so loud that Whitton could hear it. "I can taste that steak and ale pie already," he said.

He closed the back door and started to walk down the hallway. Whitton followed him. They didn't even make it halfway before Smith's phone started to ring. The ringtone told him in no uncertain terms that he wasn't going to get to enjoy one of Marge's pies anytime soon. It was the opening bars to Elvis Costello's *Oliver's Army*, and it meant that it was Detective Inspector Oliver Smyth who was calling.

Smith looked at Whitton for confirmation whether he should answer it or not.

"It might be important," she said.

"That's what I'm afraid of. My stomach is busy digesting my internal organs as we speak."

"Don't be such a baby," Whitton said. "Answer the bloody phone."

Smith did, and his fears were confirmed. A woman had been murdered in Clifton and Smith and Whitton were to cancel any plans they'd made for the evening.

CHAPTER FOUR

"This car stinks."

Lucy was sitting in the passenger seat of Darren Lewis's brother's old Mazda.

"Our Gary doesn't clean it much," Darren said. "It's better than walking."

"What is that smell anyway?"

"You don't want to know."

Darren started the engine and pulled away from the kerb outside Smith's house. It was just after seven and the streets were eerily quiet.

They turned left onto Hamilton Drive and headed east in the direction of the city centre.

"Where are all the people?" Lucy wondered. "There are hardly any other cars on the road."

"I think Boris's speech has got them spooked," Darren said. "You would have thought that the threat of lockdown would mean they'd be making the most of it, but a lot of people are scared."

"I'm scared," Lucy said. "We don't know what the future holds, and it scares me."

"We'll be alright. Shit."

Darren's eyes were fixed on the rearview mirror.

"What is it?"

"Police," Darren said. "Right behind us."

"Just stay calm, and slow down a bit."

It was too late. The lights began to flash on the police car behind them and Darren had no option but to stop the car.

"What do you think they want?" Lucy asked.

"God knows. Just stay cool."

"You haven't even got a license. My dad warned me about this."

"Let's see what they want first," Darren said.

The police car came to a halt behind the Mazda and Darren watched it in the rearview mirror.

"What are they doing?" he said. "Why haven't they got out?"

"Perhaps they're checking to see if the car has been stolen," Lucy suggested.

"Who would want to steal a pile of junk like this? They're getting out of the car. Shit. Shit, shit, shit."

Two officers, a man and a woman approached Darren's brother's car. He wound down the window when they got there.

"Is there a problem?" he asked the female PC.

"One of your rear lights isn't working," she told him.

"And your left brake light is also out," her colleague added.

Darren took an instant dislike to him. His eyes were far too close together, and his beak-like nose gave him the look of a bird of prey on the prowl.

He looked closely at Darren then his eyes fell on Lucy. His eyes narrowed and he moved closer to sniff inside the car.

"Have you been smoking marijuana?"

"Of course not," Darren said. "My girlfriend is pregnant. We don't smoke. I didn't know the lights were broken. I'll get them fixed. I only live half a mile down the road."

"Could I see your license please?" the female officer asked.

"You look a bit young to be driving, son," beak nose said.

"OK," Darren said. "I don't have a license."

"How old are you?"

"Sixteen."

"Could you step out of the car please?" the female PC asked. "Both of you please."

"Can't we work something out?" Darren said. "Like I said, I only live down the road. I'm happy to pay a fine."

"Step out of the car please."

Darren and Lucy did as they were told.

"Contrary to popular belief." It was beak nose. "You can get points on your license before you've even passed your test. Driving without the correct license can get you six points on any future license you may get. And, because you're not in possession of a valid license, you're not covered by insurance and that can accrue an additional six points. Theoretically, son you could risk the paradox of losing a license you haven't even got yet. It's a funny old world, isn't it?"

Darren wasn't laughing.

"Surely there's something we can do? We must be able to work something out. My girlfriend's dad is DS Smith."

"Smith?" the female PC said. "Really?"

"What are you implying?" her colleague said. "We turn a blind eye to you breaking the law because of who your passenger is?"

"Come on," Darren said. "I'm sorry. I'll pay the fine. It won't happen again."

The female PC seemed to be considering this, but beak nose shook his head.

"This is what's going to happen," he said. "You'll be taken in and booked."

"You're going to arrest him?" Lucy said.

"I couldn't give a hoot who your dad is, love," beak nose said. "The law is the law for everyone regardless of who they know."

"What about the car?" Darren said.

"The car will be seized, and a fee will be charged before you'll be able to reclaim it from the pound. That fee increases on a daily basis. And the car will only be released to someone with a valid driver's license and insurance. In other words, it won't be you."

"My brother is going to kill me," Darren said. "He needs the car tonight."

"Perhaps you should have considered that before you broke the law."

"You can't do this," Lucy said.

"I assure you I can. Your boyfriend will be allowed to make a phone call when we get to the station."

Lucy took out her phone. "I'm calling my dad."

"Call who you want," beak nose said. "It's not going to make a blind bit of difference."

Lucy dialled Smith's number, but after few rings it went straight to voicemail. She tried Whitton with the same result.

CHAPTER FIVE

Smith and Whitton were oblivious to Darren's predicament. Whitton had forgotten her phone in her haste to leave the house after DI Smyth's phone call, and Smith's battery had died. They were blissfully unaware that Lucy and Darren were now on their way to the station that Smith and Whitton had worked in for over a decade.

DI Smyth had told them the victim was Melissa Grange. She was twenty-three years old, and she worked as a legal secretary for one of the big law firms in the city. Melissa lived in an upmarket apartment in a complex on St Olave's Road. The four-storey face brick building looked brand new. A row of garages was attached to the property and there wasn't much room to park a car outside. Whitton had to make do with a parking spot fifty metres from the apartment. Grant Webber's car was parked closest to the building – the Head of Forensics had made it to the scene first again. Two police cars were parked behind him. An ambulance was in place further up the street.

Smith and Whitton got out of the car and walked in the direction of the flashing lights of the patrol cars. A tape had already been set up around the entrance of the building, and a few people were standing outside.
Smith and Whitton headed for the entrance.

"This is ridiculous."
A woman was arguing with PC Simon Miller by the front door.
"This is my home. You can't stop me from going inside my home."
"This is a crime scene," Smith informed her.
She looked him up and down.
"She needs to go in and feed her cat, Sarge," PC Miller said.
"The cat won't starve," Smith said. "You'll be allowed in when we say you can go in."

Billie Jones was standing by the glass door, dusting it for prints. Webber's assistant was wearing a full SOC suit, and she was also wearing a face mask. Smith wondered why she was wearing it.

"Do we know how many people are inside the building?" he asked PC Miller.

"Not yet, Sarge," PC Miller said. "I've only just arrived on scene myself."

"This happened recently," Smith said. "The boss told me that the guy from the wine bar said he came here to drop off Melissa's phone. She'd only left the bar two hours before that, so we need to find everyone who was here in the building in the past few hours. I want them all questioned, and I want that done now."

"Will do, Sarge."

"What about me?" It was the irate cat owner.

"When did you get back here?" Smith asked her.

"Five minutes ago. And I didn't expect to come home to this."

"It's OK," Whitton said. "I'm afraid it can't be helped. Is there somewhere you can wait in the meantime?"

"Are you telling me I can't even go inside my own apartment?"

"You're just going to have to be patient," Whitton said.

"Where's the man who found her?" Smith asked PC Miller.

"PC Black was one of the first here, Sarge," PC Miller said. "He suggested the bloke get checked out by the paramedics. He's in the ambulance down the street."

"Where's the DI?"

"Inside with Webber."

Smith looked at the front of the apartment building.

"Is that the only way in and out?" he asked the woman with the cat.

"There's an emergency exit round the back," she told him. "It's fire regulations apparently."

"Interesting."

"What are you thinking?" Whitton said.

"I don't know yet." Smith turned to PC Miller. "You say the bloke who found her is with the paramedics?"

"He is, Sarge."

"I want to talk to him. Come on Whitton. Webber won't thank us if we go traipsing around in there before he's finished."

Brian Welburn didn't look like someone who had just found a murder victim. In Smith's experience those first on the scene of a brutal killing usually had a particular look about them. Their faces were generally pale and often they would have a disturbing expression in their eyes, as though the horrific crime they'd borne witness to was mirrored in those eyes. But Brian Welburn displayed none of these telltale signs and this made Smith instantly suspicious.

Brian was standing outside the ambulance with one of the paramedics. He didn't seem pleased at all.

"Mr Welburn," Smith said and introduced himself and Whitton. "Can we have a word?"

"Of course," Brian said. "If it'll get me away from these do-gooders."

He started to walk away before either of the paramedics could stop him.

Smith thought he looked to be in his mid-forties. He was a stockily built man with a full beard. His eyes were blue and very alert.

"You'll be required to make a formal statement," Smith said. "But I want to ask you a few questions first."

"Shoot," Brian said.

"You were the one who found Melissa," Smith said. "Is that right?"

"She'd left her phone at the wine bar."

"Which wine bar is that?" Whitton said.

"Welburn's on Fairfax Street."

"Welburn's?" Smith said. "You own the wine bar?"

"It's not a very original name, I know, but I'm not a very original bloke. I opened the place four years ago when I left the forces."

"Army?" Smith guessed.

"Is it that obvious?"

"My boss is ex-army. You came to return Melissa's phone. Doesn't that go beyond the call of duty at the wine bar?"

"The bar was quiet," Brian said. "And I know how much Melissa needs her phone. She's never off the thing."

"Do you know her well then?" Whitton said.

"She's been coming to the bar for a few years. A lot of the city law people like to frequent the place."

"When did she leave the bar?" Smith said.

"Around four. Often we get an influx of lawyers on a Friday afternoon, although today was quieter than usual."

"Do you know if she left with anyone?"

"Some bloke."

"Could you describe him?" Smith said.

"Tall," Brian said. "About your height. And pretty slim. He had short brown hair."

"How old was he?" Whitton asked.

"I'd say about thirty."

"Had you seen this man before?" Smith said.

"Never. He wasn't one of the legal crowd. I suppose he could have been new, but he didn't look like one of them."

"What do you mean by that?"

"They have this look about them," Brian said. "It's hard to describe, but this bloke didn't look like a lawyer."

"Would you be prepared to work with a police artist?" Whitton said.

"I didn't really get much of a look at him. But I suppose it's worth a shot."

"What time did you arrive here at the apartment?" Smith said.

"Five minutes before I called the police."

"Can you talk us through the events from when you arrived until the moment you called the police?"

"I got here around six," Brian said.

"How did you get inside the building?" Whitton wondered.

"I was about to press Melissa's buzzer when someone came out. It was a man I'd seen before at the wine bar. I told him why I was here, and he let me in. I walked up the stairs and knocked on Melissa's door."

"Have you been here before then?" Smith asked.

"This is the first time."

"How did you know where Melissa lived?" Whitton said.

"Because she told me when she moved here. She's only been living here for a few months. We were chatting at the wine bar, and she told me she'd just got hold of an amazing apartment."

"You knocked on the door," Smith said. "Then what?"

"I called her name," Brian said. "I had a suspicion she wasn't alone, so I called her name and told her I had her phone. I thought that would get her attention. I expected her to come to the door, but she didn't."

"So you went inside to find her?" Whitton said.

"I didn't want to leave the phone outside, so I tried my luck with the door. It was unlocked and I went in."

"Go on," Smith urged.

"I could smell it," Brian said. "You never forget the stench of blood. It stinks like nothing else. I know – I've smelled it plenty of times. I called out again and I went into the living room. That's where I found her. Who would do something like that to her?"

"We haven't been in the apartment yet," Smith said. "Did you touch anything when you went inside?"

"What?"

"Do you remember if you touched anything?" Whitton said. "We need to know so we can let our forensics officers know."

"No, I didn't touch anything."

"So, your fingerprints won't be found anywhere inside the apartment?" Smith added.

"I touched the door," Brian said. "I had to, to open it."

"No worries," Smith took out one of his cards. "If you think of anything else, please give me a call. I'll arrange for someone to speak to you about your statement and the artist's impression of the man you saw Melissa leave with. Does the wine bar have CCTV?"

"No."

"Why not? I thought most of the bars in the city centre had cameras."

"I run an upmarket wine bar," Brian said. "My clientele are not yobos who like to cause trouble. I've never had any need for CCTV cameras."

"It was just a thought," Smith said. "We'll be in touch."

Smith and Whitton were halfway back to the apartment building when PC Miller accosted them.

"What is it, Simon?" Smith said.

"It's your daughter, Sarge," PC Miller said.

"What's wrong?" Whitton asked. "Has something happened to Laura?"

"Lucy," PC Miller said. "She's at the station. Her boyfriend has been arrested."

CHAPTER SIX

"Where are they?"
Smith hadn't even bothered to greet PC Baldwin at the front desk.
"Darren is being processed, Sarge," Baldwin said. "I thought it would be best for Lucy to wait in the canteen."
"I'll go and see how she is," Whitton said.
   "What happened?" Smith asked Baldwin.
"They were brought in a short while ago," she said. "I couldn't believe it when they came in. Apparently, Darren was stopped because his rear lights weren't working, and he was arrested because he doesn't have a driver's license."
"Who made the arrest?"
"Some new bloke," PC Baldwin said. "PC Griffin. He's not long finished his probation."
"He's going to regret this. Thanks, Baldwin. I'll go and see what the duty sergeant has to tell me."
   Sergeant Fox had been working for York Police for as long as Smith could remember. He was a quiet man who always seemed happy to stay in the background. He was standing behind his desk when Smith walked through. Darren Lewis was on the other side of the desk, giving Sergeant Fox his details.
   Smith placed a hand on Darren's shoulder and the teenager jumped. He turned around and looked Smith in the eye. Smith had never seen him look so scared. In the time he'd known the boy Smith had always known him to be confident and self-assured but here was a sixteen-year-old who was clearly out of his depth.
"I'm sorry," he said.

"We'll talk about that later," Smith said and turned to Sergeant Fox. "What's the story?"

"Underage driving," the old duty sergeant said. "Driving without a valid license and insurance."

"And he was hauled into the station for that?" Smith said.

He was absolutely furious.

"He's sixteen, for fuck's sake."

Sergeant Fox held up his hands.

"We're on the same page, Smith. It was unnecessary, but that fast-tracker seemed to think otherwise."

"Where is he?" Smith asked. "Where's the dickhead who arrested the father of my grandchild?"

"He brought the kid in, asked me to book him and headed off to get changed. His shift has just finished."

"I presume he's free to go," Smith nodded to Darren.

"I just need a few more details and he's all yours to do with as you please."

"I'll be back in a minute."

Smith hadn't set foot inside the locker room in years, but it hadn't changed a bit. There was the familiar smell of sweat and cheap deodorant, and the layers of dust on the tops of the lockers had probably been there since Smith joined up. Smith took one look at the only person in the room, and he knew instinctively this was who he was looking for.

PC William Griffin was a very short man. His brown hair was thin on top, and his piggy eyes were full of malice. His nose looked like it had been broken more than once. The beak of it almost reached his mean lips.

"I was wondering when you would make an appearance."

PC Griffin got in first.

"You fucked up," Smith told him.

"Before you start," PC Griffin said. "I know who you are, and more importantly, I know *what* you are."

"You shouldn't have arrested a sixteen-year-old boy."

"He broke the law. It's as simple as that. I couldn't care less who he knows – when someone breaks the law it is my responsibility to ensure he is made aware of it."

"There were other ways you could have done that," Smith said. "There is such a thing as discretion. Didn't they teach you that in your training?"

"Discretion does not have a place in law enforcement. The law is black and white, regardless of the circumstances."

Smith couldn't believe what he was being forced to listen to.

"Can I give you a piece of advice?" he said.

"You can," PC Griffin said. "Whether I'll take it is a different matter."

"You do not want to start burning bridges in this job. The officers who work here need to know their colleagues have their backs. Always. When that's gone, life on the job can become extremely unpleasant."

PC Griffin snorted. "Let me tell you something about burning bridges, Smith. Think about this if you will. Think about a few years down the line when you might actually have to call me *sir*."

Smith wondered whether to tell him he rarely addressed anyone as *sir*, but he decided it wasn't worth wasting his breath on. He'd come across people like PC Griffin before. They were career police officers with one thing on their minds and one thing only. Smith couldn't care less that this arrogant, fast-track PC would probably be an inspector in a few years' time. He really couldn't give a damn.

"You have a nice evening, Griffin," he said.

"I'm not scared of you."

"Why would you be? I'll let you get home. You probably have someone waiting for you there. Possibly a cat or two."

Smith was intercepted as he headed up to the canteen. A young PC he vaguely recognised approached him as he was about to go up the stairs.

"Sarge," she said. "Can I have a word?"

"Of course," Smith said.

"I'm PC Parker, Sarge. I was on patrol with PC Griffin when we stopped the car your daughter was in."

"Go on."

"The boy didn't need to be arrested, Sarge," PC Parker said. "He should have been issued with a fine and allowed to call someone to come and pick him up. PC Griffin shouldn't have brought him into the station – it was totally unnecessary. I tried to reason with him but he wouldn't budge."

"PC Griffin has a lot to learn," Smith said. "I appreciate you talking to me. What's done is done."

"There's something else, Sarge."

Smith nodded.

"I don't mean to talk out of turn, but I got the impression that PC Griffin did it on purpose."

"I'm not following you."

"I think he would have probably let the kid off with a fine, but as soon as your name was mentioned he changed."

"Could you just spit it out please," Smith said. "I haven't got all night."

"The boy told us who his girlfriend's dad was," PC Parker said. "As if it would help his cause, but it actually made things worse. It seemed to make PC Griffin more determined to make it as unpleasant as possible for the boy. It was like he was proving some kind of point."

"Thank you for bringing it to my attention," Smith said. "Don't worry yourself about it."

"I'm really sorry, Sarge."

"Don't be," Smith said. "Shit happens."

Smith wasn't just furious - he was past that stage. He was actually surprised that he'd managed to compose himself so well in the locker room. A few years ago a conversation with someone like PC Griffin would probably have ended with blood on the walls and another suspension for Smith, but he'd changed a lot since then. He couldn't quite pinpoint the exact moment things had changed, but change they had.

Whitton and Lucy were the only ones inside the canteen. Smith joined them at their table.

"What's going to happen to Darren?" Lucy asked.

"They're busy processing him," Smith said.

"Are they going to lock him up?"

"Of course not," Whitton assured her.

"He'll be allowed to come home when they're finished," Smith added.

"We might have a problem with that new PC," Whitton said.

"I've spoken to him," Smith told her. "I'm not worried about PC Griffin."

"It was like he enjoyed it," Lucy said. "He seemed to get a real kick out of it. When Darren mentioned your name something sparked in his eyes, and he changed. The young woman tried to reason with him but he wouldn't listen. She was really nice. Really kind."

"What happened to the car?" Smith asked.

"They took it to the pound," Lucy said. "Darren's brother is going to kill him. Can he stay with us tonight?"

Smith looked at Whitton and she nodded.

"Just for tonight," Smith decided. "Let's go and wait for Darren by the front desk, shall we?"

"I'm starving," Lucy said.

"Me too. We can pick up a takeaway on the way home."

CHAPTER SEVEN

"Stanley!"

Jennifer Wells turned in the direction of the voice and spotted the man across the road.

"Stanley," he shouted again.

He was holding something in his hand, and when Jennifer looked more closely, she realised it was a white stick. It was past nine and darkness had descended on the city hours ago but the man was wearing dark glasses.

"Stanley," he shouted. "Where are you, boy?"

He started to walk in the direction of the industrial estate where Jennifer worked. Tapping the stick in front of him, he walked with purpose. Jennifer decided to catch up with him. She was heading that way anyway and it was quite obvious that the man was blind.

"Excuse me," she said when she was five metres behind him.

He stopped and turned around. "Who's there?"

"It's alright," Jennifer said. "Can I help you?"

"Who are you?"

"Jennifer. I heard you calling. Who is Stanley?"

"My dog."

Jennifer thought he had a nice voice. It was very soothing.

"He ran off," the man said. "I think he caught sight of another dog and gave chase. They assured me at the centre that he wouldn't do that."

"I'll help you look for him," Jennifer said and winced. "I'm so sorry – that sounded terrible."

He laughed. "I've lost my sight – it doesn't mean I lost my sense of humour with it. He headed off in that direction."

He pointed to the road that led towards the entrance to the industrial estate.

"What are you doing out here at this time of night?" Jennifer asked as they walked.

"I live not far from here. And it makes no difference what time I go for a walk. Day or night, it's all the same to me."

"I suppose it is."

"What about you?" he said. "What's a young lady doing out all alone in a dark place like this?"

"I'm on my way to work," Jennifer said. "I work nights at one of the warehouses on the estate."

"Poor you."

Jennifer smiled. "It's not too bad, and the money is good."

The man stopped so abruptly that Jennifer almost collided with him. "You have a nice smile," he said. "It's very rare that a smile reaches a person's eyes these days, but yours does. It really does radiate in those beautiful brown eyes."

Jennifer froze. She was suddenly finding it difficult to breathe. She felt as though something was pressing on her shoulders, forcing her to keep still. It was as though the gravity around her had changed somehow.

She felt a hand on her shoulder and then a sharp pain in her chest. The *blind* man had taken off his dark glasses and he looked straight into her eyes as he pressed the knife deeper and twisted it.

"So humble," he said.

Jennifer couldn't stand on her own anymore. She felt herself falling, but there were hands on her to ease the fall. The knife was still embedded in her chest.

"So, pure, so mortified, so patient."

Jennifer registered that she was no longer standing. The warmth in her chest was now starting to cool. Icy fingers had crept inside her and they were freezing everything they touched.

"Such compassionate love for thy crucified Jesus."

The man was gazing upon Jennifer with eyes that were changing colour in front of her.

"That thou couldst obtain from Him whatsoever thou askest."

Jennifer was falling now. The cold had spread throughout her, and she could feel herself growing numb. She didn't even feel it as the knife was yanked from her chest.

The last thing Jennifer knew of was the touch of the man's hand. He took hold of her own hands and ran the tip of the knife over it. Blood flowed but Jennifer was gone by then. She didn't see the man let her go – she wasn't aware of his eyes changing colour, and she didn't see him stab himself in the arm.

* * *

"Does anyone want the last slice of pizza?"

Darren Lewis had already eaten almost a whole Americana by himself.

"I see the brush with the law hasn't affected your appetite," Whitton said. "Help yourself."

Darren did, and the slice of pizza was devoured in five seconds.

"Our Gary is going to murder me," he said.

"Nobody is going to murder anybody," Whitton said. "He'll calm down."

"He's training for the Great North Run in September," Darren said. "He sometimes likes to run at night, and he needed the car to go to a trail in the east of the city. He's going to kill me."

"Are you going to get a criminal record?" Lucy asked Darren. "This could ruin your life."

"That's not going to happen," Smith said. "It's a minor offence and Darren's age means the slate will be wiped clean when he turns eighteen."

"Thanks for bailing me out," Darren said.

"I didn't bail you out," Smith said. "I would have left you there if Lucy wasn't with you. That was a really stupid thing to do."

"I know. And I won't do it again. That fine is going to use up all my money."

"How much do you have to pay?" Lucy asked.

"Almost a grand. With the fine and the impound fees it's going to cost me almost a grand."

"I hope you've learned from this," Whitton said.

"I have," Darren said. "I've learned that the police can't be trusted. That PC was a proper prick."

"Language," Lucy warned.

"Well he was."

"For once," Smith said. "I'm inclined to agree with you. I'm going out for a smoke and then I'm hitting the sack. It's been a long day, and I've got a feeling it's going to be an even longer one tomorrow."

CHAPTER EIGHT

Smith was pounced on by DI Smyth as soon as he stepped inside the station the next day.

"Morning, boss," he said.

"I hope you sorted out what needed sorting out last night," DI Smyth said.

"It's sorted. What have I missed?"

"Not an awful lot. It appears Melissa Grange was killed sometime between four and six yesterday afternoon. She left the wine bar with an unidentified male at around four – the owner of the bar came to return her phone a few hours later and found her dead."

"Cause of death?"

"It's a strange one," DI Smyth said. "It's yet to be confirmed but Webber thinks her trachea was snapped in two. She also had a laceration in her throat, but the carotids were still intact."

"It is strange," Smith agreed. "You set out to kill someone you sever the carotid arteries. Game over."

"She also had a laceration on her forehead," DI Smyth said. "Dr Bean will be able to tell us more when he's completed the postmortem."

"Do we know anything else about the woman?" Smith asked.

"That's what we'll be looking into today. Who was she and why was she targeted? We also need to retrace her movements from the time she left the wine bar until she arrived home. It's possible someone saw her with her mystery man."

"Are we working on the assumption he's our killer? Because we've made the mistake of making assumptions before."

"It's looking likely. Uniform have been tasked with tracking down everyone who was at the wine bar between two and four yesterday."

"I spoke to the owner last night," Smith said. "There was something off about him."

"He'll be questioned again," DI Smyth said. "What was the story with your future son-in-law."

"No offence, boss," Smith said. "But fuck off."

"None taken. What happened?"

Smith told him. He told him about the arrest, and he told him about his thoughts on PC William Griffin.

"Watch out for him," DI Smyth warned when Smith was finished.

"I'm not fazed by the likes of Griffin."

"We've seen officers like him before. Straight out of university with a fast track to the top, kissing the right arses on the way up there."

"He certainly didn't kiss my arse," Smith said.

"Your arse isn't worth kissing. No, people like him can cause trouble. They're vindictive pricks who won't let anyone get in their way. He wants an office on the top floor, and he wants pips. Just stay out of his way."

"I intend to," Smith lied.

In reality he was planning on making PC Griffin's life in the police as unpleasant as possible.

"Enough about Griffin," he said. "How about we make a start on cracking a murder case?"

* * *

"Melissa Grange."

DI Smyth wrote her name on the whiteboard in the small conference room. "Twenty-three years old. She worked as a legal secretary for one of the big law firms in the city. She was single and she lived alone. We know that she left Welburn's Wine Bar yesterday afternoon at around four o'clock. The owner of the bar claims she left with an unidentified man."

"That's our killer then." It was DC Moore.

"Slow down, Harry," DI Smyth said. "It's far too early in the investigation to make those kinds of assumptions."

"It's the obvious one to make, sir," DC Moore pointed out.

"The obvious assumption is often the wrong one," Smith reminded him.

"Melissa was found inside her living room," DI Smyth carried on. "According to Grant Webber her trachea had been snapped in two. She had another wound in her neck, but it appears it was the severed trachea that was the cause of her demise."

"I've seen it before," Smith said. "You sever the trachea and you're unable to breathe. She would have been dead in a couple of minutes."

"She suffered another laceration to her forehead, but that one can't be explained."

"What else did we get from the scene?" DC King asked.

"Not much," DI Smyth said. "There was an empty wine bottle on the floor, and two glasses on the coffee table. Neither glass had been used."

"That's odd," Bridge joined in.

"The leather sofa was covered in wine," DI Smyth said. "It's possible there was a struggle, and the wine was spilled during that struggle. Uniform are busy compiling a list of everyone who was at the wine bar yesterday afternoon and we should have some names before the end of the morning. We didn't get much from the other residents of the apartment. One witness remembered seeing a man leaving the building, and he gave us a vague description. He couldn't recall much but he did remember the colour of the man's eyes. He said they were blue and rather intense."

"Intense?" DC Moore repeated. "What does that even mean?"

"What time was this?" Smith asked. "What time did he see the bloke leave?"

"Just after five."

"We need to speak to this witness again. It ties in with the timeline."

"He didn't recall anything apart from the eye colour," DI Smyth said. "He couldn't give us the height, build or hair colour."

"He wasn't pressed enough. We need to speak to him again."

"OK. We will, but right now I want to focus on Melissa herself. Who was she, and why did someone want her dead? Smith, you and Kerry can pay a visit to her place of work."

"I'm not a big fan of lawyers, boss," Smith told him.

"You're not a big fan of anybody. Bridge, you and Harry look like you could do with some exercise. Melissa's apartment is a five-minute walk from the wine bar. I want you to retrace her steps."

"It's freezing out there," Bridge complained.

"Then put a coat on. Keep your eyes peeled for any CCTV cameras. One of those cameras may have caught Melissa and our mystery man."

"Brian Welburn needs to be looked into, boss," Smith remembered. "He was far too cool under the circumstances yesterday. And I don't buy the thing about him returning Melissa's phone. What wine bar owner does that? There's more to Brian Welburn than meets the eye."

"If you'd have let me finish," DI Smyth said. "That's exactly what Whitton and Baldwin are going to do. I agree with Smith – I find it extremely hard to believe the owner of a wine bar would leave the bar to return a phone, and it's also difficult to ignore the fact that he happened to be at Melissa's apartment just after she was murdered. It's suspicious. We're still waiting for more from forensics, but there is plenty to do in the meantime."

CHAPTER NINE

"Have you always disliked lawyers?" DC King asked Smith.

"I've told you the story about how I changed sides," he said. "Dropped out of the law degree to join the police. Well that's just the half of it. In my experience when lawyers are involved in a murder investigation, aside from their usual role, everything becomes a whole lot more complicated. Information is withheld and progress is slowed down. The legal profession is probably the most paradoxical profession of all. They're bound by the statutes set out by law and yet they do everything they can to scupper that legal process."

"That's a very cynical opinion, Sarge," DC King dared.

"Cynicism comes with age, Kerry," Smith said. "You'll get there one day."

"Yes, Granddad."

"Don't joke," Smith said. "In a few months' time that's exactly what I'll be. Whitton and me will be grandparents, and I'm still trying to get my head round it."

He parked his old Sierra in the Hill Street car park, got out and took his cigarettes out of his pocket. He lit one and stretched his arms out. His phone started to ring in his pocket. The sound of *Shine on you Crazy Diamond* told him it wasn't a contact he'd assigned a personalised ringtone to. He looked at the screen and smiled.

"Dr Vennell," he answered the call.

"Fiona, please," she said. "Dr Vennell makes me sound like a wrinkly old shrink."

Dr Fiona Vennell was as far from a wrinkly old shrink as it was possible to get. She was a twenty-nine-year-old psychologist Smith had met very recently. She'd been the one who'd given him the green light to return to work and they'd hit it off from the beginning. She was almost thirty, but she looked like she was still in her teens. In fact, in one of the first conversations she'd had with Smith she'd told him she still gets asked for her ID in bars. In the same conversation she'd asked Smith for help of the oddest kind. She'd admitted she had a morbid fascination for serial killers and monsters in human form and she'd asked Smith if he would help her with some research, she was undertaking into what makes one human being kill another. Smith assumed this was the reason she was calling him now.

He wasn't wrong.

"Can you talk?" Dr Vennell said.

"Shoot," Smith said.

"I need to pick your brain."

"No psychoanalysis," Smith insisted.

"I can't promise anything."

"What did you have in mind?"

"Can we meet?"

Smith remembered the steak and ale pie he'd missed out on the night before. Pizza just didn't cut it. He decided to kill two birds with one stone.

"Same place as last time," he said.

"The Pig's Head?"

"Hog's Head," Smith corrected. "Let's say eight."

"Eight it is then. I'll look forward to it."

They ended the call and Smith realised DC King was staring at him.

"Don't ask, Kerry," he said.

He wasn't sure how Whitton was going to react when he told her he was meeting Dr Vennell again. She hadn't been best pleased the last time he met up with the beautiful psychologist. He decided he would worry about that later.

The offices of Newton and Monk were situated a stone's throw from the car park in Hill Street. The two-storey building was directly opposite the castle museum on the other side of the river Foss. Even though it was Saturday Smith knew there would be someone working at the offices today. The weekend meant nothing in the legal world.

He was surprised then, that when he and DC King were buzzed into the building there was hardly a soul in sight. The reception area was large, but there was only one desk occupied.

"Good morning," he said to the middle-aged man sitting behind it. "DS Smith and this is DC King. We need to ask some questions about one of the employees of Newton and Monk."

"This will be about Melissa," the man said. "Tragic business."

"You heard what happened to her then?"

"I found out when Mr Newton arrived this morning. Melissa was his secretary."

"Can we speak to Mr Newton?" Smith asked.

"Of course. I'll see if he can spare a moment. Please, take a seat. I'm afraid I can't offer you something to drink. We're running on skeleton staff right now."

He left the desk and walked down a corridor. He returned a short time afterwards.

"Mr Newton will see you now. Carry on down the corridor until you get to the end. His office is on the left-hand side."

Richard Newton was a big man with a big voice. He bellowed for Smith and DC King to take a seat. He wasn't concerned that they'd left the door to the office open.

"I'm afraid I'm unable to offer you refreshments," he boomed. "We're encouraging the employees here at Newton and Monk to work from home wherever possible. Do you have any news about Melissa's murder?"

"How did you find out she was murdered?" Smith asked.

"Brian. He called me last night."

"Brian Welburn?" DC King said.

"Brian and I have been friends for a few years. He has the only proper wine bar in the city. Have there been any developments?"

"It's still early days," Smith said. "Melissa was your secretary, is that right?"

"She was a real gem. She was more than just a secretary – she would go far beyond what was expected of her, and she will be sorely missed."

"Did you ever socialise with her?" Smith said.

"Now and then. Work functions and the like."

"At Welburn's Wine Bar?"

"Sometimes."

"Do you know much about her family?" DC King said.

"She rarely talked about them," Richard said. "I think her father is dead, but I believe her mother still lives somewhere in the city."

"Can you think of anybody who might have wanted to hurt her?" Smith said.

"Of course not," Richard said. "Do you think this was someone she knew?"

"It usually is. Did she socialise with anyone else from Newton and Monk?"

"Not that I'm aware of. Melissa kept work and home separate. She was a real professional. I only ever saw her out with work colleagues at specific work functions."

"You said you've known Brian Welburn for a few years," Smith said. "Would you say you know him well?"

"I suppose so. He's a good man. He's ex-forces you know."

"I'm aware of that. Did he and Melissa get on well?"

"Why are you asking me about Brian?" Richard said. "Do you think he's involved somehow? Because I can tell you now that he isn't. Brian isn't a killer."

"He spent half his life in the army," Smith reminded him.

"That's completely different. Brian did not kill Melissa."

"We're just covering all the bases. You know how it goes."

"I most certainly do," Richard said. "Is this going to take much longer, because I have a lot of work to do?"

"We'll try not to keep you for too long," Smith said. "Were you at Welburn's Wine Bar yesterday afternoon?"

"I couldn't get out of the office. I had a lot of paperwork to sign off on."

"Is it usual for your secretary to finish work so early?" DC King asked. "Brian Welburn told us Melissa arrived at the wine bar at two."

"It's a Friday tradition in the legal profession. Just as the medical world all knock off early on a Wednesday, we do the same on Fridays."

"I think that's everything for now," Smith said. "If you remember anything that you think might be important please give us a call."

Richard got to his feet. "Of course. We're all on the same team in the end, aren't we?"

Smith replied to this with a smile.

"Thank you for your time, Mr Newton."

CHAPTER TEN

"Why is it we always seem to draw the short straw?" Bridge wondered. He zipped up his coat right to the top.
"The DI should have uniforms doing this sort of grunt work," he added.
"You moan a lot these days," DC Moore informed him.
"I moan as much as is necessary. It looks like it's going to rain."
"We'd better get started then. Do you know the way?"
"Of course I know the way."

They were standing outside Welburn's Wine Bar. Whitton and Baldwin were speaking to Brian Welburn inside. It was Saturday morning, and the bar hadn't yet opened. Bridge and DC Moore started to walk in the direction of Clifton. They turned right onto the road that ran past the Museum Gardens and Bridge stopped abruptly next to the art gallery. He looked up at the modern building and sighed deeply.
"What's wrong with you?" DC Moore asked.
Bridge pointed to the CCTV camera over the entrance of the gallery.
"Are you thinking about your mate?" DC Moore said.
"Yang Chu," Bridge elaborated. "CCTV cameras were a real *thing* of his. He never failed to spot them."
"You miss him, don't you?"
"He was a good detective," Bridge said. "And a good friend."
"I heard he was a proper psycho."
"He lost touch with reality for a while, but he had his reasons. I think about what he did a lot, and I think he just broke down. He couldn't handle life anymore. I really do miss him – we all do. Anyway, that camera looks promising. It's pointing right at the pavement outside."

The art gallery was inside a massive Victorian building. The interior was at odds with the distinctive 1870s architecture of the outside. The modern style was all sharp edges and glass. The dome of the ceiling was an impressive structure of wrought iron. Display cabinets ran the length of the walls, housing ancient artefacts and modern art.

The gallery had just opened its doors and there were only a few people inside. One of them, a man in his sixties spotted Bridge and DC Moore and walked over. He was wearing a name badge that told them he worked there. The name on the badge was Albert Frogg.

"Is there anything in particular you're looking for?"

Bridge took out his ID and explained why they were there.

"What's this about?" Albert asked.

"Just routine enquiries," Bridge said. "Would it be possible to look at the CCTV footage from yesterday. Between four and five in the afternoon."

"I'll see if I can find someone to help you," Albert said and left them alone.

"I've never been into art," DC Moore said and looked more closely at one of the exhibitions on display.

It was a selection of pottery inside a glass case.

"Me neither," Bridge said. "I suppose it takes all sorts. This is the first time I've ever been in here."

Albert Frogg returned with a young man.

He looked nervous. He avoided eye contact with the two detectives. His eyes darted back and forth behind his glasses. He scratched at a goatee beard as he listened to what Albert Frogg had to say.

"Lee will be able to assist you," he said. "He's more clued up on the technological side of things here."

"Come with me, please," the man called Lee said.

Bridge and DC Moore followed him through the room and he led them inside a small office.

"Would you like something to drink?" he asked.

"No thanks," Bridge said.

He sat down in front of a laptop and tapped the keypad.

"Mr Frogg said you're interested in the camera outside the main entrance."

"The one that looks onto the road outside," Bridge confirmed. "Can you access the footage from four yesterday afternoon."

"No problem," Lee said.

It took him less than ten seconds.

"What exactly are you looking for?" he said.

"A man and a woman," DC Moore said.

"Is it alright if I leave you to it? We've got a consignment of ceramics arriving soon, and I need to make sure the display units are ready."

"Of course," Bridge said. "Thank you for your help."

They watched the footage of the road outside the gallery. The image was clear – the cameras were obviously very good. Nothing much happened for the first five minutes. The odd car drove past and a man with a dog walked by, but that was about it.

"Perhaps they didn't come this way," DC Moore suggested.

"They will have done," Bridge insisted. "It's the most direct route from the wine bar to St Olave's Road."

"The owner of the wine bar said they left around four," DC Moore said. "If they came this way, we would have seen them by now."

"He said *around* four," Bridge said. "Not four on the dot. This looks promising."

At 16:11 two people appeared on the side of the screen. Bridge and DC Moore watched as they passed by the art gallery and disappeared from view.

"Did you see what he did?" DC Moore said.

"Can you rewind it?" Bridge asked.

DC Moore tried, but no matter which keys he tapped he wasn't able to rewind the footage.

"I'll go and see if that Lee bloke can help us," he said and left the room.

It took Lee less than a few seconds to do it for them. He took it back to the moment the couple appeared and pressed play. He got up to leave but something on the screen caught his attention.

Bridge noticed it. "What can you see?"

"I think I recognise them," Lee said.

He paused the footage and took a closer look.

"Do you know who the man is?" DC Moore asked.

"He looks familiar," Lee said. "You can't really see his face, but there's something about him that rings a bell."

"We need you to think hard," Bridge said.

Lee frowned. "I can't remember where I've seen him before."

"OK," Bridge took out one of his cards. "If anything does occur to you, I want you to give me a call. Immediately."

Lee nodded. "Can I get back to work?"

"Of course."

Bridge and DC Moore watched the footage from the beginning. The couple were arm in arm at the start of the clip, but as soon as they passed the optimum camera angle one of them broke contact. Judging by the height of the figure it looked like a man, but it was impossible to make out any distinguishing features. The other figure was definitely a woman. And when her face was in profile it was quite possible it was Melissa Grange. The face on the screen was definitely similar to the photographs the two detectives had seen of her, but the identity of her companion wasn't clear. The moment they passed the art gallery he unlinked his arm from Melissa's and pulled a hood over his head.

They watched the footage again, this time in slow motion.

"He knew about the camera," DC Moore said.

"I think you're right," Bridge agreed. "The second they passed the gallery he raised his hood. The bastard knew about the bloody CCTV camera."

CHAPTER ELEVEN

"Are you sure I can't offer you something to drink?" Brian Welburn said. "We do a delicious non-alcoholic cocktail."
"No thanks," Whitton replied for herself and Baldwin.
They were sitting opposite Brian in the lounge of Welburn's Wine Bar. It was not yet open for business but there was still plenty of activity going on inside. Shelves were being stacked behind the bar, and the hum of a vacuum cleaner could be heard close by.

"I don't know what else you want from me," Brian said. "I spoke to you outside Melissa's apartment – I spoke to more officers about the clientele who were in the bar yesterday, and I've given my statement. What else is there to say?"
"There are just a few more questions we need to ask you," Whitton said. "There are some things that don't add up."
"I'll be happy to help, but I don't know what else you want me to tell you." He scratched his arm and rolled up the sleeve of his shirt. There was a plaster on the forearm halfway down.
"What happened there?" Whitton asked him.
"I dropped a bottle of wine and cut myself when I was cleaning up the glass. It's an occupational hazard."

"You said that Melissa left the bar at four yesterday," Baldwin said.
"That's right. It might not have been precisely four o'clock, but it was somewhere around that time."
"And she left with a man?" Whitton said.
"That's right."
"But you didn't really get a good look at him," Whitton said.
"I've already told you I didn't," Brian said.

The sound of the vacuum cleaner was getting louder.

"For Pete's sake," Brian said and got to his feet.

He walked over to the young man hoovering the floor.

"Turn that damn thing off. Can't you see we're trying to have a conversation here."

"Sorry, Mr Welburn," the man said.

The vacuum cleaner was turned off and the man retreated in the direction of the bar.

Brian sat back down. "Sorry about that. No brains, youngsters these days. Where were we?"

"Melissa arrived at the wine bar at around two yesterday," Whitton said. "Is that correct?"

"Yes," Brian said.

"Did she come in on her own?"

"I can't remember."

"But you can remember the time she came in," Baldwin said.

"What is this? Am I being interrogated?"

"Not at this moment," Whitton said. "How can you be so sure about the time she got here?"

"It could have been a bit later," Brian said. "But she normally arrives at two. Ask any of my staff. Two on a Friday afternoon. You can set your watch by her."

"OK," Whitton said. "She arrived at two. You're not sure if she was alone when she came in. She left two hours later with a man you didn't recognise. Do you remember when they hooked up?"

"Hooked up?" Brian repeated.

"If she left with him, it's safe to assume they engaged in a conversation beforehand. That's how it usually works."

"I wasn't paying them much attention. I had other customers to look after."

"You told us the wine bar wasn't particularly busy," Whitton reminded him.

"And yet you didn't notice the man who left with Melissa."

"I don't like the accusatory tone in your voice," Brian said.

"I apologise," Whitton said. "It's an occupational hazard."

Brian paused for a second before answering. He looked straight into Whitton's eyes.

"No, I didn't notice him," he said eventually.

"You only realised Melissa was with someone when they left," Baldwin said.

"Correct. How many times do we have to go over this?"

A middle-aged woman approached their table.

"Sorry to interrupt," she said. "The delivery from Porters has just come in, and it's a couple of cases short."

"Deal with it, Mary," Brian said. "Can't you see I'm in the middle of something here?"

"Mary France?" Whitton said.

The woman nodded. "That's right."

"We've been trying to get hold of you. You were working here yesterday afternoon, weren't you?"

Another nod.

"We need to talk to you."

"Are you finished with me?" Brian asked Whitton. "Because if you are, I have a short order to sort out. It seems I'm the only one capable of such a mammoth task."

With that, he stood up and marched away.

Mary sat down in his place.

"Is he always like this?" Whitton asked her.

"He doesn't normally get angry," Mary said. "I think this thing with Melissa is getting to him."

"Were they close?" Baldwin said.

"They weren't that close, but I suppose they were friends. Melissa came here a lot. She was one of the regulars."
"Why didn't you answer our calls?" Whitton said.
"I only realised you were looking for me when I got back from my boyfriend's house. I stayed over last night but I left my phone at my flat."
"You're here now," Baldwin said.

"How long have you worked here?" Whitton said.
"A couple of years. I only work part-time. I'm studying French and German at university."
"You must have known Melissa then." Baldwin said.
"I knew her to say hello to."
"Yesterday afternoon she left with a man," Whitton said. "Do you know this man?"
"I've never seen him here before."
"Can you describe him."
"Tall," Mary said. "Easily six foot. Brown hair. Not bad looking, I suppose. He had really nice green eyes."
Whitton looked at Baldwin and received a shrug of the shoulders. The man seen leaving Melissa's apartment building had intense blue eyes according to the eyewitness.

"Are you sure about the colour of his eyes?" Whitton asked Mary.
"Positive. I was working behind the bar when he came to get some drinks. He looked right at me and that's when I noticed them. He really did have pretty green eyes."

CHAPTER TWELVE

"We've got two conflicting witness accounts," DI Smyth said.
The team were back in the small conference room for an afternoon briefing.
"Mary France," DI Smyth continued. "She was working at Welburn's Wine Bar yesterday afternoon, and she claims the man who left with Melissa had green eyes."
"Pretty green eyes," Whitton elaborated.
"And Howard Moore," DI Smyth said. "Who is a resident in the same apartment building as Melissa saw a man leaving at around five yesterday. He is adamant that this man had intense blue eyes."
"Two different blokes then."
"Not according to the artists impressions our two witnesses were able to help us with."

DI Smyth turned on the projector screen at the back of the room and tapped the keypad of his laptop. Two images of composite sketches appeared on the screen and the room fell silent.
DC Moore was the first to speak.
"It's the same bloke."

The resemblance between the two images was striking. Both witnesses had worked with the same police artist, and the two men staring at them right now did look like they could be twins. The only difference between them was their eye colour.

"One of them must be mistaken," Smith said. "Both of these men have thin noses and high cheekbones. Their mouths are identical. One of the witnesses must have got it wrong about the eyes."
"Mary and Howard are both adamant," DI Smyth said.
"I got the impression Mary was telling the truth," Baldwin said. "She said his eyes were really pretty and green."

"And Howard Moore was positive too," DI Smyth said. "It was the eyes he remembered most. Intense blue eyes."

"Perhaps he wears contacts," DC King suggested.

"It's possible," DI Smyth said.

"We got a hit with the CCTV footage from the art museum," Bridge said. "A couple were walking past at ten past four yesterday."

"That ties in with the time Melissa left the wine bar," Whitton said.

"The woman bore a striking resemblance to her," DC Moore said. "But you couldn't get a good look at the bloke. I think he was aware of the camera."

"He was wearing a hoodie," Bridge said. "And the moment they passed the museum he raised the hood."

"This was carefully planned," Smith decided.

"How do you figure that out?" DC Moore said.

"He knew about the CCTV camera. I think he knew about Melissa Grange's habits."

"The man who helped us with the footage thinks he knows him from somewhere," Bridge said. "But he couldn't recall where he's seen him before."

"That's very helpful," Smith scoffed.

"He's promised to give us a call if it comes back to him," DC Moore said.

"The owner of the wine bar said Melissa came there every Friday at two," Whitton said. "He told us you could set your watch by her."

"He's been watching her," Smith said. "He knows her routine. He knows she spends a couple of hours at the wine bar every Friday and he knows she walks the short distance home afterwards. We need to see how far back that CCTV footage goes."

"How is that going to help us?" DC Moore asked.

"How is it he knew about the camera, Harry?" DC King said. "He's probably walked the route Melissa walks and that's how he knows."

"We might get lucky with the previous footage," DI Smyth said. "See if anyone is acting suspicious – looking to see if there are any cameras."

They were prevented from discussing this any further when PC Black came into the room.

"What is it, Jim?" DI Smyth asked.

"Sorry to interrupt, sir," PC Black said. "But the body of a woman has been found in a wheelie bin close to the industrial estate in Murton Way."

* * *

The Loner hadn't always been that way. As a child he'd been gregarious and fun-loving. His mother and father doted on their only son, and even though money was tight he was never aware of it. The three of them would holiday in Scarborough or Bridlington and those were happy times.

He's wiped those memories from his internal database now. He has no recollection of the previous version of himself and he doubts that even the most highly trained hypnotist would be able to bring the memories back. Those childhood images and sounds have been securely locked away in the deepest recesses of his mind, never to see the light of day again.

It was easier than he imagined to disassociate himself from the rest of the world. A loner doesn't have to prove himself – he doesn't feel the need to feign interest, and he certainly doesn't have to fit into the picture of conformity that's considered the norm. Being permanently alone is rather enlightening, and it is a state of being that very few people can achieve. *The Loner* doesn't consider himself to be special, but he does believe it takes a special kind of will to be able to do what he does.

He recalls the exact moment when his decision was made, but he rarely thinks about it. It was a period in his life he doesn't care to dwell on. His mother would always say *what's done is done*, and it's a motto *The Loner* likes to live by. The past cannot be changed, but the future is riddled with opportunities.

The wound on his arm was irritating him. It was itching and he wondered if he'd stabbed himself too deeply. It probably needed stitches, but he knew that would complicate matters. He removed the plaster and poured a decent amount of antiseptic onto the inflamed skin. The burn was reassuring. He wiped it clean with a cloth and applied a fresh plaster.

He got up and walked over to the window. The street outside was strangely quiet. People were staying at home, and that suited him fine. He still had a lot of work to do. His mother and father would be proud of him now. He debated whether to tell them about his progress, but he opted not to. He would discuss it with them when he was halfway there. They weren't going anywhere, after all. They were still languishing in the chest freezer in the spare room. They were exactly where they'd been since he'd frozen them in time a year ago.

CHAPTER THIRTEEN

"Where's Webber?"

It was the first question Smith had asked the woman in uniform at the scene of the latest murder. Grant Webber was nowhere to be seen. For once the Head of Forensics hadn't arrived on the scene first.

"He's on his way," the young PC said.

It was PC Palmer.

Smith looked up and down the road. There wasn't much to see. They were about half a mile from the industrial estate in Murton Way. The path that led to the estate ran past a number of fields. A row of green wheelie bins were lined up against the fence that separated the path from the fields. The body of an unknown woman had been found in one of them when the man responsible for emptying the wheelie bins had been on his rounds. The body had been left where it was found. The garbage disposal truck was parked just up the road. A man was sitting in the front.

"The man who found her is over there, Sarge," PC Palmer said.

She pointed to a short man who looked to be in his fifties. He was talking to an equally short man. It was Smith's most recent nemesis – PC William Griffin. Smith walked over to them.

"A word please, PC Griffin."

He walked away, leaving the young PC with no option but to follow him.

"What is it?" he said when he caught up.

"Have you got a pair of gloves?" Smith asked him.

PC Griffin smiled a smug smile, and pulled a pair of black nitrile gloves from his pocket.

"I never go anywhere without them."

"I expected as much," Smith said. "It's a good job you've thought ahead, because I have a job for you."

"What?"

"I want you to check the other wheelie bins," Smith told him. "The woman was found in the one on the far left and it's possible the killer left something behind in the others."

The smile was wiped from PC Griffin's face in an instant.

"You want me to go rooting around in garbage?"

"They need to be checked," Smith said.

"What exactly do you think I'm going to find?"

"Probably nothing," Smith said. "But it needs to be done. And those gloves look just the job. On you go."

PC Griffin seemed to be mulling this over. His piggy eyes narrowed, and he licked his lips.

"What are you waiting for?" Smith said.

The beak-nosed PC snorted and made his way towards the row of wheelie bins.

Smith walked over to the man who'd found the body. He introduced himself and asked him if he was OK.

"It's not something you expect to come across on a Saturday afternoon," the man said.

His name was Gordon Hill and he'd been working for the council for over ten years.

"How often are the bins emptied?" Smith asked him.

"Once a week."

"It's a strange place to have a load of wheelie bins," Smith said. "This isn't a residential area, is it?"

"It's the trash from some of the warehouses," Gordon said. "I know it seems like an odd setup but the rubbish from there is transported here and we collect it every Saturday. It's all about health and safety. Hygiene and all that."

Smith wasn't sure what else to ask him. Gordon had stumbled across a dead body – end of story.

"Did you touch her," he asked anyway. "Did you move the body in any way."

"God, no," Gordon said. "I left the bin alone as soon as I realised what was in it. The lid was half up you see. She'd been stuffed in, but the lid wouldn't close properly."

"There's another man in the truck," Smith said. "Who is he?"

"Dave. He was the one who called it in. I told him what I'd found, and he refused to get out of the truck."

"One of the other officers is going to take a statement from you. You're going to have to stick around I'm afraid."

"This is the last stop on our rounds anyway," Gordon said.

"I'll arrange for someone to come and speak to you," Smith said and walked towards the car that had just pulled up.

It was Grant Webber. The Head of Forensics got out. Billie Jones got out of the other side.

"What time do you call this?" Smith said.

"I was in the middle of something," Webber said. "Where is she?"

Smith pointed at one of the wheelie bins. PC Griffin was two bins down. His sleeves were rolled up and his arms were covered in something sticky and black.

"What the hell is he doing?" Webber asked.

"Grunt work," Smith said. "He's an arrogant prick and I thought he needed knocking down a peg or two."

"There's something not quite right about you," Billie commented.

"I'll take that as a compliment. The body hasn't been touched. I'll leave you to it. Give me a shout if you find anything to ID her."

Webber nodded. He opened the boot of the car and took out his equipment.

Smith walked further up the road and took out his cigarettes. He lit one and took in the scene. There wasn't much around apart from fields. The industrial estate could be seen to the north.

"This isn't where you were killed," he said out loud.

He reckoned the killer knew about the wheelie bins and brought the body here afterwards.

He was about to be proved wrong.

"Sarge," PC Palmer shouted. "I think I've found something."

She was looking at something on the ground about ten metres further up the road. Smith went to see what she'd found.

"That looks like blood," PC Palmer pointed to the stain on the pavement.

Smith crouched down to get a better look.

"I think you could be right."

A section of the pavement had been stained dark brown. More spots of brown were dotted around the biggest stain. Off to the side was an almost perfect imprint of a human hand.

"Go and tell Grant Webber about this," Smith told PC Palmer. "Well spotted."

His cigarette had gone out, so he lit it again and took a long drag. Further up the road PC Griffin was busy with the last bin. Smith smiled when he saw that his uniform was covered in a mystery slimy substance. It would definitely need a wash after this.

CHAPTER FOURTEEN

"And then there were two," DI Smyth said. "Two dead women roughly the same age."

The woman in the wheelie bin had been identified as Jennifer Wells. Webber found a driver's license in her purse. She was twenty-two years old, and she worked night shifts at a warehouse in the industrial estate in Murton Way.

"Are we working on the assumption they're connected?" DC Moore asked.

"It's too early to tell," DI Smyth said. "I don't believe they are. Melissa Grange was murdered at home. She was killed in a very unusual way. Early indications show that Jennifer Wells was murdered the old-fashioned way. A blade to the heart. Webber found a deep laceration on her hand, but it's possible that wound was defensive. For now, we'll investigate them as two separate instances."

"Do we know if the two women were acquainted?" Whitton said.

"Not yet. But it's unlikely they moved in the same circles. Melissa had money. Her parents left her extremely wealthy when they passed away."

"The lawyer we spoke to told us her mother is still alive," Smith remembered.

"That's not true. Mr and Mrs Grange have been dead for a number of years."

"That's how she could afford a fancy place in Clifton," DC King figured out. "I was wondering how she bought an apartment like that on a legal secretary's salary."

"Jennifer Wells still lived with her parents in Tang Hall," DI Smyth carried on. "She worked shifts as a line operator at a warehouse. Socially the two women were on opposite sides of the spectrum."

"What else do we know about the wheelie bin woman?" Bridge said.

"We'll refrain from calling her that," DI Smyth said. "If you don't mind. She usually started work at ten when she was working nights, and she didn't show up at the warehouse last night."

"Why didn't anybody raise the alarm?" DC King wondered. "If she didn't make it to work, why didn't anyone miss her?"

"According to the man we spoke to at the warehouse," DI Smyth said. "It's not uncommon for Jennifer to miss a shift – especially on a Friday night. In fact, she was on her final warning for precisely that reason."

"What about her parents?" Smith said. "Surely they'd be worried when she didn't come home from work."

"She sometimes went straight to her boyfriends' after her shift on the weekend. They didn't think anything of it."

"This is all a bit too convenient," Smith said out of the blue.

"What are you thinking?" DI Smyth said.

"A woman is killed on her way to work. She works nights and she walks to work. She's not the most reliable employee, and she sometimes doesn't go home to her folks' house on a weekend."

"Are you suggesting the killer knew all of this?" DC Moore asked. "That's impossible."

"Anything is possible if you pay enough attention," Smith argued. "Jennifer was killed on her way to work. There was a lot of blood on the pavement further up from the wheelie bin where she was found. The killer knew precisely what her movements would be. Melissa was killed by a man who knew her Friday routine too. These murders are connected."

"I disagree," DC Moore said. "These women couldn't be more different. And the MOs were completely different too."

"Both murders were carefully planned, Harry. Every aspect of the killing was meticulously thought out beforehand. He watches them and he gets to know their routines. He knows things about them – he knows enough about them to be able to carry out the murders without leaving anything behind. He does not leave anything to chance."

"I disagree, Sarge," DC Moore said. "You're making this into something it isn't. There's nothing that links the victims together. The MOs couldn't be more dissimilar, and if it is the same killer it means he's killed two women in the space of a few hours. That's very unusual for a serial killer. It's highly unlikely we're looking at the same man."

"Moving on," DI Smyth said. "Webber has his work cut out for him, and the results from the post-mortems are going to take time, so we'll concentrate on the victims. And for the sake of simplicity, Smith we'll look at the murders as two separate incidents. There is nothing to suggest this is the work of a single killer."

"Fair enough," Smith said. "We'll have to agree to disagree for the time being. Jennifer Wells's boyfriend. He's the first thing on the agenda."

"Right. According to her father his name is Gary Powell, and he also lives in Tang Hall. We will be speaking to Mr Powell during the course of the day."

"What about witnesses?" DC King said. "If we believe Jennifer was killed on her way to work, there will have been people around. It's just before shift change at a lot of the warehouses on the estate. It's possible someone saw something on their way to work."

"We'll be appealing to anyone who was in the area last night," DI Smyth said.

"Jennifer started work at ten," Bridge said. "The walk from Tang Hall to Murton Way would probably take about fifteen minutes, which means she would have probably set off around half-nine if she wanted to get there in plenty of time. It's possible the killer followed her."

"I'm more inclined to think he was waiting for her," Smith argued. "He's been watching her and he knew roughly what time she would be where he wanted her."

"And he just jumped out of nowhere and attacked her? I don't think that's what happened."

"Do we know if she usually walked to work alone?" DC King said.

"That's a very good question, Kerry," Smith said. "We need to find out."

DI Smyth's phone started to ring on the table in front of him. He looked at the screen, answered it and put it on speakerphone.

"Sorry to bother you, sir." It was PC Simon Miller. "But there's a man at the front desk who has some information I thought you'd be interested in."

"What is it?" DI Smyth said.

"He works at the warehouse next door to where Jennifer worked. He heard about the murder this morning and he remembers seeing something odd last night when he was driving to work. It wasn't far from the row of wheelie bins. He claims there was a man walking up the path."

"Can he give us a description of this man?" DI Smyth asked.

"Not really, but there was something he thought was really strange. He actually slowed down in his car when he drove past. The man was blind, sir. He said there was a blind man walking up the road in the middle of the night."

CHAPTER FIFTEEN

Karen Salway walked her Yorkshire Terrier every morning, but on Saturdays she liked to treat him to an extra special outing. Karen would leave the house later than usual, but the walk was a much longer one, and it wasn't unusual for the eight-year-old Yorkie to be so exhausted on the return trip Karen would have no option but to carry him the rest of the way.

She always walked the same route. Starting at her bungalow on Bland Lane in Knapton she would walk the whole length of the main road that dissected the small village in two and she would head north in the direction of Moor Lane. Sometimes she would stop at the dog park on the way – Sam liked socialising with other dogs, but Karen decided to give it a miss today. The weather was glorious, and she wanted to take advantage of it.

She stopped for a breather just past the A1237 and sat down on a bench on the bridleway. Sam pulled on his lead. He wasn't ready to stop just yet. "You'll thank me for it later," Karen told him.
She unzipped her backpack and took out a bottle of water. She finished half of it in one go and poured the rest into a bowl which she placed on the path next to Sam. The dog wasn't interested. He didn't want water – he wanted to carry on walking.

They passed only three other people as they walked. A man with a scruffy looking mongrel, and a couple out for a romantic stroll. The bridleway narrowed as they made their way west. Karen could hear the hum of quad bikes in the distance. The quad track wasn't far from here and it sounded like there were quite a few of them out today. A light aircraft flew overhead. It was flying very low. The airfield was also close by.

Karen took another break by one of the streams that zigzagged across the terrain in this part of York. These tributaries of the river Foss spread out for miles across the fields. Small lakes were dotted here and there, and it was one of these lakes that Karen was heading for.

She and Sam had the place to themselves and that suited Karen just fine. She loved the peace and quiet, only a stone's throw from the hustle and bustle of the city.

Sam started to bark, and Karen stopped walking. She turned around to see what had caught his attention and saw someone walking towards her. It was the man with the mangy mongrel. He was walking quickly – the dog was on a lead behind him, and it was struggling to keep up. Karen pulled Sam closer and moved over to the side of the path. The man kept walking towards them. As he passed, he nodded a greeting to Karen and she found herself smiling back.

Sam continued to bark.
"That's enough, you," Karen said. "The dog's gone. You don't want to play with a scruff like that anyway."

Another aircraft flew overhead, and Karen tilted her head to watch it. The drone of the engine was loud, and it drowned out the whoosh as the crossbow bolt raced towards Karen's neck. She registered the burn as it entered her throat, made short work of the thyroid cartilage and exited out of the back. Karen's initial reaction was to take a sharp intake of breath, but the crossbow bolt had cut off her air supply. She wasn't in much pain – there are very few nerve endings in this part of the neck, but she knew she was in trouble, nevertheless.

She was feeling lightheaded, and she knew she wouldn't be able to stand for much longer. She let go of Sam's lead and managed to ease herself to the ground. She made the mistake of lowering her head, and her chin came to rest on the back of the crossbow bolt. There was pain now.

Sam started to bark again, and Karen saw the mongrel from earlier. Its owner was nowhere to be seen. Her eyelids were heavy as she watched her beloved Yorkshire Terrier circling the old dog.

"So humble."

The voice came from behind her, but Karen no longer had the strength to turn around.

"So pure."

The sound of his voice was oddly soothing. Karen listened and gave in to the sleep that was tugging at her. Her eyes closed and she drifted away.

She didn't hear the rest. She didn't hear him finish his prayer, and she was also unaware of his gentle touch as he held her hand and ran the blade of his knife across her wrist.

* * *

The man sitting in the interview room had introduced himself as John Roberts. He worked as a forklift truck driver at a logistics company on the Murton Way industrial estate. Smith thought he looked tired and when he explained that he hadn't slept after working a night shift Smith understood why.

"Thank you for coming in," he said. "Are you sure you wouldn't like something to drink?"

"I only drink coffee," John said. "And if I drink one now, I'll never be able to get off to sleep when I go home."

"You work at the industrial estate in Murton Way, is that right?"

"Lewis Logistics. It's a big distribution operation."

"And you work nights?"

"Sometimes," John said. "I do shift rotation. I worked ten 'til six last night."

"Can you tell me exactly what you saw last night as you were driving to work."

"I didn't think I'd seen right at first. I had to slow down and do a double take. It was a blind man, and he was walking up the path in the middle of the night."

"How did you know he was blind?" Smith asked.

"He was wearing dark glasses," John said. "Who wears sunglasses in the dark? And he was tapping one of those white sticks in front of him."

"Did you not think to stop and ask him if he was alright?"

"He seemed to be coping very well from what I could see," John said. "He was walking in a straight line, and he walked with purpose. Like he knew exactly where he was going."

"Which direction was he heading in?" Smith said.

"He was walking towards the industrial estate."

"Where exactly was this?"

"Just past the bins," John said. "About fifty metres past the row of wheelie bins."

"Did you see anyone else? Was there anyone else walking close by?"

"Not that I remember."

"What time was it?" Smith said. "Can you remember the exact time when you saw the blind man."

"Probably around half-nine. I like to get to work a bit early and grab a coffee before my shift."

"Could you describe this man?" Smith said.

"It's not very well lit around there," John told him. "But I think he looked quite young. A bit younger than you, and he was about your height too. Pretty tall."

"Is there anything else you remember about him?"

"There is one thing," John said. "When I first saw him and I realised he was blind, I thought it was strange. I mean, what blind person takes a walk at night without a guide dog?"

"It is odd," Smith agreed.

"But then something else occurred to me and the more I thought about it during my shift the more it made sense. It was the way he was walking. He was walking all wrong. Blind people walk a certain way, don't they? Even if they're familiar with the route they're walking they still exercise a certain amount of caution."

"And this man didn't?" Smith said.

"Not at all. That's what struck me when I was at work. If I didn't know any better, I'd say he wasn't even blind. I wondered if he was just some kind of nutter pretending to be a blind man."

CHAPTER SIXTEEN

"I think I know how he did it with Jennifer Wells."
Smith was sitting opposite DI Smyth inside his office.
"He pretended to be blind. He made contact with Jennifer by making her think he couldn't see."
"I've seen everything now," DI Smyth said. "If you'll excuse the pun."
"It's actually brilliant when you think about it," Smith said. "Who would even suspect something like that? You'd never suspect that someone would pretend to be blind, and what better way to appear to pose no threat. You wouldn't feel threatened by someone who can't see, would you?"
"Did you get the impression that this witness definitely saw what he thinks he saw?"
"Absolutely, boss," Smith said. "It makes sense. Our killer knows Jennifer's routine. He knows the shifts she works and he knows which way she walks to work. He also knows exactly what time she'll show up by the wheelie bins. He leads her to believe he's blind and she feels safe with him. Who knows, perhaps she even offered to assist him in some way. They get chatting and he strikes. He kills her and stuffs her in a wheelie bin. We're going to have our work cut out for us with this one."
"So I'm starting to believe," DI Smyth said.
"And I still think the two murders are connected."
"I know you do, but it's far too early in the day to work on that assumption. Until we have more information at our disposal, we're not going to go down that road. Nothing from the scenes suggest this is the work of the same killer."
"Murderers change their MOs all the time," Smith reminded him.
"I'm well aware of that."
"What now?" Smith said.

"Whitton and DC King have gone to speak to Jennifer Wells's boyfriend," DI Smyth said. "Hopefully he can help in some way."

"He didn't kill her."

"I didn't say he did. But until we've spoken to him, we can't rule him out."

"This one is special, boss," Smith said. "I've got a horrible feeling about this one."

"You say that about all of them."

"The blind man thing is rattling me. This isn't just some sicko who gets off on killing woman – this is a killer with a vivid imagination. The blind man idea was ingenious."

"Let's not get ahead of ourselves," DI Smyth said. "Let's not set up a fan club for this nutcase just yet."

"He's going to be hard to catch. That's all I'm saying."

"I'm not really sure how to proceed," DI Smyth admitted. "We've put the word out, and we've asked the general public for any information but that will probably reap nothing. Forensics and Pathology is going to take time, and we now know that the victims weren't acquainted. Do you have any suggestions?"

"Motive," Smith said.

"I thought you might say that."

"When we have a series of murders where the victims aren't connected," Smith said. "It makes things a bit tricky. But it also narrows down the possible motives."

"I'm not following you."

"Look at the *Electrician* murders," Smith said. "All the victims were chosen for a specific reason. They shared a history, and the killer was a big part of that history. This one is different. His victims are strangers to him. They weren't selected because of who they are – they were chosen because of what they are – easy targets. He's been keeping an eye out for a long time.

He watches his prey closely – he does a lot of reconnaissance work, and he only strikes when he knows beyond a shadow of a doubt that he will be able to carry out the murders without getting caught."

"You still haven't touched on a possible motive," DI Smyth pointed out.

"There aren't many to consider. Perhaps he's one of the rare serial killers who kill for the sake of it. Maybe he gets off on the thrill of it, but I don't think that's it with this one. This one is too cautious to be a thrill-seeker. Everything he does is done for a specific reason. He has an agenda – I just haven't figured out what that agenda is yet."

"Do you believe he will kill again?" DI Smyth asked.

"I've got a sinking feeling he will," Smith said.

"A little bird told me about your treatment of PC Griffin at the scene in Murton Way," DI Smyth said out of the blue.

Smith was shocked. "Where did that come from? Who is this little bird?"

"That's not important. Is it true?"

"He needs to learn how things work in this job, boss. He's an arrogant prick and he needed knocking down a peg or two."

"Stay away from him," DI Smyth said.

"I'm not stressed about a weasel like Griffin."

"Then you're a bigger fool that I thought you were. The man can make trouble for you, and I get the feeling he won't hesitate to do so. You're lucky he hasn't already lodged a complaint about your little stunt with the wheelie bins."

"It was a valid request," Smith insisted. "The woman was found in a wheelie bin. It wasn't unreasonable to ask him to check the others."

"That was a job for the forensics officers," DI Smyth said. "And you know it."

"I gave him an order because I believed it was justified to give that order."

"Shut up," DI Smyth said. "You are to stay away from PC Griffin unless it can't be helped. And that is a real order."

"Fair enough."

"I mean it, Smith."

"I'll stay away from him," Smith promised.

"Make sure you do."

"I'll be off then."

"Where are you going?" DI Smyth asked.

"It's been a while since I set foot in the New Forensics Building," Smith told him. "I reckon it's about time I did something about that."

CHAPTER SEVENTEEN

Gary Powell lived in one of the tower blocks on the Tang Hall estate. The area had been tidied up since the last time Whitton was there. Tang Hall was a notorious hot bed of crime once upon a time, but from the initial impression Whitton got of the place as she and DC King drove up it was clear that things had changed.

"This used to be a no-go area," Whitton told DC King when they got out of the car. "Even for the police."

"It doesn't look that bad," DC King said.

"We had a riot here not so long ago. There was a string of murders not far from here, and things really kicked off. It looks like the place has been cleaned up since then."

"There's a housing estate like this one in every city," DC King said. "In Bradford it was Toller Lane. Nobody I worked with wanted to be called out to Toller Lane."

They walked up to the block of flats and stopped by the entrance. There was a row of buzzers on the wall next to the door. Whitton found the one with Gary Powell's name on it and pressed it.

"Come on up," a man's voice said over the speaker shortly afterwards.

The door buzzed and Whitton pushed it open.

"Is he expecting us?" DC King said.

"He's expecting someone," Whitton said. "But it's not us. I didn't let him know we were coming."

Gary's flat was on the second floor, so they took the stairs. They walked down the corridor and stopped outside number 12. Whitton knocked on the door and the expression on the face of the man who opened it told her he definitely wasn't expecting a visit from two women.

"What do you want?"

Gary looked to be in his late twenties. His hair was shaved, and his blue eyes were full of suspicion.

Whitton took out her ID. "DS Whitton and this is DC King. Can we come in and have a chat?"

"Now isn't a good time," Gary said.

"I'm afraid it can't be helped. Shall we talk inside?"

"I need to make a phone call first."

He closed the door in their faces, and it took Whitton by surprise.

"He's up to something dodgy," DC King whispered. "I bet you anything he's on the phone to whoever he was expecting, to tell them to back off."

"Things haven't changed that much on the Tang Hall estate after all," Whitton said.

The door opened again, and Gary invited them in. He asked them to take a seat in the small living room. The place was surprisingly tidy.

"Is this about Jenny?" he asked.

"You heard about what happened?" Whitton said.

Gary nodded. "Her dad phoned earlier."

"We're very sorry about Jennifer," DC King said.

Another nod. "I should go round to see Don and Louise. I just don't know what I'm going to say to them."

"Are they Jennifer's parents?" Whitton said.

"Right. What happened to her? Don just said she was found close to the industrial estate where she works."

"We're not sure yet," Whitton said. "When was the last time you saw Jennifer?"

"Probably a few days ago."

"Could you be more specific?" DC King said.

"It was Wednesday. When she's on nights we don't see each other much. Ten 'til six is a shit shift."

"How long have you and Jennifer been together?" DC King asked.

"About a year. What exactly happened to her? I kept telling her it wasn't safe to be walking to work on her own at night."

"Did she walk to work every night when she was on that shift?" Whitton said.

"She did. I even offered to walk with her, but she said she was fine on her own."

"So, she walked alone?"

"I knew something like this would happen."

"What makes you say that?" DC King said.

"You hear about it all the time, don't you? Women getting attacked at night."

"How did Jennifer seem to you the last time you saw her?" Whitton said.

"What do you mean?" Gary said.

"Was there anything bothering her?" DC King said.

"She was the same as usual. Why are you asking me how she was? Some bastard killed her – what's her state of mind got to do with that?"

"We're just trying to get a fuller picture of what happened," Whitton explained. "It's possible that whoever attacked her had been watching her. Did she mention anything like that to you?"

"No," Gary said. "Are you telling me someone has been stalking her?"

"It's possible," DC King said. "She didn't say anything to you about it? She didn't get the feeling that someone had been watching her on the way to work?"

"I just told you, she didn't."

"Where were you last night?" Whitton said.

It was clear Gary wasn't expecting this. His eyes darkened and he fixed Whitton with an icy stare.

"It's a question that needs to be asked," DC King said. "It's better if we can rule out as many people as possible very early on in an investigation."

"You can't think I killed her," Gary said. "She was my girlfriend, for fuck's sake."

"Could you please just answer the question," Whitton said.

"I went out to the Goat's Arms. It's a pub on Tang Hall Lane. Just off the Hull Road."

"I know it," Whitton said. "What time did you go to the pub?"

"Probably around eight. I was there until closing."

"Can anybody corroborate this?" DC King said.

"Probably," Gary said. "I didn't kill Jenny. I could never hurt her."

"We're going to need the details of the people you were with last night," Whitton said.

"I didn't kill her," Gary said again.

"What do you do for a living?" Whitton asked.

"This and that," Gary said. "I do some odd jobs, and I'm pretty handy with a car engine."

"I think that just about covers everything," Whitton said. "We may need to talk to you again, and we'll need the details of the people you were with at The Goat's Arms last night."

"Are you going to catch him?" Gary said. "Are you going to catch the bastard that killed Jenny?"

"Yes," Whitton replied without thinking. "We're going to catch him. I promise you we will catch him."

CHAPTER EIGHTEEN

The building that housed the finest forensic brains in the city had always been referred to as the New Forensic Building. It was over a decade old now, but the name had stuck. It was an ultra-modern high-tech structure even by today's standards, but it had become such a familiar sight on the York skyline that the term *new* seemed inappropriate somehow.

Smith took the lift to the third floor and stepped out into the corridor. This was where Grant Webber did most of his work. This was where the majority of the forensic evidence that led to the convictions of some of the most devious minds in the city was brought to light. Smith had lost count of how many investigations had been resolved here.

He hadn't forewarned Webber about his visit, but he knew that the Head of Forensics would smell a rat if he did. Smith never made an appointment – he preferred to pop in, unannounced and uninvited and this time was no different. He made his way down the corridor to the main lab. He was sure that this is where he would find Webber.

He wasn't mistaken. He went inside and saw that Webber was concentrating on something on the screen of the laptop on his desk.
"Afternoon," Smith said when he was halfway to the desk.
"To what do I owe the pleasure?" Webber said without turning around.
"I've missed the place, that's all. What are you looking at?"
"Something that leads me to believe that both women were killed by the same perpetrator."
"I've been saying that all along. What have you found?"

He looked at the screen of the laptop. On it were two photographs, side by side. Both depicted some kind of injury.
"The one on the left is a photograph Billie took of the wound on the forehead of the first victim," Webber said.

"Melissa Grange," Smith elaborated.

"The first victim," Webber insisted.

He rarely referred to murder victims by their names. He found it easier to focus on the science if he dehumanised them.

"And the photograph on the right is the laceration in the hand of victim number two."

Jennifer Wells, Smith thought.

He wasn't like Webber at all. He liked to be reminded that the victims were very much human. He preferred to see them as people with families and friends. People who were going to be missed.

"If you look closely at the edges of the wounds," Webber said. "You can see similarities in the shape of the damaged skin."

"I must need my eyes testing," Smith said. "Because I have no idea what I should be looking for."

"Let me enhance the images," Webber said.

He tapped the keypad and enlarged both photographs.

"The area of the skin where it's split open is what's important," he continued. "Do you see the jagged pattern on the outer edges?"

Smith could see it now. The deep cut on Melissa Grange's head was roughly an inch long and the skin on the outside of the wound was rippled. He spotted the same thing on the photograph of Jennifer Wells's injury.

"I think the same weapon was used to inflict both wounds," Webber deduced. "I cannot be a hundred percent certain, but it was probably a knife with a serrated blade."

"Have you told Kenny about this?" Smith said.

"Dr Bean has been informed," Webber said. "He'll be able to tell me whether the second victim was stabbed with a similar weapon, but I think I know what he's going to find. You're looking at a single killer."

"If you weren't so damn ugly, I'd kiss you right now."

"And if you were to do so," Webber said. "You would be leaving here in an ambulance."

"I was right," Smith said. "I knew it."

"As much as confirming the reliability of your gut instinct leaves a sour taste in my mouth," Webber said. "This is a step forwards."

"It certainly is," Smith agreed. "Do you have anything else to tell me?"

"You might want to ask yourself why he did this?"

"Why make the lacerations?"

"From a killing perspective," Webber said. "They were unnecessary. They served no purpose in ending the lives of these women."

"Is it possible they happened by accident?"

"No," Webber said. "An accidental laceration would be irregular in its shape and size. It would be messy. These wounds are not defensive, - they're almost identical. Dr Bean will be able to give you more details about the depth and size but in my opinion the cuts were made to serve a purpose."

"Interesting," Smith said.

"It most certainly is."

"How are you doing?" Smith said out of the blue.

Webber looked at him now. "What sort of question is that?"

"It's the sort of question one bloke asks another bloke when he wants to know how he is."

"I'm doing just fine, thank you," Webber said.

"Do you fancy grabbing a few pints some time?"

"That sounds like a great idea. Is there anything else I can do for you?"

"I think I've got enough to be thinking about. At least now I can tell the boss that I was right."

"I'm sure DI Smyth will look forward to it."

Smith's phone started to ring. The ringtone made him smile.

"Speak of the devil. His ears must have been burning. I'll stick it on speakerphone."

"Where are you?" DI Smyth asked.

"Still busy at the New Forensics Building," Smith told him. "Webber has confirmed that I was right. We're looking at a single killer. Both Melissa Grange and Jennifer Wells were murdered by the same man."

"There's been another one. A couple out for a walk found a body near the quad track halfway between Knapton and Hessay."

"Another woman?"

"Another woman," DI Smyth confirmed. "She was killed very recently. The couple remembers seeing her earlier walking her dog. It looks like someone shot her through the neck with a crossbow."

CHAPTER NINETEEN

According to Smith's GPS the closest place to park his car was at the coffee shop in Hessay. From there he would have a two-hundred metre walk to the location where the body of the woman had been found. The New Forensics Building was on the opposite side of the city, and it took him twenty minutes to get there. The cars already parked in the car park of the coffee shop told him Whitton and Bridge had beaten him to it. A police car was also parked there. Smith had offered to give Webber a lift, but the Head of Forensics had politely declined the offer. He still hadn't arrived on the scene.

Smith set off on the path the GPS on his phone told him would lead him to the third dead body to be found in the space of twenty-four-hours. It was early afternoon – the sun was directly overhead, but it wasn't doing much to warm up the day. Smith took out a cigarette and smoked as he walked. It wasn't long before he spotted what was obviously the place where the woman had been found. The police tape was already in place to secure the scene. Two officers in uniform were busy taping an area around the outer cordon. One of them was PC Griffin. DI Smyth's words were still fresh in Smith's head, but he pushed them to the side. This was a scene of a murder. This was his department.

He made his way over to Bridge and Whitton.

"Where's the boss?" he asked.

"Stuck in a meeting with Chalmers and the Super," Whitton told him. "Covid stuff."

"Lucky him. What have we got?"

"Dead woman," Bridge said. "A man and a woman were out for a stroll when they found her. She was walking her dog according to them. A Yorkshire Terrier that's developed a bit of a crush on Kerry. She's playing with him now."

"The DI said something about this happening very recently."

"The couple remembered seeing the woman about an hour before they found her," Whitton said. "They were heading in the opposite direction. They also remember seeing a man walking his dog."

"Where are they now?" Smith asked.

"Harry is looking after them," Bridge said. "The woman seems OK, but the bloke has taken it badly."

"Webber is on the way."

Right on cue a very red-faced Grant Webber appeared. It took him a while to get his breath back before he could speak.

"I'm out of shape. Where is she?"

Smith pointed to the police tape.

"Who was first on the scene?"

"PC Griffin and PC Black," Bridge said. "It looks like she was shot with a crossbow. It went straight through her neck."

"That's quite a shot to make," Webber said.

He walked off in the direction of the police tape.

A dog started to bark somewhere close by. Smith turned to look in the direction it had come from and the scene that met him caused him to grin like a deranged sailor. A small Yorkshire Terrier was barking at one of the uniformed officers. The feisty creature had clearly taken a dislike to PC William Griffin. The beak nosed officer was holding his hands up in defence.

Smith walked over to them. DC King appeared and managed to get hold of the dog's lead. Smith bent down and scratched his head.

"Good boy," he said. "You're a good boy."

"That thing almost bit me," PC Griffin said. "It's vicious."

"Make yourself useful," Smith said. "You're not paid to entertain dogs. Go and make sure nobody contaminates the scene."

"I'm not paid to get harassed by stupid dogs either."

"He's obviously a good judge of character," Smith said and turned to PC King. "What's his name?"

"Sam," she said. "It says Sam on his collar."

"The poor thing."

PC Griffin was still hovering around.

"Get out of here," Smith said. "Before I let the hound of hell loose again."

PC Griffin glared at him but did as he'd been instructed.

"Is that the couple who found her?" Smith pointed to the man and the woman sitting on a wooden bench.

DC Moore was standing next to them.

"That's right, Sarge," PC King said. "I think the bloke needs to see a doctor. He doesn't look well at all. There's an ambulance on the way."

Smith walked up to them. He greeted DC Moore and told the couple who he was. The man and the woman looked to be in their early twenties. The woman was pretty with sparkling blue eyes. Even though it was still only March her face was very tanned. Her companion was deathly pale in comparison. All the colour had drained from his face, and he looked like he was going to pass out at any moment.

"Are you alright?" Smith asked him.

"It was a bit of a shock," the woman replied for him. "Gordon is terrified of blood. He can't bear the sight of it."

"There's an ambulance on the way."

"The other officer said that ten minutes ago," the man called Gordon managed.

Smith learned that the woman was called Susan Brown, and she and Gordon walked the paths around here regularly.

"You told my colleagues that there was a man walking his dog," Smith said.

"He was just behind us," Susan said. "And he was acting really strange."

"What do you mean by that?"

"He was walking quickly. With the dog behind him. He overtook us and a moment later he suddenly stopped and turned around."
"That is strange," Smith agreed. "Where was this? Where on the path did he suddenly make his U-turn?"
"About two hundred metres from where we are now."
"OK," Smith said. "Could you talk me through the timescale involved. You passed the woman and the Yorkie. How soon after you went past her did the man overtake you?"
"Not more than a few minutes," Susan said.
"So he must have passed her too."
"I suppose so."
"And then he doubled back shortly after that?"
"That's right. Do you think he's the one who did that to her?"
"I'm just trying to get an idea of what happened," Smith said. "Could you describe this man?"
"I can tell you the dog looked like it needed attention," Susan said. "It was a scruffy thing."
"What about the man."
Smith wasn't interested in the dog.
"He was a bit older than me I think," Susan said. "I'm twenty-three. He was tall like you, and he walked like he was in a hurry."
"What about his face," Smith said. "Can you describe his face?"
"I suppose he wasn't bad looking. Nice skin. And he had unusual eyes. He looked right at me when he walked past, and I remember he had really nice green eyes."

CHAPTER TWENTY

"It's the same man."

Nobody disagreed with Smith this time. The man Susan Brown described was very similar to the man two other witnesses recalled seeing close to where the other women were killed.

The third victim hadn't been identified yet. There was nothing on her person to give them any idea of who she was.

"It looks like she died from the damage caused by the crossbow bolt," Smith continued. "Straight through the neck."

"That was quite a shot," DC Moore commented.

"That's what Webber said," Smith told him. "And that leads me to believe this isn't the first time he's fired such a weapon. Shooting someone smack bang in the middle of the neck would require practice."

"Where does someone even get their hands on a crossbow?" DC Moore said.

"Internet," DC King said. "It's not against the law to own a crossbow."

"We should look into shooting clubs," Bridge suggested. "Perhaps he belongs to a club."

"He doesn't," Smith said.

"How can you be so sure?"

"He does not belong to any shooting club. He wouldn't risk it. It's one of the first things we suggested, isn't it."

"Are you saying he knows how we operate?" DC Moore said.

"It's looking that way."

"Can a crossbow bolt be linked back to the weapon that fired it?" Whitton wondered.

"I don't think so," Smith said. "I don't think it's like a bullet that's unique to the gun it was fired from."

"It'll be easy enough to check," Bridge said.

"Until we know who the third victim is," Smith said. "We can't be sure whether he's been watching her, but I think he has. I think this woman takes that walk regularly and our killer is aware of this. The couple who found the body told me they walk those paths all the time, but they can't recall ever seeing the man before."

"That contradicts what you just said about him watching the victim," Bridge pointed out. "If he's been stalking his prey, it's likely the couple would have seen him before."

"Not necessarily," Smith said. "He pretended to be blind to lull Jennifer Wells into a false sense of security. I think he brought the dog along with him today to do something similar. I think it was some kind of misdirection."

"Susan Brown said his eyes were green," Whitton said. "That's two witnesses who say green and one who insists the eyes were blue. Which one is it?"

"Both," Smith said.

"Are you suggesting he was wearing contacts?" Bridge said.

"No. It's his natural eye colour."

"What?" DC Moore said. "Blue one day, and green the next? I've never heard anything so ridiculous in my life."

"It's very rare," Smith said. "But it does happen. There have been cases where a person with a certain condition has eyes that change colour depending on their mood."

"Are you serious?" DC Moore said.

"I am, Harry. Something occurred to me earlier and I did some digging. The witness who was adamant the man he saw had intense blue eyes saw him after the fact. He remembers seeing him leave the apartment where Melissa Grange lives. That was after he killed her."

"His eyes change colour after he's killed," DC King cottoned on.

"I think they do," Smith said. "The woman who saw him with Melissa in the wine bar told us he had green eyes. Melissa was still alive then. And the woman who saw him walking the dog also mentioned his green eyes."

"Because it was before he carried out the murder," DC King said.

"And I'll bet a month's salary that had she seen him afterwards, she would have described his eyes as being intense and blue."

"That is totally weird," DC Moore said.

"We live in a weird world, Harry."

"Killing excites him," DC King said.

"You're weird," DC Moore told her.

"We live in a weird world," Smith said once more. "But Kerry's right. His eyes change in tune with his moods. They're intense and blue after he's killed because, as Kerry said it excites him. He gets off on it, and I'm starting to wonder if we are dealing with a serial killer who kills for the sake of it after all."

DI Smyth came into the room and the look on his face told Smith that the meeting with Chalmers and Superintendent Smyth hadn't been much fun.

"Good meeting, boss?" Smith said.

"What do you think," DI Smyth said. "The Super is getting totally OCD with these new guidelines. I've got a feeling things are going to change for the worse for the foreseeable future. What have I missed?"

Smith filled him in. He told him about the third victim, he outlined Webber's findings, and he mentioned his conclusion about the confusion around the colour of the killer's eyes.

"Horner's syndrome," DI Smyth said when he'd finished.

"What's that?" Bridge asked.

"There was a boy in my class at school," DI Smyth said. "He had slate-grey eyes, but they changed to green when he was particularly excited. I remember he was never able to lie to the teachers – his eyes always gave him away."

"And we think our killer has this syndrome?" DC Moore said.

"It's not common," DI Smyth said. "But it does happen. And going on the witness accounts it's very possible in this instance. Do we have anything else from a forensic perspective?"

"Not much apart from the similarities in the wounds found on the victims," Smith said. "There was a handprint on the ground in Murton Way. A perfect handprint, but unfortunately Webber couldn't pull any prints from it."

"He was wearing gloves," Whitton deduced.

"It looks that way," Smith said.

"Gary Powell has an alibi for the time Jennifer Wells was killed," Whitton said. "He was in the Goat's Arms at the time. It's been confirmed by more than one person."

"I knew he had nothing to do with it," Smith said.

"Have we had any luck with the CCTV footage from the art gallery?" DI Smyth asked.

"The manager of the place has promised to get the footage to us as soon as possible," Bridge said. "He hasn't a clue how to retrieve it, but he said he'll get the bloke who works there to send it over as soon as he comes back to work. He went home sick apparently."

"We need that footage now," Smith said. "Get someone to assist the manager if you have to. Send that friend of yours. He's helped us in the past."

"Barry isn't answering his phone," Bridge said.

"We need that footage," Smith said.

"Going back to the wounds on the victims," DI Smyth said. "Does Webber have any theories about them?"

"Nothing concrete," Smith said. "He's confirmed they were intentional, and they were also not what resulted in the deaths of the women."

"Perhaps they're some kind of calling card," DC King suggested.

"It's possible," Smith agreed.

"Did Webber find anything on the latest victim?" Whitton asked.

"A laceration on her wrist," Smith said. "Similar size and depth to the others."

"I wonder what they mean," DC Moore joined in.

"It beats me, Harry," Smith said. "Melissa Grange had a cut on her forehead – Jennifer Wells had a laceration on her arm, and the latest victim had a wound on her wrist. I have no idea why he does that."

"Stigmata," DC King said a few seconds later.

"What on earth are you talking about?" It was DC Moore.

"Stigmata," DC King repeated. "The wounds Jesus suffered when he was on the cross. There have been reports throughout history of people who claim to have suffered similar wounds without any explanation."

"I think you're clutching at straws there," DC Moore said.

"There are six main ones," DC King carried on, regardless. "The head, hands, wrist, feet, back and chest."

"And we just happen to have three victims with three of those exact wounds," Smith said. "I think you could be onto something there, Kerry."

"Are you suggesting we're looking for some kind of religious nut?" DC Moore said.

"If the injuries these women were subjected to represent the wounds that Jesus suffered when he was being crucified," Smith said. "It's something we need to consider."

"But if that's the case," Whitton said. "It means he's only halfway there. It means he's going to kill three more women."

CHAPTER TWENTY ONE

Steven Lemon was an avid reader of true crime. He devoured volumes of accounts of real-life murders. Steven knew more about the depraved individuals in criminal history than anybody he'd ever met, and he'd been following the online reports on the recent murders in the city with a keen interest. Based on what he'd previously read, he suspected that the killer York CID would later dub *The Loner* wasn't finished yet. He also knew that until he was stopped in his tracks the women of the city weren't safe.

Almost every documented serial killer in history shared one common trait with the others. These murderers tended to target similar victims. They had a *type*. John Wayne Gacy murdered teenage boys and young men. The Killer Clown raped, tortured, and killed more than thirty young men and boys, and he never deviated from his choice of victim.

Ted Bundy was responsible for the deaths of a similar amount of people, but his victims were all young women. Jeffrey Dahmer's preference was similar to Gacy's – he killed and dismembered over a dozen young men and boys. And based on this knowledge, Steven Lemon knew that statistically he wasn't at risk from the serial killer who was prowling the streets of York.

So, when he opened the door to the tall man with the striking green eyes, thoughts of murder were the furthest things from his mind. The young man introduced himself as Detective Constable John Hill and showed Steven his warrant card to confirm this.

"What's going on?" Steven asked him.

"Just a routine door-to-door. I'm sure you're aware of the recent murders in the city."

Steven could feel his heart speeding up. He'd read a lot about true crime, but he'd never been in the position to be involved in it. He invited DC Hill in and offered him some coffee.

DC Hill declined the offer.

"Take a seat," Steven said in the living room. "How can I help you?"

"We've had reports of a prowler in the area," DC Hill said. "A person matching the description of the man we believe may be involved in the recent string of murders has been seen close to here. Have you noticed anything suspicious recently? Anyone hanging around who looked out of place?"

"I don't think so," Steven said.

A strange noise stopped the conversation. It was a quiet tapping sound.

"Is there someone else here?" DC Hill asked.

"My mother," Steven said. "She's bedridden, and she'll be wanting her cup of tea. She can wait."

"Are you sure you haven't seen or heard anything out of the ordinary?"

"Not that I can recall. How is the investigation progressing?"

"They're not going to catch this one."

Steven thought this was a strange thing for a police detective to say.

"Can I see your ID again?"

He didn't know why but something inside him was telling him this situation was all wrong. This detective was wrong. Steven's stomach was warming up and he could feel acid burning in his throat.

The *detective* sensed his discomfort. He knew from the instant he looked into Steven's eyes that he'd been unmasked.

"Get out," Steven said. "Get out before I call the police."

"Of course. I apologise for disturbing you."

DC Hill stood up. Steven did the same. He walked towards the door, but he was stopped halfway there by an intense burning pain in his lower back. He was aware of a dull pain as the knife was removed but he didn't feel it as it was thrust into his right kidney. The first stab had severed his spinal cord at its base.

Steven slid to the floor and watched as the man with the green eyes removed the sock from his right foot. He didn't feel a thing as the blade etched a deep wound into the top of the foot.

"So humble," the man with the green eyes began.

He looked at Steven when he recited the prayer, and the last thing Steven Lemon registered was the bizarre spectacle of the man's eyes changing colour in front of his face.

* * *

Smith got the feeling he'd been sent on a wild goose chase. DI Smyth had come up with the idea to try and find people in the city who suffered from Horner's syndrome. Smith didn't believe the killer would have advertised the fact. The research he'd done told him there was nothing that could be done about the rare condition. There was no cure, and according to the sites he'd perused it wasn't a life-threatening illness. It was a rare condition with unusual symptoms – end of story. It wasn't something you would bother your GP with.

DC King had suggested a public appeal. Smith thought this was a much better idea. Appealing to the general public about men whose eye colour changed with their mood would be much more productive in his opinion. DI Smyth had disagreed, and now Smith's eyes were burning from poring over web pages about Horner's syndrome.

After three hours of this he decided to call it a day. It was after six and he was dog tired. He also remembered he'd made plans with Fiona Vennell. He'd promised to meet the young psychologist in the Hog's Head later. He still hadn't mentioned it to Whitton, and he knew he needed to tell her. He shut down his laptop and left the office. It had been a complete waste of three hours of his time.

He found Whitton in the canteen. She and Baldwin were drinking coffee at the table by the window. Smith got himself a cup and joined them.

"The Horner's syndrome thing was a pointless exercise."

"Tell me about it," Whitton said. "I don't know what the DI was thinking. Our killer is hardly likely to advertise something like that."

"I've been summoned to a meeting with Dr Vennell later," Smith came out with it. "Do you want to join us? A bite to eat and a few pints at the Hog's Head. I seem to remember missing out on a pie last night."

"I'll give it a miss thank you," Whitton said.

"Are you sure?"

"I'm knackered, and I feel like a night in. You go and enjoy yourself with your teenage shrink."

Baldwin looked at her as though she'd grown another nose. "Is there something I've missed?"

"You have to see this woman," Whitton said. "She's like Dougie Howser, only in female form."

Baldwin started to laugh.

"She's twenty-nine," Smith reminded Whitton. "And she's highly respected in her field."

"And she also looks like a supermodel," Whitton reminded Smith.

"You two are weird," Baldwin told them. "I'm off. I'll see you in the morning."

"Are you sure you don't mind me going out?" Smith sipped his coffee.

"Of course not. What is it she wants to see you about?"

"She wants to pick my brains. Probably about past cases. And maybe she can help me with the present one, because this one is really starting to piss me off."

"All of them piss you off," Whitton said.

"I've got a feeling another woman is going to be killed very soon," Smith said. "Another woman is going to fall victim to this psycho and there's nothing I can do about it."

He didn't know then that *The Loner* had already claimed another victim, but it wasn't a woman he'd killed. It was a forty-six-year-old man who still lived at home with his mother. He was also unaware that the bedridden old lady would be instrumental in the future progress of the investigation.

CHAPTER TWENTY TWO

Fiona Vennell was already there when Smith arrived at the Hog's Head. It was a busy Saturday night and she'd managed to grab the only free table in the pub. Smith had never seen the place this busy before. The bar staff were struggling to keep up and the waiters and waitresses were working harder than any of them had ever worked before.

Smith sat down opposite Fiona. "Good evening, Dr Vennell. Sorry I'm late."
She shook her head. "What have I told you about the Dr Vennell thing."
"Sorry," Smith said. "Fiona it is then. It's busy tonight."
"Lockdown is imminent," Dr Vennell said. "And I think people are making the most of the freedom before it's taken away from them. Would you prefer to go somewhere else?"
"Nowhere else makes steak and ale pies like Marge's. Do you want something to drink?"
"I've already ordered," Fiona told him. "Theakston wasn't it?"
"Am I that predictable?"
"Predictable is good. How are you?"
"You promised not to psychoanalyse me," Smith said.
"Enquiring about a person's wellbeing is not psychoanalysis."
"In that case I'm as good as can be expected, considering there's a nutjob out there killing women."
"Nutjob?" Fiona repeated. "Is that a technical term?"
"How else would you describe him? He's killed three women, and we have reason to believe his eyes change colour when he's finished stopping their hearts."
"Interesting."

The drinks arrived, and Smith ordered two steak and ale pies. He was informed that due to the backlog in the kitchen, there would be a long wait.

"What was it you wanted to talk to me about?" Smith asked.

He took a long drink of his beer and when he placed it back on the table, he realised he'd downed almost half a pint in one go.

"You're thirsty," Fiona stated the obvious. "I wanted to ask your opinion on something I'm working on."

"Shoot."

"I'm writing a thesis on motives for murder."

"Then you've come to the right person," Smith said. "Motive is my baby."

"If you go by conventional wisdom," Fiona said. "There aren't many possible motives for wanting to end a person's life."

"Hatred," Smith said. "Revenge, financial gain, jealousy and love."

"I forgot you wrote the textbook on the subject."

"Far from it," Smith said and finished his beer. "But those five are the classic motives for committing murder. There are deviations to the norm – and often the motives cross over but ultimately they all lead back to the classic ones."

"In your experience," Fiona said. "What is the most common motive? Which one have you come across the most?"

"That's a tough question. And it's one I really can't answer. Perhaps another beer will help refresh my memory."

He ordered two. The first one had hit the spot, and he didn't feel like waiting forever for a drink. More people had come inside the pub, and those who wanted food were being told to wait for an available table.

"I think it would have to be revenge," Smith said.

"I had a feeling you would say that," Fiona said.

Their eyes met and Smith smiled at her. She seemed even younger tonight. Her skin was flawless, and her eyes sparkled. Smith could see why Whitton thought she was gorgeous. He was starting to think the same.

"Revenge comes in all shapes and sizes," he said. "And very often it's accompanied by bits and pieces of the other classic motives. Why do you want to avenge something? Are you getting revenge for yourself, or is it for someone close to you? Someone you love. Is it because of a hatred of a person? Or is it someone you envy? Motive is the most complicated aspect of murder."

"And it's a subject you're most passionate about?"

"It's not passion," Smith said. "It's the foundation of every murder investigation, without exception. It should be the starting place in every case. You can discuss *how*, *when* and *where* until the cows come home, but it's only when you analyse the *why* that you start to understand the mind of the killer, and only then will you get the answers you're looking for."

He stopped there and Fiona didn't comment on his thoughts. Instead, she tilted her head as though she were appraising a piece of art in a museum. She smiled and Smith found himself smiling back.

"You're an interesting man, Detective Smith," she said.

"I've been called worse things."

"And you have intense blue eyes."

Smith broke eye contact first.

"Speaking of eyes," he said. "Are you familiar with Horner's syndrome?"

"Of course," Fiona said. "Emotional triggers cause the eyes to darken or lighten. Hormones are released which affect the appearance of the retina."

"Have you ever come across someone with the condition?"

"I treated a man with something similar. It wasn't Horner's but his eyes would change slightly when I asked him certain questions. Especially when we discussed his childhood."

"What colour were his eyes?" Smith asked.

"Green."

"And they became blue when he was triggered?"

"They did."

"I need a name."

"And you know I can't give it to you."

"Patient, doctor confidentiality can be broken under certain circumstances," Smith reminded her.

"This man is not your killer."

"How can you be so sure of that?"

"Because he's dead. The patient I was referring to died two years ago. He was sixty-four. What are your thoughts on this murderer?"

"He's killed three women in the space of twenty-four hours," Smith told her. "Different MOs each time. It's clear that he's been preparing for this for a very long time. He watches his victims, and he knows their routines inside out."

"Are you getting close to him?"

"We're nowhere near that point. We have no likely suspects, and that in itself is unusual. What's also unusual is the timescale involved. It's very rare for a serial killer to kill with such urgency."

"Have you considered why he's done that?"

"I have," Smith said. "But I haven't been able to come up with an explanation. He's managed to kill three women in less than a day without leaving anything behind. He's exceptional."

"That's a peculiar way to put it."

"It's what he is," Smith said. "And I think he's going to be hard to stop."

"What else can you tell me about him?" Dr Vennell said.

"He has quite an imagination. He pretended to be blind to lull the second victim into a false sense of security. He took a dog with him to carry out the third murder, and he somehow charmed his way into the flat of the first. I get the impression he's exceptionally good at making women feel at ease."

"Serial killers are often charmers," Dr Vennell said.

"Is there anything you can help me with?" Smith asked. "Based on what I've told you."

"I might have a theory on why he's been so hasty."

"I'm all ears."

"It all boils down to necessity," Dr Vennell said.

"I'm not following you."

"Things are about to change."

"My Super said something similar yesterday," Smith said.

"Soon, new regulations are going to be implemented. It's no secret that lockdown is imminent and it's possible your killer has realised the implications of this."

"When the curfew comes in, it'll be much harder for him to get his victims where he wants them."

"Precisely," Dr Vennell said. "For him, killing is necessary. He has to kill these women, and he has a plan that needs to be carried out. Lockdown will cause him huge problems, so he's restricted in the time he has to fulfil his desires. I think it's as simple as that."

The food arrived, and Smith tucked in without saying anything further. He polished off the pie in record time. He finished off his second pint of Theakston and his phone started to ring. The screen told him it was Whitton. He answered it and after a brief conversation he ended the call and sighed deeply.

"Bad news?" Fiona asked.

"I have to go," Smith said. "Work. I'm sorry."

"It can't be helped."

He took out his wallet and realised it didn't have any money in it. He shouldn't have been surprised. He never carried cash.

"Dinner is on me," Fiona said. "I was the one who invited you remember."

There was still a full pint of beer on the table.

"Help yourself to the Theakston," Smith said.

Fiona stood up and leaned over to hug him. She held on for much longer than Smith felt comfortable with. He could smell the shampoo in her hair and her perfume was something familiar. She broke the embrace and followed up with a kiss to his lips. Her lips were open slightly when she kissed him, and he could feel the moisture on them.

"We'll finish this another time," she said.

Smith almost ran out of the pub to where Whitton was waiting. He really wasn't sure what had just happened, but he knew instinctively that Dr Fionna Vennell had overstepped the mark. Smith was clueless where women were concerned but even he knew that there was more to that parting embrace than a couple of friends saying their goodbyes.

CHAPTER TWENTY THREE

It was PC Simon Miller who took the initial call, and it was the most bizarre call he'd ever taken. An elderly woman had phoned the police because her son hadn't brought her a cup of tea and that meant something was wrong. PC Miller had explained that it wasn't really a police matter, but Rachel Lemon had insisted that it was. She'd explained that her son, Steven always brought her a cup of tea at six on the dot. Without exception he was there with the hot cup of tea, but today he hadn't. Therefore, something had happened to him.

PC Miller had always had a soft spot for old people – he was very close to his grandparents, but he knew that resources were tight, and he couldn't justify sending out a couple of uniformed officers because an old woman hadn't had her tea.

But then the conversation took a different turn. Mrs Lemon informed PC Miller that there had been someone in the house earlier. Someone had paid her son a visit and the snippets of the conversation she managed to hear were rather disturbing. In the end, PC Miller decided it wouldn't do any harm to send a couple of officers to the address Mrs Lemon gave him. He would find someone close by and ask them to go and take a look. He reasoned it would probably take no more than five minutes.

The phones were quiet for the next twenty minutes and then PC Miller got another call. This one was from one of the uniforms who'd gone to check Mrs Lemon's house. They'd arrived at the house to find a body in the living room. The man had been stabbed multiple times and he was lying on his back on the carpet. His mother Rachel was in bed upstairs.

* * *

"You smell like a brothel."

Smith wasn't expecting those words from his wife when he got into her car outside the Hog's Head.

"I wouldn't know what a brothel smelled like," he said.

"Well, now you do."

"Dr Vennell did go a bit over the top with her goodbye hug," Smith said. "It actually took me by surprise."

This was an understatement. Smith was still in shock.

"It must be your irresistible Australian charm."

"There's nothing I can do about it. Women throwing themselves at me is something I just have to live with. What have we got?"

"Dead male," Whitton said. "Steven Lemon. Forty-six years old. His elderly mother phoned the switchboard because he hadn't brought up her six o'clock cup of tea."

"You're kidding me?"

"That's what I was told."

"And they took it seriously?" Smith said. "They sent someone round for that?"

"It's lucky they did. Steven was lying in the living room. It looks like he's been stabbed to death."

Steven Lemon lived in Foxwood. It was a five-minute drive from the Hog's Head, but five minutes were enough for Whitton to tell Smith about the rest of the peculiar call to the station.

"The mother claims there was someone in the house earlier. She said Steven had a visitor and she thinks it was a policeman. She overheard parts of the conversation."

"Where was she at the time?" Smith asked.

"She's bedridden most of the time, but apparently there's nothing wrong with her hearing. She said something about Saint Rita's prayer."
"Who on earth is Saint Rita?"
"Your guess is as good as mine."
"It sounds like she's a bit senile," Smith said.

He realised that this wasn't the case when he met the old woman. Rachel Lemon definitely had all her faculties intact. Physically, she wasn't in the best shape, but there was nothing wrong with her mind. Smith and Whitton had left Grant Webber to it in the living room and gone straight up to talk to the victim's mother.

The first thing that hit Smith was the smell in the small bedroom. He knew it well – it was an odour that had been in the background of his life once upon a time. It was the unmistakable peppery reek of marijuana. He wondered if Mrs Lemon liked to have a toke or two. The smell inside the room was completely at odds with the décor. Framed pictures of biblical scenes were dotted around the room. A statue of Christ on the cross stood on the dressing table and another cross had been hung on the wall behind the bed, perhaps to ward off evil.

Rachel was sitting up in bed. She'd finally managed to get her cup of tea and she was sipping it slowly. A blanket was covering her legs, and she was wearing a T-Shirt that surprised Smith.
"You've got great taste in music," he nodded to the Led Zeppelin shirt.
"I saw them once when I was younger," she said. "I remember the gig at Earl's Court. Jimmy Page looked right at me during the solo in Stairway to Heaven. That was back in 1977."
"That must have been something," Smith said.
"It certainly was. The young man in the uniform told me Steven is dead."
"I'm afraid so," Smith said.
"We're very sorry, Mrs Lemon," Whitton said.

"We all have to die sometime. He's with the good Lord now."

"You told the other officer that Steven had a visitor earlier," Smith said.

"It was one of your lot," Rachel said. "Or at least I think he said he was a police detective."

Smith knew for a fact that none of his colleagues had come here earlier.

"Did you hear what they were talking about?" Whitton asked.

"Bits and bobs," Rachel said. "Would you be a dear and put this on the table for me?"

She handed Whitton her teacup.

"Of course," Whitton said and did as she was asked.

"It's the arthritis," Rachel said. "It's a real bugger. I take weed every now and then, and that helps, but it always comes back."

"Marijuana?" Whitton said.

"Marijuana, weed, dope, spliff. Whatever you want to call it. The doctor suggested I take it in capsule form, but where's the fun in that? Anyway, old habits die hard, if you know what I mean."

"You don't go to a Zeppelin gig without smoking the odd joint," Smith said.

"You're a sharp one."

"Can you remember what time the man you thought was a policeman came to the house?" Whitton asked.

"Just before six," Rachel said. "I know it was then because Steven always brings my tea up at six. He never misses a day."

"But he did today," Smith said.

"I tapped on the floor with my stick, but he still didn't come up."

"Can you tell us what you heard?"

"Something about a door-to-door. The policeman mentioned a door-to-door. I wondered if that's why Steven forgot about my tea."

"Why would you think that?" Whitton said.

"Because he's a crime freak," Rachel said. "He's always watching those true crime things, and he reads nothing but grisly mystery stories."

"Can you describe his voice?" Smith said. "The man you thought was a police detective – what was his voice like? Do you think he's a local?"

"It sounded like he could be from around here," Rachel said. "His accent was definitely from somewhere in Yorkshire."

"Did you hear anything else?" Smith asked.

"Steven raised his voice. I heard him shout to the man to get out."

"Do you have any idea why he did that?"

"None at all. But he said it more than once. He told the man to get out and then it was quiet. Until…"

"Go on," Smith urged.

"I heard the other man begin Saint Rita's prayer."

"Who is Saint Rita?" Whitton said.

"Saint Rita of Cascia. It's a sanctuary in Italy. I went there once. It was very moving. Saint Rita is the patron saint of loners."

"What is this prayer you spoke about?"

Rachel closed her eyes and pressed her arthritic hands together.

"So humble. So pure, so mortified, so patient. Such compassionate love for thy crucified Jesus that thou couldst obtain from him whatsoever thou askest. It's the loneliness prayer."

"Are you absolutely sure that's what you heard?" Smith said.

"Positive. My joints and bones may be buggered, but there's nothing wrong with my ears."

"What does the prayer mean?" Whitton asked. "Excuse my ignorance, but I'm not really religious."

"Each to their own," Rachel said. "There's a book in the bottom drawer down there. It's got a picture of Rita in it. Pass it to me, will you."

Smith fetched it for her. She opened it up somewhere in the middle and pointed to a painting of a woman who looked like she'd seen better days. Her clothes were ragged, and she was covered in scars.

"That's Rita of Cascia," Rachel said. "The patron saint of loners."

"What happened to her?" Whitton said. "Was she attacked?"

"Stigmata," Rachel explained.

Smith and Whitton looked at each other. DC King had brought up something similar only a few hours ago.

"The suffering of Christ was suffered by Saint Rita too," Rachel said. "She had scars of unknown origin on her head, hands, wrist, feet, back and chest."

"Excuse me for a moment," Smith said.

He left the room and went downstairs. Webber was looking at something by the front door.

"Does he have lacerations on his feet?" Smith asked him.

"On his right foot," Webber said. "Exactly the same as the ones found on the other victims."

"They're representative of stigmata," Smith said. "That's…"

"I know what stigmata are," Webber interrupted.

"He's diversified," Smith said. "We thought he only targeted young women, but it's quite clear that we were very wrong."

CHAPTER TWENTY FOUR

Smith was dog-tired after the conversation with Rachel Lemon. The elderly lady had changed the perspective of the entire investigation and Smith's brain was finding it hard to process what he'd been told. Why had the man who killed Steven recited a prayer known as the loner's prayer? What was the significance of that in the greater scheme of things? Smith knew it was important. He couldn't deny that in light of what they now knew about the wounds on the victims. Four people had been slayed and all of them had wounds that represented the wounds of Christ on the cross, but what exactly did it mean? Why was this so important to the most prolific serial killer Smith had ever dealt with?

He could feel a headache coming on and he hoped it wouldn't grow into a full-blown migraine. He hadn't suffered one for a while but they always knocked him for a six when they did show their ugly face. He made a mental note to take some of the painkillers he'd been prescribed when he got home. The last thing he needed right now was a migraine. He was planning on taking the pills and heading straight to bed. He needed a good night's rest.

He realised that wasn't going to happen as soon as he and Whitton stepped foot inside the house. Darren Lewis was standing at the top of the stairs with a wild look on his face.

"Lucy's bleeding."

Those two words made Smith forget about his headache in an instant. He raced up the stairs, two at a time with Whitton close on his heels. They found her on the floor of the bathroom, doubled up with pain.

Whitton crouched down next to her. "What happened?"

"It hurts," Lucy said.

"When did it start? Why didn't you call us?"

"It's only just started," Lucy said and winced. "There's a lot of blood."

"I'm calling an ambulance," Smith said.

"We'll take her in my car," Whitton said. "It'll be quicker."

"I don't want to lose my baby," Lucy said. "I can't lose my baby."

"We're going to get you to hospital," Whitton said. "Can you stand up?"

Lucy managed to get to her feet. Her face was stained with tears, and her eyes were red.

"Come on," Whitton held her hand. "We'll help you down the stairs."

"I'll pack her some things," Smith said. "In case she has to stay overnight."

Darren Lewis helped him. The teenage boy was visibly shaken. Smith patted him on the shoulder.

"It's probably nothing serious. It's quite common to have some bleeding."

"She's in agony," Darren said. "I don't know what we'll do if we lose the baby."

"Don't think like that," Smith said, and stuffed a T-shirt into the bag.

Darren removed it. "She won't wear that one."

He replaced it with a T-shirt with a dragon print on it.

Whitton made it to the hospital in six minutes. Smith had phoned ahead, and a team of medical staff were waiting for them when they arrived. Lucy was placed on a stretcher and wheeled inside. Darren watched her go. His mouth was open, and his eyes were blank. He looked like he'd been frozen in time.

Whitton put her arm around him. "She'll be alright. She's in good hands."

"Do you think it could be from stress?" Darren wondered. "Do you think it's because of me getting arrested?"

"I don't think so," Smith said. "The doctors will find out what's wrong. Let's go inside."

They went into the canteen and sat down at a table. Smith's headache was worsening, and he realised he'd forgotten to take any painkillers when he got home. The emergency with Lucy had made him forget all about it.

"Do you have any paracetamol?" he asked Whitton.

"Are you getting a migraine?" she said.

"Not if I can help it."

"I've got some," Darren said.

He reached inside his jacket pocket and took out a blister pack. He handed them to Smith.

Smith popped two in his mouth and chewed on them. "Thanks. Why do you carry painkillers around with you?"

"Lucy sometimes gets cramps," he said.

Smith found himself smiling. Whatever he thought about the sixteen-year-old boy, it was becoming very clear that he really did care deeply for Lucy.

"Why is it taking so long?" Darren asked twenty minutes later.

An untouched can of Coke stood on the table in front of him.

"They probably need to do some tests," Whitton said. "That can take time. Drink your Coke – you've had a bit of a shock, and the sugar will help."

Darren humoured her. He opened the can and took a small sip.

A short while later, a doctor Smith recognised approached their table. She was one of the medical staff who had treated him during one of his many stays in hospital. He couldn't recall the precise time he'd been admitted, but there were many of them and they all blurred into one right now.

"Is she going to be alright?" Whitton asked.

The woman introduced herself as Dr France and assured her that Lucy was going to be fine.

"Why was she bleeding?" Darren said. "That was a lot of blood. It wasn't just a bit of spotting."

Dr France smiled at him. "You've done your homework. Are you the father of the baby?"

Darren nodded.

"Well, you'll be glad to know that mother and baby are doing just fine. The bleed was due to cervical insufficiency. It's when the cervix opens too early in preparation for birth. It's not uncommon, and it doesn't usually pose a threat to the mother or the baby."

"So, she's going to be alright?"

"We're going to keep her in overnight just to be on the safe side," Dr France said. "But she'll be allowed to go home tomorrow. We'll discuss the dos and don'ts then."

"Dos and don'ts?" Darren repeated.

"There are a number of important things you need to be made aware of, so this doesn't happen again. Like I said we'll talk about it tomorrow."

"I want to know now," Darren insisted.

"There are some precautions you need to take," Dr France said. "It would be best if you would refrain from engaging in sexual intercourse until..."

"Tomorrow will be fine to discuss this in more detail," Smith interrupted.

Dr France smiled at him. "Of course."

"Can we go in and see her?" Darren asked.

"Lucy is sleeping now," Dr France said. "I suggest you all go home and do the same. I assure you she's in good hands."

"Thank you," Smith said.

Whitton thanked her too.

Darren went a step further. The teenager got up and wrapped his arms around the perplexed looking doctor.

"Thank you," he said. "You don't know what this means."

"I'm starting to get a good idea," Dr France said. "You can let go now."

"Sorry," Darren said and sat back down.

"We'll speak in the morning," Dr France said. "Go home and get some rest."

They were halfway to the exit when Smith had an idea. He stopped in his tracks and took out his phone.

"Who are you calling?" Whitton asked.

"Kenny. I'm suddenly wide awake and those headache pills seemed to have done the trick. I'll see if Kenny's here. I want to have a word with him."

CHAPTER TWENTY FIVE

Smith was in luck. Dr Bean was still at the hospital. He told Smith he was in his office, and he would be happy to spare a few minutes. Whitton and Darren had gone home. Smith told her he would get a taxi when he was finished speaking to the Head of Pathology.

He knocked on the door and went inside the office. Kenny Bean was dressed in a black shirt and white jeans. The effect was rather comical.
"Kenny," Smith said. "Is this the new uniform?"
"I was just about to knock off for the night," Dr Bean told him. "And this happens to be what I wear when I'm not dissecting the dead."
"It suits you," Smith said. "How are you?"
"A lot healthier than the people I have the pleasure of working on. What can I do for you?"
"I just wanted to know if you've got anything for me. Anything important."
"That depends on what you consider important. Take a seat."

Smith sat down at the desk. Dr Bean sat down opposite him.
"What brings you here tonight?" he said.
"A couple of terrified teenagers," Smith said.
He told Dr Bean about what had happened to Lucy.

"And I don't mind admitting I was shitting myself for a while too," he said when he'd finished.
"You do lead a colourful life," Dr Bean said. "And you're soon to be a grandfather. I shall have to learn to treat you with a bit more respect when that time comes. Granddad. Unbelievable."
"It certainly is," Smith agreed. "What have you got for me?"
"Your man is no stranger to the human anatomy," Dr Bean said. "I presume the killer is a man."
"Without a shadow of a doubt."

"He knew exactly where to make the incision that destroyed the first victim's voice box. The larynx isn't an easy thing to locate unless you're schooled in that kind of thing."

"Are you suggesting he's had some kind of medical training?"

"It's possible, or he may have simply done extensive research. The initial incision destroyed the larynx, but it also served to make severing the trachea easier. This was done manually, and that is virtually impossible."

"How did he do it then?" Smith said.

Dr Bean placed a hand on his throat. "The larynx is here. And the trachea is situated just below that. The wound to the upper neck will have weakened the cartilage there and made it possible to snap the trachea. I believe he took hold of her hair and yanked her head back."

"Nasty," Smith said.

"Victim number two was more straightforward," Dr Bean carried on. "That one would have required nothing more than a basic knowledge of the anatomy of the chest and everyone knows where the human heart is located. A single stab wound was enough. Her heart will have stopped beating within a couple of minutes."

"The crossbow is bugging me," Smith said. "A bolt through the neck in broad daylight is unbelievable."

"That's an understatement," Dr Bean said. "And it's something I've never come across before. That was an exceptional shot. Smack bang in the middle of the neck. Added to that, she would have had to be gazing skyward for it to be possible."

"Perhaps she was looking at a bird in the sky."

"Perhaps," Dr Bean said. "But it really was an amazing shot. I did a bit of archery in my youth, and I never came across anyone who could make such a shot."

"I never had you pegged as a Robin Hood," Smith said.

"Unfortunately, I was more of a Friar Tuck. That's why my archery career was extremely short lived."

"What can you tell me about the strange wounds on the victims?" Smith said. "Can you tell if they were inflicted after they died?"

"No. But I can confirm they were made either shortly before or shortly after the victims' hearts stopped beating."

"Can you also confirm the cuts were made by the same weapon?"

"It appears so. The shape of the wounds suggests a serrated blade was used, and all of them were extremely similar in shape and depth. The second victim was stabbed with a similar knife."

"When will you have a report on the latest victim?" Smith asked.

"When I've completed the post-mortem of course."

"Fair enough. I've taken up enough of your time. I don't suppose you could give me a lift home?"

"Where's your car?"

"Parked outside my house. I was in the middle of a discussion with a shrink friend of mine when I got called out to the latest murder, then we had the emergency with Lucy."

"Shrink friend?"

"It's a long story," Smith said.

Fiona Vennell's excessive embrace was still fresh in his head, and he didn't really want to talk about it.

"Can I give you some advice?" Dr Bean said outside Smith's house twenty minutes later.

"Of course," Smith said.

"I'd change your aftershave if I were you. That feminine scent really doesn't suit you."

"I'll bear that in mind," Smith said. "Thanks, Kenny. I appreciate it."

He got out of the car and went inside the house.

Whitton was still up. She was in the kitchen with a cup of coffee. Darren Lewis was nowhere to be seen.

"Darren's sleeping upstairs," Whitton said. "Do you want some coffee?"

"I shouldn't really," Smith said. "I don't want to encourage a migraine, but a coffee would go down well right now. I'll risk it."

He made a strong cup and sat down opposite Whitton.

He ran his hand through his hair. "What a day."

"You can say that again," Whitton said. "Just when we thought it was time to switch off for a few hours, Lucy gives us the fright of our lives."

"Darren really does care about her, doesn't he?"

"So I'm starting to see."

"I'm wondering if maybe he should move in here for a bit."

Whitton looked at him as though he'd just told her he was giving up beer.

"Did I just hear right?"

"It makes sense," Smith said. "We all know that lockdown is coming, and that will probably mean Lucy and Darren will be separated. If he moves in here, he'll be there for her when she needs him."

"Who are you?" Whitton said. "And what have you done with my husband? Do you realise what you're suggesting?"

"I think it's the right thing to do."

"You seem to be forgetting that we only have three bedrooms."

"And you seem to be forgetting that Lucy and Darren are expecting a baby."

"Are you saying they should share a room?" Whitton said. "Share a bed? They're only sixteen."

"And they're about to become parents," Smith said.

"Has it also slipped your mind that Darren was arrested yesterday? Not only are we endorsing two teenagers sharing a bed, we're harbouring a criminal. We're police officers, Jason – what are people going to think?"

"Since when did I give a shit about what people thought?" Smith said. "Think about it. It makes sense. And I reckon Lucy will feel less stressed with Darren here. They really do love each other."

"You never cease to amaze me. I'll give it some thought."

"Don't think too long," Smith said. "Lockdown is on its way and it's coming soon."

"I'm off to bed," Whitton said. "Are you coming?"

"I'll just finish my coffee and have a quick smoke There's far too much stuff banging around in my head right now, and I need to try and shut it out if I'm going to be able to sleep."

Whitton kissed him on the cheek. "Night night."

Smith opened the back door and went outside. The sky was clear and the air cool. He lit a cigarette and inhaled deeply. He really did have a lot on his mind. It had been a crazy day. He sat on the bench and closed his eyes. It hadn't been a rollercoaster ride of a day, it felt more like he'd been on a dodgem car with someone else driving. Snippets of the events from the past twenty-four hours came and went. Images of dead women with identical wounds bounced around inside his head. He also couldn't shift the picture of Lucy lying on the stretcher as she was wheeled inside the hospital.

PC Griffin's piggy eyes and beak nose appeared and left as suddenly as they had arrived and then another face came into view. It was a pretty woman with sparkling eyes. Dr Vennell was all he could see, and her face was refusing to budge. Smith could even smell her. He could smell the scent of her shampoo and the sweet, cloying odour of her perfume.

He opened his eyes and realised he'd dropped his cigarette on the ground. He wasn't sure if he'd nodded off for a moment. Or had he been dreaming while he was still awake? He couldn't be sure. He picked the cigarette back up and relit the end. He took a few long drags, stubbed it out and went back inside the house. He wasn't sure if he would be able to sleep but he knew he needed to rest. He brushed his teeth and lay down next to Whitton. Within seconds he was overcome by a deep, dreamless slumber.

CHAPTER TWENTY SIX

Smith leaned over in bed and his hand fell on something warm. It wasn't Whitton – the rising and falling of the fur told him it was one of the dogs, and the loud snoring could only come from one particular breed. Theakston had somehow managed to get up onto the bed. Smith realised there was still life in the aged Bull Terrier yet.

He sat up and scratched his old friend on the head.
"You're taking the piss, boy."
Theakston opened one eye but refused to budge. Smith got up and left him where he was. If he'd managed to get up by himself, he was more than capable of getting down again. He did what he had to do in the bathroom and went downstairs.

Whitton and Darren Lewis were already up. The smell of coffee filled the kitchen. Smith made himself a cup and sat down.
Darren looked up from his tablet. "Boris is addressing the nation tomorrow."
"It's the Prime Minister to you," Whitton told him.
"Boris suits him better. He doesn't act like a Prime Minister."
"What's he addressing the nation about?" Smith said.
"The lockdown," Darren informed him. "It looks like the Coronavirus Act is coming into effect and restrictions are going to be enforced. The schools are going to close."
"We don't know that yet," Smith argued.
"Don't you watch the news?" Whitton said.
"Not if I can help it."
"Lockdown is a reality. People are going to have to stay at home. Pubs and restaurants will close, and curfews will come into place."
"When exactly is this thing happening?" Smith said.
"Probably by the end of the week," Darren guessed.

"Then we have four days to prevent two more people from being murdered."

"Jason," Whitton warned. "This is not a topic to discuss at the breakfast table."

"Let's change the subject then," Smith decided. "Whitton and me were talking last night, Darren."

The teenage boy turned to look at him. "What were you talking about?"

"We haven't made up our minds yet," Whitton said.

"I have," Smith said. "We were wondering if you would like to move in here for a while. The lockdown is going to mean you'll never see Lucy, and I don't think that would be good for either of you."

"Are you serious?" Darren said.

"I am. It's clear that you care for her, and I think it would be better for you to go through whatever this lockdown entails together."

"That's awesome. I didn't expect this."

"There are going to be rules you'll have to abide by," Whitton said.

"I'll do whatever you say."

"The main reason I'm even suggesting this," Smith said. "Is that I know you too well. You'll think nothing of breaking curfew to sneak out and see Lucy, and this way you don't have to do that."

"It's not going to be easy," Whitton said.

"Me and Lucy will be together," Darren said. "That's all I care about."

"You'll be together twenty-four-seven," Whitton added. "It's going to be a big change for you. It's going to be a big change for all of us."

Smith patted the boy on the shoulder. "If you haven't killed each other by the second week I'll be impressed. I don't think I could bear to be with Whitton every hour of the day. No offence, dear."

"None taken," Whitton said. "The feeling's mutual."

"I'm going out for a smoke."

"You two are not right in the head," Darren said.

"And you're going to be stuck here with us," Smith said. "I'll leave you to think about that."

The sun was making an appearance in the sky overhead, and it was bitterly cold. Spring hadn't quite arrived yet. Smith lit a cigarette and stretched his arms. The conversation with Dr Vennell came back to him. When he'd asked her why she thought the killer carried out the murders in such a hurry, she hadn't even hesitated before she'd replied.
It all boils down to necessity.
She'd suggested that he'd been so hasty because he understood the implications of the impending lockdown. He knew the restrictions would make life very difficult for him. They had less than a week to catch the most exceptional killer Smith had ever come across, and he wondered if that was even possible.

They had four victims. Four people had been killed in a very short space of time. The MOs for all four murders were very different, and the meticulous orchestration of the murders suggested that this had been in the planning stages for a very long time. They had no likely suspects and the forensic evidence they'd gathered was laughable.

And they were still lacking a motive. Nobody on the team had come up with a plausible reason why these four people were killed. They weren't acquainted with one another, and they came from different walks of life. There was absolutely nothing that linked the four victims together, and Smith was starting to wonder if this was going to be the one who was going to get away with it. He reasoned that it had to happen one day.

"Fuck that," he spoke to the sky.

He was damned if he was going to start thinking like that. Somewhere in his city were two people who were going to have their lives cut short in the next few days. Somewhere in York two people were oblivious to the fact that they were soon to become victims of the worst serial killer the city had ever encountered. They were about to die. One of them would have a wound carved into their back, and the other would be found dead with a similar laceration in their chest.

CHAPTER TWENTY SEVEN

Smith and Whitton arrived at the station the same time as Bridge. Smith's car had refused to start again, and he'd had to travel to work with Whitton. They'd been informed by someone at the hospital that Lucy had been given the all-clear to go home. Smith wasn't sure when they'd be able to get away from work, but after a brief phone call with Darren Lewis the teenager had offered to go and collect her in a taxi. At least Smith didn't have to worry about him *borrowing* his old Sierra.

Bridge walked over to them, and it was when he got closer that Smith noticed the inane grin on his face.
"What's wrong with you?" he asked.
"There's absolutely nothing wrong with me," Bridge said. "All is well in the world."
"Would you take that smile off your face," Whitton said. "It's rather unsettling."
"This smile is here to stay. I am a happy man right now."
"Are you going to let us in on the secret," Smith said. "Or do I have to beat it out of you?"
"That won't be necessary. I asked Billie to marry me. The women of York are going to weep – Rupert Bridge is soon to be officially off limits."
"God help us all," Smith said.
"Did she say yes?" Whitton asked. "Did Billie accept your proposal?"
Bridge's smile faded slightly. "Not exactly. But she said she'd think about it, so it's only a matter of time."
Smith walked away. He went inside the station shaking his head.

Baldwin was manning the front desk.
"Anything to report?" Smith asked her.
"All's quiet on the murder front," she said.

"Do we have any new leads? Has anyone phoned in with any information?"
"Not a sausage, Sarge. Uniform didn't get anything from the door-to-door in Foxwood. None of Steven Lemon's neighbours remembered seeing a man they didn't recognise in the area around the time he was killed."
"How does he do it?" Smith wondered. "He's killed four people, and we have no witnesses. That's virtually impossible in a city like this."
"It's still early days, Sarge."
"That's what worries me," Smith said. "This one hasn't just appeared out of nowhere – he's exploded onto the scene and murdered four people. Why is it nobody has come forward with any information? Someone must know who he is. We've been quick off the mark with the public appeals. We've given the public a hell of a lot more than we usually give them, so why has it resulted in a big fat zero?"
"Perhaps he's not from York," Baldwin suggested. "It's possible he doesn't know anybody here."
"A loner," Smith mused.
"Sarge?"
"Thanks, Baldwin," Smith said. "You could be onto something there."
He smiled at her and walked off in the direction of the canteen.

Whitton and Bridge walked over.
"Where did Smith go?" Whitton asked Baldwin.
"Canteen probably," she said. "He's in one of his *Smith* moods again."
"You should be used to that by now," Bridge said. "Is everybody else here?"
"The DI hasn't arrived yet, but Harry and Kerry have been here since the crack of dawn."
The phone started to ring, and Whitton and Bridge left her to answer it.

Smith was sitting at his usual seat by the window when Whitton and Bridge came into the canteen. He was looking at something on his mobile phone.

Whitton sat next to him. "What are you looking at?"

"Mrs Lemon was spot on with her recital of St Rita's prayer," Smith said. "She spoke it word for word."

"What does it mean?" Bridge said.

"It's the loner's prayer," Smith told him. "And it's significant. We're looking for a loner."

"It should be right up your alley then," Bridge pointed out. "It might take a loner to catch a loner."

"I'm not a loner."

"If you say so." It was Whitton.

"It makes sense," Smith carried on. "We've got a man who's killed four people in a very short space of time. We have no witnesses and that makes me think he's not known in the city. Nobody has come forward with any information about him, and I think that's because we're looking for someone who keeps themselves to themselves. He can plan his murders in peace. He doesn't have to run the risk of a friend or family member stumbling across something incriminating because he doesn't have any friends or family. He lives alone and he socialises with nobody."

"Where do we even start to look for someone like that?" Bridge said.

"We don't," Smith said.

"We don't look for him?"

"It would be pointless," Smith said. "We concentrate our efforts elsewhere. Why is he the way he is? Why has he shut himself off from society? Something probably happened to him to make him that way. Humans as a species are a sociable bunch. It's not natural to want to be alone all the time."

"I hate to stop you in your tracks when you're clearly on a roll," Whitton said. "But there's nothing to confirm he is actually some kind of loner. He could have friends and family for all we know. It's possible he might just be very good at keeping his activities secret."

"No," Smith disagreed. "That prayer means something to him. Why recite a prayer associated with loners if it's not significant?"

"Do we know if he spoke the words of the prayer before, during or after the murder?" Bridge said.

"He said it afterwards," Smith said. "It's the only possible explanation."

"I agree on that," Whitton said. "His victims would start to smell a rat if he spoke the words before he carried out the murders."

"And that means he sticks around," Smith said. "Most killers get the hell away when the deed is done. This one doesn't – he recites a prayer, and that's risky. That prayer is extremely important to him, and that's where our focus needs to be."

"Don't you think it's weird that he killed someone whose mother just happened to be familiar with his prayer?" Bridge put forward. "I suppose it could just boil down to coincidence."

He looked at Smith, expecting a reaction. He didn't get one.

"Mrs Lemon is very religious," Smith said. "I'm not. It's possible that prayer is known to a lot of people. We need to look into it."

DC Moore burst into the canteen. He was out of breath, and he was very red in the face.

"Have you been out for a morning run, Harry?" Smith asked him.

"We've got another victim, Sarge," DC Moore panted.

"Take a few deep breaths," Whitton said.

DC Moore breathed in deeply and waited a moment.

"A woman," he said. "She was out for a morning stroll when she was attacked."

"Attacked how?" Bridge said.

"She was dragged into the bushes and stabbed, Sarge," DC Moore said. "But someone saw the whole thing."

"Is she OK?" Whitton asked.

"She's in a bad way," DC Moore said. "But she's still alive. He was interrupted, Sarge. A passer-by rushed in and caught him in the act."

Smith got to his feet.

"This is the break we've been waiting for. So far, we haven't been able to find a single witness, and now we have two."

CHAPTER TWENTY EIGHT

Vixmead Greens was a small park just east of Middlethorpe. Smith had never been to this part of the city before. The park was no more than a number of fields surrounded by trees. It was within these trees that the killer Smith had secretly dubbed *The Loner* had lain in wait for his fifth victim.

Her saviour was a young man out for a run. He was close by when he heard a muffled cry. He arrived just in time to witness the woman being dragged into the trees and he'd rushed to help her without giving it a second thought. The attacker fled in the direction of Middlethorpe Hall, and the man had let him go. He was more concerned with the woman. He'd called an ambulance and the police had been informed. The first officers arrived on the scene ten minutes later.

Smith and DC King walked towards the police cars parked on the field. DC King wasn't sure if her little Honda would be able to handle the terrain and she'd parked at the side of the dirt road at the entrance to the park. Whitton and Bridge had gone to the hospital where the woman had been taken. Early indications were, she'd been stabbed in the chest, but it was still unclear how serious her injuries were.

Smith experienced a brief feeling of déjà vu when they got closer to the cars. PC Griffin was standing next to one of them. He was bent over the bonnet, writing something in a notebook.

"That bloke is really starting to piss me off, Kerry," Smith said.

"I get a bad vibe from him," DC King said. "I don't know what it is about the man, but he gives me the creeps."

"He's a nasty piece of work. I saw that the moment I laid eyes on him."

"Don't look now, but he's seen us and he's coming over."

PC Griffin intercepted them before they'd reached the police cars.

"PC Black and I were the first responders," he said to Smith.

He didn't even acknowledge DC King.

"Good for you," Smith said. "Has Webber been informed?"

"Of course. It was the first thing I did before securing the scene."

"Where's the man who scared off the attacker?" DC King asked.

PC Griffin looked her up and down. "I don't believe we've been introduced."

"Come on, Kerry," Smith said. "We're wasting time here."

He walked off, leaving a wide-mouthed PC Griffin in his wake. DC King followed after him.

Smith made a beeline for PC Black.

"What do we know?" he asked him.

"Morning, Sarge," PC Black said. "A man out for a run caught the bloke in the act. He heard her moaning and he saw her being dragged into the trees."

"Do we know how she's doing?" DC King said.

"I haven't heard anything back from the hospital, but the bloke who found her reckons there was a lot of blood."

"Where is he?" Smith said.

"I thought it was best to stick him in the back of one of the cars," PC Black said. "PC Griffin was giving him a hard time."

"PC Griffin has got a lot to learn."

"What's his problem, Sarge? He acts like he's running the show."

"Unfortunately, he probably will be in a few years' time," Smith said. "The rubberneckers are starting to arrive. Can you make sure they don't contaminate the scene?"

"Will do, Sarge."

They found the man who'd interrupted the attack, in the police car parked closest to the river and when Smith saw who it was, he did a double take. It was Gary Lewis. The hero of the day was the brother of Lucy's boyfriend. Gary was a petty criminal and he'd had a few run ins with the police over the years, but there was also another side to him. Smith had witnessed it first-hand. A woman had been murdered earlier in the year and Gary hadn't hesitated to rush to her aid. He hadn't thought twice about intervening when he realised she was in trouble. Unfortunately he'd been too late in that instance. Smith hoped this time would be different.

"Gary," he said. "Could you step out of the car, please."
Gary obliged. "That has to be the first time I've been asked to step *out* of a police car."
"Do you two know each other?" DC King said.
"It's a long story," Smith said. "Are you alright, Gary? Do you have any injuries?"
Gary shook his head. "The bastard legged it as soon as I got there. I probably could have caught him, but I was more worried about the woman."
"You did the right thing," Smith said. "Can you talk us through what happened."
"I was out for a run," Gary said. "I'm training for the Great North Run in September. I prefer to run on the paths around the river, and I was running past the stream when I heard this noise. It sounded like someone gasping for air. I went to see what was going on and I saw the woman getting dragged into the trees over there."
He pointed to the cluster of trees and the bushes behind them.

"What did you do then?" Smith said.
"What do you think?" Gary said. "I went to help her. I ran in, but it was too late – she was covered in blood. Is she dead?"
"She was taken to hospital," DC King said. "She was badly injured, but she's still alive."
"You said the man ran off," Smith said. "What direction did he go in?"
"Towards Middlethorpe Hall," Gary said. "Like I said I probably could have

caught him, but I let him go and phoned for an ambulance."

"Did you get a good look at him?" Smith said. "Can you describe him?"

"He was tall, and he was quite skinny. Brown hair."

"Was there anything else you remember about him? What was he wearing?"

"A tracksuit and a hoodie. He looked like a normal bloke out for a run. I told the policeman all of this."

"I want you to work with a police artist," Smith said.

"Fine. Would it be possible…"

"We can arrange for it to be done at home," Smith interrupted. "I appreciate you're not a big fan of police stations."

"I've put all that behind me," Gary said. "I swear I have."

"Glad to hear it. You did a brave thing today. It's possible you might have saved that woman's life."

Gary shrugged his shoulders. "I'd do it again if I had to."

"Kerry," Smith said. "Could you find out if there's any news from the hospital."

"No problem, Sarge," DC King said.

She walked away and took out her phone.

"Have you got your car back yet?" Smith asked Gary.

"I was planning on fetching it later."

"Darren shouldn't have been driving."

"The little shit," Gary said. "It's a good job he stayed over with you. I wanted to kill him."

"He told you where he was?"

"He phoned me. He shouldn't have been arrested you know. I get that he doesn't have a license, but that was a bit over the top. The old man is mad as hell. He's talking about lodging a complaint."

"He'd be well within his rights to do so."

"Do you think it's worth a shot?"

"It was a minor offence," Smith said. "Darren is sixteen and he shouldn't have been arrested."

"I'll tell my dad you said that."

Smith nodded. "I'll arrange for an artist to come to you sometime this morning. It's vital we get it done while the events are still fresh in your head. Is there anything else you can remember about this man?"

"It was all over pretty quick," Gary said. "I shouted out and he legged it. I hope the woman is going to be alright."

"Me too," Smith said. "I'll be in touch. And good luck with the training for the Great North Run."

Neither of them knew then that Gary's training was all in vain. The 2020 Great North Run wasn't going to happen. It would be one of many major events that would be cancelled that year.

Smith spotted DC King and made his way over to her. She was talking to someone on her phone. He watched as she ended the call and turned to face him. The expression on her face told a story of its own, and when she gave him a subtle shake of the head his heart felt like it had dropped further in his chest. The woman Gary Lewis had tried to rescue hadn't made it. *The Loner* had claimed his fifth victim.

CHAPTER TWENTY NINE

The Loner was finding it hard to think straight. All thoughts were obscured by the thick fog inside his head. He'd arrived home thirty minutes ago, and he hadn't stopped walking up and down since he got there. He'd already done half a dozen circuits of the house and he was still pacing the rooms without being able to stop.

He'd made a mistake. He'd made a terrible mistake, and he didn't know how to handle it. It wasn't supposed to be like that. The young woman took that walk every Sunday. Every week, she would spend the early hours of the Sabbath walking around the fields of Vixmead Greens and every time *The Loner* had observed her, she'd been alone. The man shouldn't have been there, and the consequences of his presence were going to be far reaching.

There wasn't time for modifications to be made. There wasn't enough time to re-plan, and it was making him feel sick. The interfering bastard in the park had disrupted what was meant to be. He had meddled in something that was none of his business. There hadn't been time to finish the job. The mark of the Christ hadn't been made, and the prayer of St Rita hadn't been spoken and that wouldn't do.

The Loner stopped in front of the mirror in the hallway. He observed his reflection in the glass and smashed his fist into it with such fury that his features shattered in front of his face. Just before his face was obliterated The Loner caught a glimpse of his eyes, staring back. They were fierce and green.

He needed help. He needed advice from someone who could help – someone who wouldn't judge. There was too much judgment in the world. He unlocked the door to the spare room and flicked up the light switch. The fluorescent globe flickered to life and lit up the only thing inside the room. *The Loner* regarded the chest freezer for a moment before retrieving the key from his pocket. He turned the key in the lock and lifted the lid. A crow shrieked outside the window. *The Loner* opened the curtains and saw it in the tree at the back of the garden. It was looking right at him – its black eyes stared unblinking, judging him. *The Loner* closed the curtains and turned his attention back to the freezer.

The police hadn't even bothered to check what was contained inside the freezer when they'd paid him a visit. After his parents disappeared and a busybody neighbour had pointed the finger of suspicion in his direction, they'd carried out a cursory check and left him in peace. Had they searched more thoroughly things would have been very different. *The Loner's* mother and father didn't look like they once had – they were now preserved in various freezer bags, but had the police stumbled across the contents of the chest freezer things would have turned out very differently indeed. The neighbour disappeared soon after that.

"Have you missed me?"

He wasn't sure if he was talking to his mother or his father. A year inside a freezer tended to distort the features somewhat. Their heads had been placed at the bottom of the freezer anyway. That was important.

"I have a problem."

The Loner went on to outline his predicament. He told his mum and dad what he'd managed to achieve in the last few days, and he also told them about the mistake he'd made in Vixmead Greens.

"The mark of Christ wasn't made," he said. "And she didn't hear the prayer."

The frozen pieces of his parents offered no comment on this.

"I need your advice," *The Loner* said, much louder than he intended.

"I need your help," he said in a softer tone.

He could feel his face heating up and something was changing inside his head.

"We'll say it together," he said. "Let's talk to Saint Rita together."

He placed both hands inside the freezer and closed his eyes. The skin on his fingers were drawn to the ice on the outside of the plastic bags containing his mother and father and he ignored the pain as the cold crept up his arms.

"So humble," he began.

He recited the prayer and his breathing slowed. The ice on the bags started to melt and the warmth spread throughout his body. He finished the *prayer of the loner* and closed the lid of the freezer. Nothing had changed though. He was calmer now, but he knew that if he looked into the shattered glass of the mirror a pair of green eyes would be staring back at him.

He slammed his hands down on the top of the freezer and let out a silent scream. The crow outside screamed too, but his yell was loud. *The Loner* left the spare room and went downstairs. He retrieved the crossbow from the cupboard in the kitchen and loaded a bolt. He returned to the spare room and shifted the curtain to the side. He opened the window wide and focused his attention on the crow. The black bird was mocking him, taunting him. Its coal-black eyes never left his.

The Loner took aim and fired. The crow didn't hear it until it was too late. The bolt hit it right between the eyes and it dropped silently to the ground.

* * *

"She just lost far too much blood."

DI Smyth looked at the faces of the detectives on the team. All of them looked utterly dejected. The woman who'd been attacked in Vixmead Greens had died shortly after arriving at the hospital. The medical experts had tried their best to bring her back, but the injuries to her chest were severe and it was estimated that she'd spilled more than half of the blood inside her. There was no way she was going to survive an attack like that.

"She was our only proper witness so far in the investigation," Bridge said. "She could have given us a description of him."

"We still have Gary Lewis," Smith reminded him.

"No offence," DC Moore said. "And I know he's the brother of your daughter's boyfriend, but he's hardly an upstanding citizen, is he?"

"What else would you call him, Harry? How else would you describe someone who realised a woman was in trouble and rushed to help her without thinking of his own safety? He didn't think twice. In my book that is a prime example of an upstanding citizen. The guy deserves a fucking medal."

"I just meant…"

"I know what you meant. He's been in trouble with the law a few times, so that makes him a menace to society. Well, you're so far of the fucking mark it isn't even funny."

"That's enough," DI Smyth said. "We're all a bit on edge right now, but this isn't helping. It's very possible Gary Lewis will be able to give us a better description of this man than the one we already have."

"What do we know about the victim?" Smith asked when he'd calmed down a bit.

"Sally Dean," Whitton said. "Twenty-four years old. Bridge and me met her parents at the hospital. They're devastated, as you can imagine."

"Her mother seemed to take it better than her dad," Bridge said. "We got a bit more out of Sally's mum. Apparently, she liked to go for a walk every Sunday morning. She worked six days a week in a shop and Sunday was the only day she had free."

"She preferred to walk alone," Whitton added. "And she tended to stick to the same route."

"He's been watching her," Smith decided. "The bastard has been watching her too, hasn't he?"

"It's highly likely he has," DI Smyth agreed. "All of the victims share one thing in common. They follow the same routine for certain aspects of their lives. Melissa Grange liked to unwind every Friday at the wine bar. She spent two hours there and walked the short distance home afterwards. Jennifer Wells worked nights and she always walked to work alone. Karen Salway walked her dog by Knapton every Saturday, and the latest victim, Sally Dean walked the paths in Vixmead Greens on Sunday mornings."

"You're forgetting Steven Lemon," Smith said. "Not only is he the only male victim, he's the only one that didn't follow a set routine."

"He brought his mother a cup of tea at six on the dot every day," Whitton reminded him.

"How would *The Loner* know this?"

"I agree," Bridge said. "Unless this psycho is a friend of Mr Lemon's, how would he know about the six o'clock cup of tea?"

"What did you call him?" DI Smyth said.

"What?" Smith said.

"Just now, you called him something."

"I called him *The Loner*, boss," Smith said. "Because that's precisely what he is. Our killer has stayed off the radar for so long because he doesn't have any family or friends. He's a loner."

CHAPTER THIRTY

Ralph Richards had been a familiar face at Full Sutton correctional facility for over a decade and a half. Ralph had seen his fair share of hardened criminals – he'd witnessed altercations between inmates that had ended badly, and he'd also experienced things much worse than that. Eighteen months ago, a man had arrived to start a six-month sentence for assault and something about him had sounded warning bells in Ralph the moment he laid eyes on the man.

He wasn't an imposing figure. He wasn't at all like some of the inmates who came to Full Sutton built like tanks and left the prison even more beefed up, but there was definitely something about him that unnerved the seasoned prison officer. He recalled one incident in particular. The inmate in question had been accused of stealing another man's cigarettes. He was brought into the office to discuss the matter and he'd vehemently denied it. He didn't even smoke, but that meant nothing to Ralph. Cigarettes were hard currency in a place like Full Sutton, and it was possible he'd taken them to exchange for something else.

Halfway through his questioning the man's whole demeanour began to change. He became agitated and, in hindsight Ralph realised he might have pushed him a bit too far. He admitted he probably did come down rather too hard on him. The inmate began to display signs that he might become aggressive – his body language changed, and his face began to flush. But it was his eyes that Ralph remembers from that day. His eyes didn't simply alert Ralph to the fact that he was extremely displeased with the accusations that were being thrown at him – they changed dramatically. They changed colour. When the inmate came inside the office, his eyes were green but by the end of the conversation they were deep blue.

Ralph had been following the developments in the murder investigation in York. He liked to keep abreast of ongoing investigations. He liked to be prepared for what he was likely to expect afterwards. A lot of the criminals brought to justice by York CID ended up as Ralph's problem. Many of them were shipped off to Full Sutton afterwards.

It was the public appeal that grabbed his attention most and he was wide awake when he watched the press liaison officer appeal to anyone who knew of any men whose eyes changed colour to contact York Police. Ralph took it straight to Barry Coleman. Barry was the custodial manager of Full Sutton correctional facility, and he was also an old friend and colleague of DCI Bob Chalmers.

* * *

Chalmers found Smith in his office. He was looking at something on his laptop.
"You're not paid to surf the Internet for porn."
"Afternoon, boss," Smith said without turning round. "I've never seen the point of Internet porn. Are you lost?"
"Cheeky bastard," Chalmers said. "Drop whatever it is your doing. You're coming with me."
This time Smith turned around. "Where are we going?"
"Road trip to Full Sutton. I've just got off the phone with an old friend and you're going to want to hear what he has to say."
"Can't he say it over the phone?"
"Probably," Chalmers said. "But I haven't seen Barry Coleman in months, and it gives me a great excuse to get out of here. The Super is doing my bloody head in with his lockdown crap. We'll go in my car if that's alright with you."
"No worries," Smith said. "The Sierra wouldn't start this morning anyway."

"How's your daughter doing?" Chalmers asked as they drove. "I heard she was rushed to hospital."

"She's been allowed to come home," Smith said. "It gave us quite a fright. She was bleeding but apparently it was something to do with the cervix opening in preparation for the birth. Sometimes it opens early. The doctor said she's going to be fine."

"That's good news. Are you ready? Are you ready to become a grandparent?"

"It doesn't sound right," Smith said. "I never expected to be a granddad in my thirties."

"It's funny how things turn out."

"What about you?" Smith said. "How is Mrs Chalmers?"

"She has good days and bad days," Chalmers said.

His wife had been diagnosed with breast cancer and she was determined to fight it naturally. The doctors had tried to persuade her to go the chemotherapy route, but Mrs Chalmers had refused.

"I still haven't got used to the new diet," Chalmers said. "But I told myself she wasn't going to go through this alone. If I have to forego a fry-up in the morning, so be it. You should see the concoctions we drink for breakfast. Green juice. Percolated toad springs to mind."

Smith laughed. "It sounds lovely. I must admit you're looking good on it."

"I feel good," Chalmers said. "Although I don't tell Mrs Chalmers that. When we've beaten this thing the first thing I'm going to treat myself to is a Full English. Tell me about the case. Where are we at with that?"

"Not as far as I'd like to be," Smith said. "This one is exceptional. He's killed a man and four women, and we have only one promising witness."

"That's very unusual," Chalmers stated the obvious.

"He's been watching his victims for a very long time. He knows their routines inside out, and he chooses them carefully. What is it Barry Coleman has to tell us?"

"It's not Barry," Chalmers said. "It's one of the other prison officers. You've met him before. Ralph Richards."

"The fat bloke?"

"Very politically correct," Chalmers said. "But yes – he does have a bit of a weight problem."

A sign on the road told them that Full Sutton was half a mile further up the road and soon the grim building that housed some of the worst criminals in Yorkshire loomed up ahead. Chalmers slowed down and stopped by the side of the road.

"Why are you stopping here?" Smith asked him.

"Smoke," Chalmers said. "We won't be able to smoke inside the prison, and Mrs Chalmers won't let me smoke in the Beemer. I might have to subject myself to a rabbit food diet, but I'm buggered if I'm giving up the fags.

They got out of the car. Chalmers lit a cigarette and offered the pack to Smith.

He declined. "No offence, boss but your smokes smell like camel shit."

He lit one of his own.

"Are you going to catch this one?" Chalmers said.

"I'm going to do everything I can," Smith said.

"That's good enough for me. Do you need help?"

"As in extra bodies?"

"Something like that."

"I don't think it'll make any difference," Smith said. "Extra bodies are only useful when we've got something to put them to work on. Leads are a bit thin on the ground right now."

"Hopefully the lard arse prison officer can change that."

"Very politically correct."

"Let's get going," Chalmers said. "Barry is expecting us."

CHAPTER THIRTY ONE

Barry Coleman could have been Chalmers's brother. They were as unlike as possible in appearance – Chalmers was tall and lean, whereas Coleman was a short squat man, but if you closed your eyes you would have great difficulty telling them apart when they spoke. Smith imagined working with both of them would have been rather entertaining. They were Yorkshiremen through and through.

Coleman invited them into his office and offered them some coffee. Smith and Chalmers accepted his offer.

"How are things in the correctional services industry?" Chalmers asked.

He took a sip of his coffee and smiled. It was much better than the coffee from the machine at the station.

"Worse than ever," Coleman said. "I'm looking forward to the day they put me out to pasture. The scumbags have more rights than the prison officers these days. Can you believe we have to attend seminars on how to spot the warning signs of bullying. This country has gone soft. The scrotes shouldn't have broken the law in the first place if they didn't want to be bullied."

Smith realised that Barry Coleman hadn't changed a bit since he last saw him.

"What about you?" he asked. "How's life as a DCI treating you?"

"I'm on the same page as you," Chalmers said. "I'll not be sorry to see the back of York CID."

"He doesn't mean that," Smith said.

"I bloody well do," Chalmers said. "I believe Ralph came to you about a man whose eyes change colour when he's agitated."

"I'll give him a buzz," Coleman said.

He picked up a phone and asked Ralph Richards to come to his office.

The portly prisoner officer hadn't changed much either. If anything, Smith thought he looked like he'd put on even more weight. They greeted one another and Ralph managed to squeeze into one of the chairs around the desk.

"I saw it on the evening news," he said. "A public appeal asking anyone if they knew of any men whose eyes changed colour."

"And you know someone who fits the bill?" Smith said.

"I'll never forget him. He gave me the willies the moment he was brought in. There was something about him that really creeped me out."

"Who is he?" Chalmers asked.

"His name is Levi Wright."

"What was he in for?" Smith said.

"Assault," Ralph said. "He was sentenced to a six-month stretch, but he got out after three. Good behaviour, would you believe."

"Are you sure his eyes changed colour?" Smith said.

"It's one of those things you never forget," Ralph said. "I've been a prison officer here for over fifteen years. I've seen my fair share of drama, but this was in another league altogether. Another inmate accused him of nicking his fags. Levi denied it of course. He would, wouldn't he? The other bloke wanted it put on record, so we had no choice but to go through the motions. Levi was questioned and it was during that interrogation that it happened. I've never seen anything like it before."

"What colour are his eyes?" Smith said.

"Green, and they changed to blue when he got agitated. In hindsight, I might have been a bit hard on him."

"You were as hard as was necessary," Coleman said.

"Do you have his file?" Smith asked.

"Of course," Coleman said. "And I took the liberty of making a copy for you."

"Thank you. I appreciate it."

Coleman handed it to him, and Smith opened it up. He'd brought along the artist sketches made from the descriptions given by the resident of Melissa Grange's flat and the waitress from the wine bar. He took these out and lay them on the table.

"I suppose there are some similarities between them," Chalmers said. The photograph of Levi Wright was a typical police mug shot. It depicted a wild-eyed man staring directly at the camera. Smith looked carefully at it and then he scrutinised the artist's impressions. The lips of the man in the mug shot were fuller, and the eyes narrower but the shape of the nose was the same.

"Do you remember his height and build?" Smith asked.
"He was tall like you," Ralph said. "And slim. Do you think this is your man?"
"It's very possible. Where was he arrested?"
"Bramham," Coleman said.
"Why didn't he serve his time in Armley in Leeds?" Chalmers said.
"Leeds was full. It's always overcrowded, so he was brought here to Full Sutton."
"Do you know the details of the assault?" Smith said.
"Only the bare minimum," Coleman said. "You'll have to speak to Leeds if you need any more info."
"We'll do that. Can you remember anything else about this Levi Wright. You said he was released after only serving three months."
"Apart from the cigarette incident," Coleman said. "He was a model prisoner. Never caused any trouble."
"He was cleared of nicking the fags anyway," Ralph Richards said. "I think that's why he got so rattled when he was accused. Another inmate owned up and the whole thing was forgotten about."
"And Levi Wright kept his nose clean?" Smith said.

"He stayed in the background," Coleman said. "Kept himself to himself."
"Was he friends with any of the other prisoners?" Smith said.
"Now you ask, no. He always ate on his own and he rarely socialised with the others in the yard. He was a solitary soul. A real loner."

CHAPTER THIRTY TWO

"A loner," Smith said.

He'd asked Chalmers if he minded making a slight detour to Bramham on the way back to the station. Chalmers had explained that Bramham was thirty miles west of York, but he'd gladly agreed, nevertheless. The more time he could spend away from Superintendent Smyth the better.

"It's him," Smith said.

"Don't get ahead of yourself," Chalmers said. "We don't know that yet."

"Come on, boss," Smith said. "How much more do you need? His eyes change colour with his mood. He's a loner – our killer recites St Rita's prayer after killing his victims. She's the patron saint of loners. Levi Wright is our guy."

"Are you finally going to trade in that old banger of yours?" Chalmers changed the subject.

"Nope," Smith said. "There's still life in the Sierra yet."

"You've had that piece of scrap metal since I met you. And it was a piece of scrap metal even back then."

"There is nothing wrong with that car," Smith insisted.

"Besides the fact that it doesn't work."

"It's probably something simple. I'll ask Darren's brother to take a look at it. Gary is pretty clued up where cars are concerned."

"Gary Lewis?"

"That's the one."

"Frank Lewis's kid?"

"What about it?"

"Associating with the criminal fraternity is generally frowned upon in the job," Chalmers said.

"Frank Lewis is hardly a criminal mastermind," Smith pointed out. "He's a petty thief and a fence. He hasn't been in trouble for months."

"A leopard doesn't change its spots. Just be careful. And I'd keep an eye on your kid's boyfriend too. The apple doesn't usually fall far from the tree."

"You need to ease off on your idioms, boss," Smith said. "You're turning into a cliché."

"Cheeky bastard. I'm just giving you a friendly warning. Once a criminal – always a criminal."

"Speaking of criminals," Smith said. "Darren was arrested yesterday." Chalmers slowed down a bit. "Are you serious?"

"He came to pick Lucy up in his brother's car and he was stopped because of a faulty rear light. When they found out he's only sixteen, he was arrested for driving without a license and insurance."

"You're taking the piss, aren't you?"

"I'm not," Smith said. "It was a new bloke. PC Griffin is his name and the officer who was with him at the time told me Griffin did it as soon as my name was mentioned. Darren told PC Griffin who his girlfriend's dad was, and the other PC said this made Griffin determined to make an example of the kid."

"I haven't had the pleasure of this PC Griffin," Chalmers said.

"You've met plenty of his type. Career officers, straight out of university. He'll no doubt be an inspector in a few years. But he's bad news for the job. The DI warned me to keep away from him, but someone needs to show the prick how it works in this job."

"The DI could have a point," Chalmers said. "This Griffin berk sounds like someone who won't hesitate to cause trouble if it's within what's written in the guidelines. Stay away from him, and do not wind him up."

"I can't promise anything."

After being told by the bored-looking man behind the desk at Bramham police station that they were in the wrong place, Chalmers and Smith headed west to Leeds. According to the old PC the case with Levi Wright was dealt with by the officers there. Leeds Police headquarters was situated in a modern building a stone's throw from the football stadium on Elland Road. Chalmers found a spot in the car park and turned off the engine.

"It's been a while since I was in this neck of the woods," he said.

"What brought you to Leeds Police HQ? Smith asked.

"It wasn't work related. I came to Elland Road to watch the Minstermen get walloped by Leeds a few years back."

"Football?"

Chalmers sighed. "How long have you lived in York?"

"I've never seen the point of football. Grown men in shorts kicking a ball around doesn't really appeal to me."

"I give up."

They got out of the car, and Chalmers took out his cigarettes and lit one. Smith did the same.

"I've got a feeling we're getting closer," he said. "Levi Wright is our man. He's *The Loner*."

"If he is," Chalmers said. "He's made a massive leap in a very short space of time. The assault can't have been serious if he was out within three months. Why has he suddenly decided to kill five people?"

"I think he's been planning this for years," Smith said. "This didn't just happen overnight. He's been working up to it for a very long time, and that's why he's got away with it. Is someone expecting us?"

"Barry Coleman has a lot of clout here. I spoke to him while you were talking to the old fossil in Bramham, and he's paved the way for us. We need to speak to someone called Hatfield. She's a sergeant and she was working here when Levi Wright was brought in."

Smith's phone started to ring in his pocket. The ringtone told him it was DI Smyth. He let it go to voicemail.

"Aren't you going to see who that is?" Chalmers said.

"It's the DI," Smith told him.

"How do you know that?"

"He has his own ringtone. *Oliver's Army*. It's an Elvis Costello song."

"Oliver's Army," Chalmers said. "I like that. It's very apt."

He stubbed out his cigarette and looked at Smith.

"You did tell the DI where you were going, didn't you?"

"You abducted me so quickly," Smith said. "I didn't get the chance."

"You're such an idiot sometimes."

"I'll give him a call when we're finished here."

CHAPTER THIRTY THREE

"Does anybody know where Smith went?" DI Smyth asked the four people sitting round the table in the canteen.

It was Whitton, Bridge, DC King and DC Moore.

"He was in his office the last time I saw him," Bridge said.

"He wanted to do some research into Saint Rita," Whitton said. "He wanted to find out more about the loner's prayer."

"Well he's not there now," DI Smyth said. "And he's not answering his phone."

"He's probably off on another of his lone wolf missions," Bridge said. "This *Loner* case is starting to get to him. It's starting to consume him."

"If anyone can catch a loner it's Smith," DC King said. "It takes one to know one and all that."

"If anyone hears from him," DI Smyth said. "I want to know. What's the next plan of action?"

"We were hoping you would tell us, sir," DC Moore said. "We're a bit stuck."

"We've got nothing from Forensics," Whitton said. "No fingerprints, fibres, nothing. There was nothing at any of the scenes that can help us. All we know from Pathology is how the victims were killed and how he mutilated them."

"The only promising witness is Gary Lewis," Bridge added. "And he only got a brief look at the man. His description ties in with what the other eyewitnesses have told us, but it still doesn't give us much to go on. We know the victims aren't connected in any way so talking to their families and friends isn't going to give us anything. I really don't know where to look next."

A phone beeped and DI Smyth took it out of his pocket. He'd received a message. He opened it up and read it.

"That's interesting," he said.

"What is it?" Whitton said.

"That was Dr Bean," DI Smyth said. "He's scheduled the post-mortem on the latest victim for this afternoon, but he gave her a quick once-over when she was brought in. Sally Dean died due to massive blood loss – that's pretty clear, but that's not the interesting part. Dr Bean could find no indication that Sally had any lacerations like the others. The only wound Dr Bean found was the stab wound that killed her."

"He was interrupted," DC King said. "He was stopped before he could cut her."

"If we follow the pattern Smith suggested," Whitton said. "Sally Dean ought to have been cut somewhere on her back. There were six locations of the wounds of Christ on the cross – the head, hands, wrist, feet, back and chest, and so far all the victims have been subjected to these wounds. But *The Loner* didn't get the chance to finish the job with Sally. Gary Lewis interrupted him."

"What difference does it make?" DC Moore said. "She's still dead."

"Smith thinks the wounds are important to him," DC King said. "As is the *loner's prayer*. It's possible this is going to rattle him. He doesn't kill for the fun of it. The murders mean something to him, and the rituals of the wounds and the prayer are instrumental in his plan."

"You're talking gibberish," DC Moore said.

"Kerry's right," Whitton said. "The ritual is important to him."

"I still don't see how it's relevant to the investigation," DC Moore wasn't budging. "He didn't get the chance to finish what he started, so what? What's he going to do about it now?"

"I suppose Harry's right," Bridge said. "It's pointless dwelling on it."

* * *

Dr Bean was taking a well-earned break in his office. He'd recently bought a new coffee machine and he was looking forward to sampling one of the blends that came with the machine. He selected a strong espresso and inserted the capsule into the slot. He pressed the button to start it up and nothing happened. He checked to see if it was plugged in and realised that it was. He couldn't understand why the coffee machine wasn't working. He removed the capsule and reinserted it, but the light on the front still didn't come on.

"Damn you, modern technology."

He glared at the coffee machine and left the office. One of his assistants was very tech-savvy and she would be able to tell him what he was doing wrong. Sarah Monk had been tasked with the job of cleaning down the autopsy room. Everything inside the room needed to be disinfected. The table and floor had to be scrubbed down, as did the cameras, laptop and the instruments used in the examination of the body. It was a particularly unpleasant job, but it had to be done. Dr Bean was due to perform the postmortem on the body of Sally Dean in an hour and there could be nothing inside the room that could compromise the examination.

He was halfway to the autopsy room when he heard a scream. It sounded like it came from a woman, and it sounded like she was in the mortuary freezer room. Dr Bean had no idea why someone would be in there. He headed straight for it and another scream filled the air when he reached the outer door. He pushed it open and shivered. The temperature in here was at least twenty degrees cooler than in the corridor.

Sarah Monk was backed up in the corner of the room and she wasn't alone. A man was standing stock still in front of her. He was wearing an identical lab coat to hers.

"What is going on in here?" Dr Bean said.

The man turned around and Dr Bean took a step back. The knife he was holding was long and the serrated blade looked extremely sharp.

"What do you want?" Dr Bean said.

"Sally Dean."

The man took a step closer. Dr Bean took another step back.

"Sally Dean," the man repeated. "Where is she?"

"I'm calling security," Dr Bean told him.

The man fixed his green eyes on him and turned around. Before Dr Bean could stop him, the knife was against Sarah's throat. A trickle of blood ran down her neck.

"Alright," Dr Bean said. "Sally Dean is in there."

He pointed to one of the compartments a few feet to his left.

"Open it," the man ordered.

Dr Bean did as he was asked.

"Now stand in the corner with her."

"Are you alright?" Dr Bean asked Sarah.

She was holding her hand to her neck. The wound wasn't deep, but the blood was still flowing.

"He just pushed me in here," Sarah whispered.

The mystery man had opened the freezer compartment, and he was bent over the lifeless body of Sally Dean. She was on her back and her frozen eyes were staring straight up. Dr Bean watched as she was turned onto her side, and he winced as the knife carved an incision into her back.

"So humble..."

Dr Bean and Sarah were forced to listen to the prayer in its entirety. Later, the Head of Pathology would describe it as the most terrifying moment of his life.

When he was finished the stranger in the lab coat turned to look in Dr Bean's direction. His facial expression was one of utter calm. His eyes looked serene but there was something very wrong about them. They were no longer green – Dr Bean was forced to look away from the blue eyes that were boring holes in his head.

CHAPTER THIRTY FOUR

Sergeant Penny Hatfield was a short woman with friendly eyes. Smith thought she looked to be in her late-forties, perhaps early fifties and the smile she gave him when they were introduced was a genuine one. She'd been informed of the nature of their visit, and she was well prepared. She led them to a small office and asked them if they would like something to drink. Smith and Chalmers both declined the offer.

"I've been following the case on the Internet," she said.
"We've been a lot more open with information," Smith said. "We've given the press much more than we usually do."
"Sometimes it's the general public who are our biggest asset."
"You're not wrong there," Chalmers said. "What can you tell us about Levi Wright?"
"I took a look through the case files when I heard you were coming," Sergeant Hatfield said. "Just to refresh my memory, and there really isn't much to tell. Mr Wright was arrested in Bramham. It's a town about five miles from here."
"He was arrested for assault, wasn't he?" Smith said.
"It was a typical pub brawl. Nothing unusual about it."
"But he did time for it." Chalmers said.
"I wasn't expecting him to get jail time," Sergeant Hatfield said. "According to the arrest report Mr Wright got into a fight with another man outside the pub. He broke the man's nose, and he inflicted a few other, minor wounds. Mr Wright also sustained injuries, but they weren't as serious as the other bloke's."
"I'm surprised he went to prison for it," Smith said. "Did he have any previous convictions?"
"Nothing. He was squeaky clean before the assault. I heard later that it was

his behaviour in court that landed him a prison stretch."

"What happened?" Smith said.

"He rubbed the judge up the wrong way," Sergeant Hatfield said. "And you do not do that. He probably would have got off with a slap on the wrist and a fine, or maybe a bit of community service, but he really wound the judge up. He had a smirk on his face throughout and I think the judge made an example of him."

"He was out after three months," Chalmers said. "Good behaviour."

"That figures."

"What was he like?" Smith said. "Can you remember what he was like?"

"I recall he was quite a charmer," Sergeant Hatfield said. "And he was cooperative and polite the whole time."

"When did the assault take place?" Chalmers said.

"Around eighteen months ago. I remember it was just after I became a grandparent for the first time."

"You don't look old enough to be a grandmother," Smith said.

Chalmers snorted. It went unnoticed.

"I've got two of them now," Sergeant Hatfield said. "A grandson and a granddaughter."

"Do you still have his details on file?" Smith asked. "We need his address."

"Of course," Sergeant Hatfield said. "I have to say this though – he didn't give me the impression he was capable of murder."

"Murderers are often difficult to spot," Smith said. "I've learned that the hard way."

"There is something you might be interested in," Sergeant Hatfield said. "Not long after he was released from prison, we got a call from the man who lived next door to him. He was convinced Mr Wright had killed his parents."

"Why would he think that?" Chalmers said.

"He told us they'd disappeared. One day they were there and then they were gone."

"Did you take him seriously?" Smith said.

"We had no choice. Hold on."

She got up and left the room without offering an explanation.

"I thought you were the only one who did that," Chalmers said.

"Did what?" Smith said.

"The *hold on* thing," Chalmers said. "Leaving you wondering what the hell you're thinking. I bet you she says things like, *I'll let you know when I've figured it out* too."

"I like her."

"Of course you do," Chalmers said. "She's a female version of you. She's even a grandparent."

"I know you're the superior officer here, boss," Smith said. "But fuck right off."

Sergeant Hatfield returned with a young officer in uniform.

"This is PC Dewbury. He was one of the officers who attended the call out to Mr Wright's house."

PC Dewbury looked at Smith and his mouth opened wide. "You're Detective Smith."

"Well spotted," Smith said.

"I've been a fan of yours for years, Sarge. I want to get a spot in CID. I want to be just like you."

"God help us all." It was Chalmers.

"You went out to Levi Wright's house," Smith said. "Because the neighbour suspected he'd killed his mother and father. Why did the neighbour think this?"

"He just said one minute they were there," PC Dewbury said. "And then they were gone."

"What did Levi Wright have to say about this?"

"He said he didn't know where they were. He came home one day, and they were gone. Some of their belongings were missing and it seems they'd taken their passports too."

"But he didn't mention whether they were planning on going away?" Chalmers said.

"He did say something about them talking about it," PC Dewbury said. "He said his dad was always talking about how much the weather was getting him down, and he wanted to go somewhere warmer, so we assumed that's what they'd done."

"Did you check inside the house?" Chalmers said.

"We did, sir. And there was nothing in there to suggest anything untoward had taken place. No sign of a struggle, nothing. The neighbour kept calling, and one day the calls suddenly stopped. There wasn't much more we could do. Nothing suggested that Mr Wright had done anything wrong, and it looked like the neighbour had realised he was being a bit melodramatic. He did tell us he wasn't happy about living next door to a convicted criminal. That's probably what made him overreact a bit. Mr Wright's parents are probably sitting on a beach somewhere warm, end of story."

"We're going to need his address," Smith said.

"Of course," Sergeant Hatfield said. "I don't know if he still lives in his parents' house though."

"Wasn't he on license when he was released?" Chalmers asked. "He'd have to inform his supervising officer about a change of address if he was on license."

"He was, but only for three months. He's no longer obliged to inform his supervising officer of his movements."

Sergeant Hatfield wrote the address on a piece of paper and handed it to Smith.

"This is in Tadcaster," Smith said. "How far is it from Tadcaster to York?"

"Fifteen miles, max," Chalmers said.

"An easy commute then."

"What are you thinking?"

"I'll let you know when I've figured it out," Smith said.

PC Dewbury started to giggle.

"Is something funny, son?" Chalmers said.

"Sorry, sir," PC Dewbury said. "But I thought Sergeant Hatfield was the only one who said that."

Chalmers smiled at Smith. "What did I tell you?"

CHAPTER THIRTY FIVE

Whitton had never seen Kenny Bean so distraught. She'd known the amiable Head of Pathology for years now and his demeanour rarely changed. Even when he was dealing with the grisly aftermath of a brutal murder, he remained upbeat, but now he looked like a man on the verge of tears. His face was deathly pale, and his eyes were devoid of expression. Whitton and Bridge were sitting with Dr Bean and Sarah Monk in his office. The Head of Pathology had figured out the coffee machine but the espresso he'd been so looking forward to was growing cold on the desk in front of him. Sarah had a bandage around her neck.

"How are you feeling?" Whitton asked.

"Numb," Dr Bean said. "I thought I'd seen everything but clearly I was wrong. That was truly evil."

"I thought he was going to kill me," Sarah said.

"Can you talk us through what happened?" Bridge said.

"I was on my way to the canteen to grab something for lunch," Sarah said. "When the man stopped me and asked where the cold room was."

"Had you seen this man before?" Whitton asked.

"Never. He said he was new, and he'd been told to meet the Head of Pathology in the cold room. I smelled a rat straight away. He was wearing a lab coat, but I knew he didn't work here. I know everybody who works here, and nobody calls it the cold room."

"What happened then?" Bridge said.

"He took out a knife," Sarah said. "He said if I made a sound, he would slit my throat. He said it so calmly, but he said it in a way that made me believe him. He told me to walk slowly to the *cold* room and he followed close behind. When we got there, he shoved me inside. That was when I screamed."

Dr Bean placed a hand on her shoulder. "It's alright. It's over now."
"He told me to stand in the corner of the room," Sarah continued. "And he asked me where Sally Dean was. I didn't know. I didn't know which compartment she was in, but he didn't believe me. He thrust the knife in front of my face, and I screamed again. That's when Dr Bean came in."
"I couldn't work out my new coffee machine," Dr Bean said. "So I came looking for Sarah. I knew she'd be able to help. I heard the screams and that's how I ended up in the freezer room."

"He kept asking where Sally Dean was," Sarah said. "Dr Bean threatened to call security, and that's when he cut my neck."
She rubbed the bandage on her throat.
"I had no choice but to tell him which compartment Sally was in," Dr Bean said. "He told me to stand with Sarah and then he mutilated the corpse."
"He made an incision in her back, didn't he?" Whitton said.
"How did you know that?" Sarah asked.
"It's part of his ritual. He makes a mark corresponding to one of the wounds Jesus suffered on the cross then he recites the loner's prayer. We believe the ritual is of paramount importance to him, but he was interrupted before he could carry it out with Sally Dean. The prayer is a big part of that ritual."
"That was the bit that spooked me the most," Dr Bean said. "The words were completely at odds with his actions. *So humble, so pure, so patient*. It was absolute madness."
"His eyes changed colour," Sarah said. "I've never seen that happen to anyone before."
"They change when he's excited," Bridge told her. "They change from green to blue after he's killed."
"I'm never going to forget that," Sarah said. "I'm going to have nightmares about that for years."
"We're going to catch him," Whitton said. "I promise you we will catch him."

"Did you see which direction he headed in when he left the freezer room?" Bridge said.

Sarah shook her head.

"I think we were in shock," Dr Bean said. "We weren't paying much attention."

"It's OK," Whitton said. "That's OK. The hospital has CCTV, doesn't it?"

"There are cameras in the busy areas," Dr Bean said. "And there is CCTV outside too."

"I'll see if I can find someone to help you," Sarah offered.

She stood up.

"Someone else can do that," Bridge told her. "You've been through a terrible ordeal."

"I don't mind," Sarah said. "It would be better to have something to do, otherwise I'd just end up mulling over what happened."

"Thank you," Whitton said. "It's very possible one of those cameras will give us a better idea of what he looks like."

"He was so calm," Dr Bean said when Sarah had left the room. "So calm and in complete control. I got the impression he was a man with nothing to lose."

"What do you mean?" Bridge said.

"It's hard to explain. He was absolutely driven by what he came here to do, and nothing was going to get in his way."

"He was taking a big chance coming here today," Whitton said. "And he's deviated from his usual MO. In all of the murders he's made absolutely sure he's one step ahead the whole time. He's planned the murders taking everything into account. He watches his prey for months and he gets to know their routines."

"He hasn't made a single mistake," Bridge added. "We've never come across anyone like him before. He could quite easily have been caught today, and

I'm finding it hard to understand why he came here."

"I think I know the answer to that," Dr Bean said. "If you're right and he's motivated by the marks of Jesus on the cross it means he has one more to go."

"He's going to kill someone," Whitton said. "And he's going to carve up their chest."

"He had the perfect opportunity to do just that today," Dr Bean said.

"You or Sarah," Bridge guessed.

"That's right," Dr Bean confirmed. "He had us right where he wanted us. What was there to stop him from killing one of us right there in the freezer room today?"

CHAPTER THIRTY SIX

Levi Wright's house was a typical semi-detached property in a row of similar houses. Situated in the far east of Tadcaster the property had a bird's eye view of the viaduct and the River Wharfe from the upper floor. There was a car parked outside and Smith wondered if they were in luck. In his opinion Levi Wright was the man they were looking for – Levi was *The Loner*.

After ringing the bell a number of times, he realised there was nobody home, and when the door to the house next door opened and a man walked towards the car, he also knew the vehicle didn't belong to Levi Wright.

Smith walked up to him. He was a short man with a thin moustache.
"Can I have a word?" Smith said.
"Make it quick."
Smith showed him his ID. "We're looking for the man who lives next door."
"I wouldn't have a clue where he is."
The man told him his name was Brian and he'd only lived on the street for a couple of months.
"Do you know your neighbour well?" Chalmers asked.
"Not at all," Brian said. "I see him coming and going, but we've barely spoken two words since I moved here. Sometimes I don't see him for days."

Smith remembered what Sergeant Hatfield had told them about the neighbour suspecting Levi of killing his parents.
"Do you know the previous owners of your property?"
"I'm not following you," Brian said.
"The people who lived here about a year ago. Do you know them?"
"You'll have to ask the landlord about that."
"You're renting?" Chalmers said.
"It's not a crime, is it? I can't afford to buy a place."
"Do you have the contact details of the landlord?" Smith said.

"Of course."

Brian took out his phone and brought up a number. He showed it to Smith and Smith saved it to his own phone.

"Thank you. When did you last see your neighbour?"

"I heard him leave this morning," Brian said.

"What time was this?"

"Early. It was actually his car door slamming that woke me up. It must have been about seven."

"What car does he drive?" Chalmers said.

"A Ford Focus," Brian told him. "A black one."

Smith took out one of his cards and handed it to Brian.

"Can you give me a call the moment your neighbour comes home?"

"I'm off out to my sister's."

"That's fine," Smith said. "If the Ford Focus is here when you get back, call me."

"What's this all about? What has he done?"

"We're just very keen to talk to him," Chalmers said.

"Should I be concerned?" Brian asked.

"Not at all," Smith said.

Unless you're the last one on his list, he thought.

He kept this thought to himself.

"Can I go now?" Brian asked.

"Of course," Smith said. "Call me if you see your neighbour."

"What do you reckon?" Chalmers said.

"I reckon we need to organise a search of his house," Smith said.

"On what grounds? We're never going to get a warrant based on a feeling in your gut."

"It's more than that, boss. Levi Wright is our man. There are too many things pointing in his direction. We need to search the house. I'll break in if I have to."

"That is exactly what you're not going to do," Chalmers said. "All we need is for evidence to be thrown out because it was obtained illegally. We need to play this carefully."

"Let's see if the landlord can help us," Smith said. "He'll probably know more than someone who has only been living here a few months."

He didn't get the chance to call him. His phone started to ring as soon as he took it out of his pocket.

"It's Whitton," he told Chalmers.

He put it on speakerphone.

"Where are you?" Whitton asked.

"Tadcaster," Smith told her. "Me and Chalmers have been on a fact-finding mission. One of the prison officers at Full Sutton remembered a bloke whose eyes changed colour. That led us to Leeds, and an interesting chat with a lovely Sergeant there meant we ended up here."

"The DI was wondering where you'd got to."

"I was going to give him a ring."

"He finished what he started with Sally Dean," Whitton said.

"What?"

"At the mortuary. He held Dr Bean and his assistant hostage in the freezer room and made them watch as he cut Sally's back and recited his prayer."

"Is Kenny alright?" Smith said.

"He's a bit shaken up, but he'll be fine."

"How did he even get into the freezer room?"

"He threatened Dr Bean's assistant with a knife. He's moved up a gear. He was taking a massive risk going to the hospital, and I think he's going to take his final victim very soon. What's in Tadcaster?"

"Levi Wright's house. He's our man. Levi Wright is *The Loner*."

"Hold on," Whitton said. "The DI wants a word."

"If he insists."

"Where the hell have you been?" DI Smyth said.

"Long story, boss," Smith said.

He told DI Smyth about the road trip, and he outlined his suspicions about Levi Wright.

"Are you absolutely sure about this?" DI Smyth said when Smith was finished.

"Almost positive," Smith said. "It all fits. None of the appeals have given us anything because the bloke doesn't live in York. He has no friends, and he stays off the radar. We need to find him."

"What else do we know about him?"

"Hardly anything. And that's because he doesn't want us to know anything about him. But now we have a name, we can do some digging. He should be on the system somewhere. We know he did a three-month stint in Full Sutton so his details will be on record somewhere. We need to find him."

"OK," DI Smyth said. "I'll set the ball in motion."

"I want a warrant to search his house."

"On what grounds?"

"On the grounds that he's a serial killer," Smith said. "I reckon that ought to be enough."

"Hold your horses. First we find him, then we worry about a warrant."

"You're the boss."

"And don't you forget it. I assume you'll be coming back to York sometime today."

"On our way." It was Chalmers.

"Glad to hear it," DI Smyth said and ended the call.

Smith lit a cigarette and took a long drag.

"We're getting close."

"I think we are," Chalmers said.

"I just hope we're not too late," Smith added.

CHAPTER THIRTY SEVEN

"Why me?" DC Moore said and rubbed his eyes.
He was talking to himself. He was alone in one of the offices. Bridge's friend had gone to the art gallery and managed to retrieve the footage from the camera outside the entrance. Barry Stone had sent over the CCTV footage and DC Moore had been given the unenviable task of sifting through it to see if anything jumped out at him.

"Why is it always me who gets the shit jobs?"
Unfortunately for the man from London the file he'd been sent consisted of the footage from the past month, and DC Moore had only managed to get through the first couple of days. He still had a mammoth task ahead of him and he knew it was going to be an extremely long day.

He sipped his third cup of coffee and resumed watching. He reckoned he would see the street outside the art gallery when he closed his eyes to go to sleep that night.

People came and went. Night morphed into day and then the sun disappeared again. It rained – the wind blew, and the sun made another appearance, but after watching the screen for over two hours DC Moore hadn't seen anyone who matched the description of the man they were looking for.

On Friday 21st February something caught his eye, and he paused the footage. At just after four in the afternoon a man and a woman walked past. DC Moore took a closer look at their faces and decided he'd been right to pause the footage. He didn't recognise the man, but the woman was very familiar now. She'd been featured in the news a lot recently. It was Melissa Grange, alive and well.

She appeared again, a week later with a different man. On the 28th of February she walked arm in arm with a man who appeared to be a lot older than her. It was almost five pm this time.

"She liked to pick up men at the wine bar," DC Moore decided.

He wondered if the killer they were looking for was aware of this.

He carried on watching. It was getting late in the afternoon and the man Smith had dubbed *The Loner* didn't make another appearance. DC Moore wondered if he'd made allowances for this exact scenario. It was possible he knew they would look at the previous footage and it was also possible to see the camera without actually being caught by it. He could have spotted it from the opposite side of the street.

DC Moore carried on watching, regardless. Melissa Grange didn't walk past on Friday 6th March, but it was plausible that she didn't go to Welburn's Wine Bar on that day. She was back a week later with yet another man, but there was still no sign of their loner.

DC Moore admitted defeat and went to inform DI Smyth that it had been a wasted six hours. He found him inside his office. Smith was sitting opposite him.

"Melissa Grange liked to pick up men at the wine bar," DC Moore said. "She passed the art gallery on three different occasions, and each time she was with a different man."

"*The Loner* was aware of this," Smith said.

"Will you stop calling him that," DI Smyth said.

"It's what he is, boss. Why didn't anyone mention the fact that Melissa brought men back to her apartment after leaving the wine bar? It's important."

"Perhaps they didn't want to speak ill of the dead," DC Moore suggested.

"Did you get any more footage of the killer?" DI Smyth asked.

"Not a sausage," DC Moore said. "I think he's one step ahead of us. Anyone who watches CSI knows that the police go back and check what I've spent most of the day checking. And the CCTV camera is clearly visible from the other side of the road. You can see it without getting caught on camera."

"What about the bloke who works at the art gallery?" Smith said. "He said he thought he recognised the man with Melissa Grange on Friday."

"The manager of the gallery can't get hold of him," DC Moore said. "He went home sick yesterday, and he's not answering his phone. He probably went to bed and switched it off."

"We got a possible lead from the hospital," DI Smyth said. "One of the nurses remembered a man acting suspiciously, exiting the hospital just after the time Dr Bean and his assistant were held hostage. He was wearing a lab coat, but the nurse said he was in a hell of a hurry to get out. We'll have the CCTV footage from there within the hour. Hopefully it'll give us a better idea of what he looks like."

"We know what he looks like, boss," Smith said. "We've got his mug shot from when he was arrested."

"We still can't be certain it is Levi Wright."

"It's him. I know it's him. What's the progress with the search warrant for his house?"

"We still don't have enough to justify it with the CPS."

"What more do they need?" Smith said. "He matches the descriptions we've got, and his eyes change colour when he's agitated."

"It's still not enough."

"Levi Wright is our man. I haven't heard back from his neighbour in Tadcaster, and I'm starting to wonder if he knows he's been busted."

"How could he possibly know that?" DC Moore asked.

"Because he's in complete control, Harry. I've never come across a killer who has so many contingency plans in place. There will be something in that house in Tadcaster that will lead us to him."

"You've just contradicted yourself," DI Smyth pointed out. "If he has a contingency plan for every eventuality surely, he will leave nothing behind at his house to incriminate him."

"My brain hurts," Smith said. "We've been outsmarted before, but never like this. He's going to kill again. He has one more person on his list and that person is going to die very soon unless we come up with something."

"It's quite possible he's going to lie low for a while," DI Smyth said. "If he suspects we're aware of who he is he might feel it's too risky to carry out the final murder."

"He has to do it before the lockdown regulations come into effect," Smith argued. "And his little stunt at the mortuary proves he's not averse to a bit of risk when it becomes necessary. Someone is going to lose their life soon if we don't find him."

"What's everyone else up to?" DC Moore said.

"Whitton and Baldwin have gone to see the man who owns the house next door to Levi Wright's," DI Smyth said. "He owns a few properties in Tadcaster, but he lives in York. Bridge is tracking down Levi Wright's supervising officer, and I've asked Kerry to go back to the beginning to see if there's anything we've missed."

"Clutching at straws then," Smith decided.

"Do you have any better suggestions?"

"A search warrant for *The Loner*'s house would be a good start."

"I give up."

"That makes two of us," Smith said. "I'll be outside having a smoke if anybody needs me."

Smith had barely made it outside to the car park when he was pounced on by a very red-faced PC Griffin.

"You're going to regret this," the piggy-eyed PC said.

Smith lit a cigarette. "It won't be the first time. What am I going to regret now?"

"I know it was you who's behind this."

"Spit it out, for fuck's sake. I'm not in the mood for you right now."

"The boy I arrested for driving without a license and insurance," PC Griffin said. "His father has lodged an official complaint, and I know for a fact you had something to do with it."

"Was my name mentioned in the complaint?" Smith asked.

"Not exactly."

Smith blew a cloud of smoke into his face.

"Then I suggest you take your flimsy allegations and fuck off. You made a mistake arresting a sixteen-year-old and you'll come to learn that mistakes carry consequences in this job. Will there be anything else?"

"You haven't heard the end of this, Smith."

Smith took a long drag of the cigarette and started to laugh. He didn't know where it came from. The confrontation with PC Griffin had cheered him up no end. He hadn't really expected Darren Lewis's father to put in a complaint, but he was glad that he had. The arrogant PC needed putting in his place once and for all and this could be just the thing that would do it.

CHAPTER THIRTY EIGHT

Tom Green was younger than Whitton expected him to be after their brief phone conversation. She guessed his age to be mid-twenties, and he didn't look like any of the landlords she'd encountered in the past. He was a short blond man with a baby face. He invited her and Baldwin in and offered them something to drink.

"Coffee would be great," Whitton said.

"Nothing for me thanks," Baldwin told him.

They sat in a spacious living room. Whitton got the impression that the dividing wall between two rooms had been knocked down to create a single, large living space.

Tom handed Whitton her coffee. "It's nothing special I'm afraid. Instant."

"I only drink instant coffee. I believe you own a number of properties in Tadcaster."

"They were my old man's places," Tom said. "I inherited them when he passed away."

"Do you rent them all out?" Baldwin said.

He nodded. "I considered selling them when my dad died, but a friend suggested I rent them out. The housing market is crazy at the moment and first-time buyers are struggling to keep up. There's a real demand for rentals, and it means I don't have to get a proper job."

He giggled a girlish laugh.

"We're interested in the property overlooking the viaduct," Whitton told him.

"Westfield Crescent," Tom said.

"That's right. I believe the current tenant hasn't been there long."

"Brian Vole," Tom said. "He's been in the house for a few months."

"Who were the previous tenants before him?" Whitton said.

"There have been a few in the past year. I'm still relatively new at this game and I haven't quite got the hang of sniffing out the decent ones."

"Can you explain what you mean by that?" Baldwin said.

"Brian has been great so far," Tom said. "Always pays his rent on time, and never bothers me for stupid repairs, but not all of them are like him."

"Who was in the house about a year ago?" Whitton asked.

"I'd have to check for you. I keep all their details on my laptop. What's this all about? Why are the police interested in one of my houses?"

"Could you go and get your laptop please."

Tom got up and left the room. He returned with the laptop and sat back down. He booted it up and open a file on the screen.

"Len Boswell," he said. "I remember him now."

"He lived on Westfield Crescent a year ago?" Whitton said.

"He was one of the tenants I inherited from my dad, along with the house. It was even specified in his Will. He'd been there five years."

"Why did he leave?" Baldwin said.

"It beats me," Tom said. "He was a model tenant – always paid on time, but one day he didn't. I'm not one of those sharks who hassle the tenants when the rent isn't paid on the first of the month. I understand that sometimes unexpected expenses crop up, but when I still hadn't got the rent by the tenth, I went round there. Mr Boswell was gone."

"He left without letting you know?" Whitton said.

"He left quite a bit of his stuff behind too. The TV and the lounge suite were still there and there were a few other belongings of his scattered around the house."

"Didn't you think that was strange?" Baldwin said.

"Of course I did. I tried phoning him, but it went to voicemail every time. I wondered if perhaps he'd taken a trip abroad, but when I still couldn't get hold of him after another couple of weeks and the rent was still unpaid, I figured he'd done a runner."

"Didn't you think to call the police?" Baldwin said.

"It did cross my mind," Tom said. "For precisely ten seconds. No offence, but I don't have much faith in the police. It's not unusual for tenants to do moonlight flits. I've only been in the business for a few years, and I've lost count of how many people have legged it without paying the rent. I tried to get the police involved a few times and I was given the brush off every time. The police aren't interested in things like that. I was informed by one officer that it wasn't even a matter for the police. It's a civil matter apparently."

"I'm afraid that's correct," Whitton said. "So, you just assumed Mr Boswell was another tenant who'd left without giving notice?"

"What else could I think?" Tom said. "He disappeared and I couldn't get hold of him."

"Do you know the man who lives next door to your house on Westfield Crescent?" Whitton said. "Levi Wright."

"I've seen him a few times," Tom said. "But we've hardly ever spoken to each other."

"Did you know his parents?" Baldwin said.

"Only in passing. They were strange ones."

"What do you mean by that?"

"Religious nuts. My dad told me something about them a year before he died. They had these weird beliefs. No noise on a Sunday and stuff like that. One of the tenants liked to play a bit of music while he pottered around in the garden. He had a thing for seventies rock, but Mr and Mrs Wright weren't best pleased."

"They asked him to turn it down?" Baldwin said.

"They told him to turn it off," Tom said. "And they also told him he was all but a devil worshipper. Said he was heading straight to hell. They were real religious freaks. No offence. You're not religious, are you?"

Whitton ignored the question. "When was the last time you saw Mr and Mrs Wright?"

"Probably just over a year ago."

"Where did they go?"

"I haven't the foggiest idea. And I didn't really care. For all I know they went to live on one of those nutjob communes you hear about. They were a liability if you want to know the truth. Who wants to live next door to someone who complains about sod all, and damns you to hell when you don't do as they say?"

CHAPTER THIRTY NINE

Bridge had found the number for the woman who acted as the supervising officer when Levi Wright was released from Full Sutton. He was about to dial the number when his phone started to ring and the display told him it was a number not in his contact list.

"DS Bridge," he answered it.

"Hello," a man said. "We met yesterday at the art gallery. You asked me to phone you if I remembered who the man in the CCTV footage was."

"Are you feeling better?" Bridge asked him.

"What? Oh, yes. It was just one of those twenty-four-hour things."

"What can you tell me?"

"I remembered where I've seen him before."

"It's Lee, isn't it?" Bridge said.

"That's right. The man in the footage looked just like a man who came into the gallery a few weeks ago."

"Did you get his name?" Bridge said.

"No, but we did strike up a conversation. He was particularly interested in the *Sacred Spaces* exhibition."

"Could you explain what that is?" Bridge said.

"It's an exhibition that explores the changing nature of artistic expression in Italy from the 14th century onwards. It focuses on how the decoration of places of worship fostered new techniques and styles of painting. This man was truly fascinated in the exhibition."

"And you're sure it was the same man as the one on the CCTV footage? The picture was rather grainy, and you couldn't see his face."

"It could have been someone else, but there was something about the way he walked that reminded me of the man who came in to see the *Sacred Spaces* exhibition. He had a very unique gait."

"Could you elaborate on that?"

"He walked with purpose. Like he was a man who knew exactly where he was going. He looked like someone who was totally focused."

"Can you remember what you talked to this man about?" Bridge said.

"Mostly about the exhibition. I remember it clearly because he obviously knew more about it than I did."

"Did he strike you as a religious man?" Bridge said.

"He did. I recall he even made the sign of the cross when he viewed some of the art on display."

"Did he say anything to give you any idea about whether he lived in York?"

"I'm not following you?"

"Did he mention anything to suggest he was just passing through?" Bridge said. "Did he strike you as being a tourist?"

"His accent was local."

Bridge wasn't sure how this information was going to help. He thanked the art gallery assistant and ended the call. He rubbed his eyes and stretched his arms. It had been another exhausting day, and they didn't really have much to show for all the work they'd put in. He decided to put the call to the supervising officer on hold until he'd had another cup of coffee.

Smith had had the same idea. He was sitting on his own at his table by the window.

"What a day," Bridge said.

He selected a coffee from the machine and sat opposite Smith.

"Anything useful to report?" Smith asked.

"Sod all," Bridge said. "You?"

"Levi Wright is *The Loner*," Smith said. "But the DI reckons we have no grounds to search his property."

"He's right you know. We don't have much on him apart from the fact that his eyes change colour. The CPS is going to take one look at his file and laugh the request straight into the bin. The only previous he has is a six-month sentence for assault. He was out after three for good behaviour. That is not the rap sheet of a serial killer. And before you get all stroppy, I'm with you on this one. I think you're right, but we can only work with what we have on paper."

"I don't get stroppy," Smith argued.

"If you say so."

"Has Billie given you an answer yet?" Smith asked. "Has she decided whether she wants to become Mrs Bridge?"

"Not as such."

"No, then?"

"It's only matter of time," Bridge said. "Billie Jones is the one, and she'll soon realise she won't do any better than Rupert Bridge."

"Modesty doesn't suit you."

"I'm just telling you how it is. You're invited by the way."

"Invited?" Smith repeated.

"To the wedding, you berk."

"I should think so. I'm going to see if Kerry has managed to find something we didn't spot before. The DI has got her running through the events from the very beginning."

"Sometimes it helps," Bridge said.

"I sincerely hope this is one of those times. Haven't you got something you could be doing?"

"I was just taking a break before I got hold of Levi Wright's parole officer or whatever it is they call themselves these days."

"Supervising officer," Smith educated him. "It's supposed to make them sound more important."

Bridge watched him leave. He picked up his phone and brought up the number he'd been given for Sharon Cole.

The supervising officer answered straight away. Bridge outlined the reason for his call.

"What do you want to know?" Sharon said when he was finished.

"What did you make of Mr Wright?" Bridge said.

"I got the impression he was keen to put what happened behind him. He was determined to make a fresh start."

"He was only on license for a few months, wasn't he?" Bridge said.

"He was released halfway through his sentence and put on license for three months. The board ruled that their findings didn't warrant any more than that. The assault was his first offence, and he kept his nose clean while he was inside. Can I ask why you're so interested in Levi?"

"Just a routine check," Bridge said. "His name has come up in the course of an investigation and we're just ticking names off a list at this stage."

"I don't know what else you want me to tell you," Sharon said. "The last time I spoke to Levi was almost a year ago."

"Did the terms of his parole specify he would be released into the care of his parents?"

"He volunteered to go and live with them," Sharon said.

"Are you aware that his mother and father disappeared not long after he got out of prison?"

"I'm not."

"It might not be important," Bridge said. "His next-door-neighbour reported him to the police about it."

"Why would the neighbour do that?"

"We don't know. He disappeared as well shortly afterwards. The police had no option but to take it seriously and they paid Mr Wright a visit."

"And?"

"They found nothing," Bridge said. "There was nothing to suggest that Mr Wright had done anything to his mother and father. It never went any further."

"There you go then," Sharon said. "I believe you can cross his name off your list. Whatever it is you're looking into, I doubt Levi Wright is involved. He learned his lesson inside, and I don't think he'd be in a hurry to end up back there. He got his life back on track. He moved back in with his parents and found employment at the gallery."

DC Moore came inside the canteen. He made his way over to Bridge's table. Bridge stopped him from speaking with a wave of the hand.

"What did you say?" he asked Sharon.

"Levi Wright moved back in with his parents and got a job at the art gallery." Bridge could feel his face warming up.

"Which art gallery?"

"The one down the road from Clifton," Sharon told him.

CHAPTER FORTY

"It could be another art gallery?" DC King said.

Bridge had rounded up everyone on the team after the conversation with Sharon Cole. What Levi Wright's old supervising officer had told him could be the first real break they'd had in the investigation.

"There's only one art gallery in that part of town," he said.

"That's how he knew about the CCTV camera," Smith said. "He didn't have to check out the place from the outside. He works there for fuck's sake."

"I want a complete list of everyone who works at that gallery," DI Smyth said. "And I want it now."

"I think I can save us the bother," DC Moore said.

"What is it, Harry?" Smith said.

"I've got a sinking feeling me and Bridge have met him."

Bridge's eyes narrowed.

"The man who helped us with the CCTV footage," DC Moore said. "His name was Lee."

"Lee," Bridge repeated. "Levi. It's possible. But he didn't look anything like the man in the mug shot."

"He was the same height and build. Same hair colour. He was wearing glasses, and he had a beard when we saw him at the gallery, but it's possible that was to disguise his face."

"What colour were his eyes?" Smith asked.

"I can't remember," DC Moore said.

"It's your job to remember things like that."

"Shit," Bridge said. "I've just got off the phone with the bastard. He's been playing with us, hasn't he?"

"I want the number he called you on sent straight over to the tech team," DI Smyth said. "I want someone to get hold of the manager of the art gallery and I want at least one car to head straight to Tadcaster."

"He won't be there," Smith said.

"I thought you wanted his house searched," DI Smyth said.

"That was before he made damn sure we knew who was calling the shots. He's still in control and he will definitely not go back to the house in Tadcaster."

"We don't know that," Bridge said.

"*He* called you, didn't he?"

"What?"

"You said you've just spoken to him. I'm guessing that he called you."

"He did, yes," Bridge confirmed. "He told me he remembered a man matching the description of the one seen with Melissa Grange coming to the gallery a while ago. He said he was very keen on an exhibition about religion in art."

"He's fucking with us."

"You were right, Smith," DI Smyth said. "You've maintained that we were looking for Levi Wright all along. This all but proves that you were right."

"And I take no satisfaction in the fact that I was right," Smith said. "I'm just telling you we're not going to find him at home in Tadcaster."

"Where do you suggest we look?" DC King said.

"I don't know."

"Try phoning him," DC Moore suggested.

"No," Whitton said. "Send him a WhatsApp instead."

"He'll probably know that calls can be traced," DC King said.

"That's right," Whitton said. "He's not stupid. WhatsApp messages aren't so easy to track."

"What am I supposed to say?" Bridge said.

"Tell him to come out from whatever rock he's hiding under," Smith said. "Tell him we're coming for him and tell him he's going straight to hell."

"We definitely won't say that," DI Smyth said. "Bridge, when you spoke about the man in the art gallery – did he mention when it was he came in?"

"He just said it was a few weeks ago," Bridge said.

"As him if he can be more specific."

"Why not ask him if you can meet?" DC Moore suggested. "Tell him you need what he told you on record. Ask him where's convenient to come and take a statement."

"It won't work," Smith said.

"I think it's worth a shot," DI Smyth decided.

It was the hardest message Bridge had ever had to compile. If the man he was composing the WhatsApp to was in fact *The Loner*, every word in the message counted. It had to sound convincing, and it had to be enough to make the most prolific killer any of them had ever come across come out of hiding. It took him a while to write, and his trembling fingers didn't help matters. When he was finished, he re-read the words to check that everything was perfect and pressed *send*.

"Now what?" DC Moore wondered.

"Now we wait," Smith said.

"He hasn't read it yet," Bridge said. "It's been sent, but there are no blue ticks."

"He hasn't dumped the sim then," DC King said. "That's always good."

Bridge looked at the screen again. "Still no blue ticks."

"We're not going to waste time waiting for him to read the message," DI Smyth said. "Does anyone have any suggestions about how to move forward on this?"

Nobody did. All of them were convinced they'd found out the identity of *The Loner* but none of them could come up with anything to help them find him.

"It's possible he has another property somewhere," DC King was the first to speak. "I can go and do a bit of digging."

"Thanks, Kerry," DI Smyth said.

"Check to see if there's any properties registered in his parent's names too," Smith said. "Their details will be somewhere."

"I'll find them," DC King said and left the room.

"Anything?" DC Moore asked Bridge.

A quick glance at his phone told Bridge the WhatsApp still hadn't been read.

"I need to think," Smith said. "Would anybody object if I adjourned to my other office in the car park to smoke a cigarette?"

"Make it quick," DI Smyth said.

Smith was halfway out the door when Bridge called out.

"He's read the WhatsApp."

Smith stopped and turned around.

"He's writing a message," Bridge added.

Time seemed to stand still inside the small conference room. Bridge kept his eyes fixed on the screen of his phone. It told him the person on the other end of the line was writing a message and then the phone beeped and two blue ticks appeared.

"What did he say?" Smith asked.

He was still standing in the doorway.

Bridge opened the message. "Bloody hell."

He dropped the phone on the desk.

Whitton picked it up. A close up of a man's face stared back at her. He was smiling but the clownish grin didn't reach his eyes. Whitton looked at them intently. She stared into the fiercest blue eyes she'd ever seen.

The phone beeped again, and she jumped. The message consisted of just seven words. Whitton read them out.

"I'm almost done. Then I'll go. Levi."

CHAPTER FORTY ONE

Levi Wright stared at the screen of his mobile phone and when the blue ticks he'd expected didn't appear, he threw it onto the carpet. The detective had not replied to his message. He left the room and stood in front of the mirror in the hallway. It was almost identical to the one in his house in Westfield Crescent, but this one was intact. He leaned forward and removed the blue contact lenses, one by one. He blinked a couple of times and observed his true eye colour.

His mother had once described them as two emeralds ready to be plucked from a sea of sin. Those words had never left him. She told him she loved his eyes. They were special eyes – a true gift from God.

Then everything took a downward spiral.
His father had recoiled the first time the change occurred. He'd watched in horror as the emerald green morphed into the intense blue, and nothing after that was ever the same again.
You're the Devil's spawn itself, he'd proclaimed. *The seed of the Demon is in you*.
Levi can't recall what had precipitated the change.

The clock on the wall told him it was six in the afternoon. It would be dark soon, and then it would be time to get to work. He experienced a pang of regret for not bringing his mother and father here with him. It would be nice to talk to them now, but he hadn't had time. They were still locked in their eternal embrace in the chest freezer in Westfield Crescent.

The last one on the list was going to be the most taxing. There were too many variables beyond Levi's control, and it made him nervous. He'd gone through every possible scenario and every foreseeable problem in his head a dozen times, but there was always the chance that something might go wrong. The clock ticked in the background. He wondered how long it would be before they came for him.

The doorbell sounded and Levi got to his feet. He was impressed. They'd found him sooner than he expected.

* * *

"He's not likely to just answer the door," Bridge said.

"Of course he won't," Smith agreed. "Because he's not here."

He wanted to see what was inside the house in Westfield Crescent even though he knew beyond a shadow of a doubt that *The Loner* wouldn't be there. He wanted to know what secrets were hidden in the home of the most ingenious killer he'd ever come across.

DI Smyth had insisted on bringing in an armed unit. Smith had argued that it would be a complete waste of time and resources but DI Smyth, ever cautious had disagreed. If they were correct in their assumption that Levi Wright was their murderer, he was an exceptionally dangerous man and the DI didn't want to take any chances.

The armed unit were to go in first. That wasn't up for debate. Smith had simply shrugged his shoulders when he heard this. In his opinion it made no difference to him in which order they entered an empty house.

"They're going in," Bridge said. "It looks like the door was unlocked."

Smith lit a cigarette and watched as the four highly-trained armed officers went inside the house. Two more were stationed at the back.

Smith exhaled a cloud of smoke. "I'll give them three minutes."

"It's highly unlikely that he'll be in there," DI Smyth said. "But I will not take any chances. Not on my watch. You'll understand that when you finally make Inspector."

"Never going to happen, boss," Smith said. "That bird has flown. I bet you they'll be out before I've had the chance to smoke this cigarette."

If he'd put money on it, he would be worse off when, after ten minutes the first of the armed officers came back outside. Smith had managed to smoke two cigarettes in that time.

"You lose," DI Smyth told him.

"No worries," Smith said. "Shall we go and take a look?"

He headed towards the house before DI Smyth had the chance to reply. The door to the property next door opened when he got closer, and Brian Vole came outside.

"What's all the fuss about?" he said.

"I need to ask you to stay inside your house," Smith said.

Even though there was no immediate threat, he was working on autopilot.

"Please go back inside," he said. "Someone will come and talk to you when we're finished."

Brian reluctantly complied. He had the last word when he slammed the front door so hard the sound reverberated inside Smith's head for a few seconds.

"All clear," one of the armed unit told Smith.

He nodded his head and went inside. It was obvious as soon as he stepped into the living room that the house wasn't used much. A single-seater couch was all that was inside the room. There was no television and no ornaments or pictures on the walls. There was a mirror on the wall in the hallway. The glass had been smashed to smithereens. Pieces of the broken mirror were scattered all over the carpet.

Smith went into the kitchen and stopped by the fridge. Using the fabric of his T-shirt he grabbed the handle and opened it. All it contained was a half-full bottle of milk and an unopened tub of yoghurt. Both were well past their expiry dates.

Smith took in the room. The kitchen wasn't unlike his own in size and shape. A table stood against one of the walls. The sink was covered in a layer of dust and all that was in it was a single coffee cup. A row of cupboards took up the wall opposite the table. Smith wondered whether to wait for Forensics to get there before taking a look but decided not to. He opened the cupboards, one by one and stopped dead when he realised what was inside the one on the far left. He didn't touch the crossbow – he knew better than that, but he didn't need to. It was confirmed – this was the house of *The Loner*.

Grant Webber came in with Billie Jones.
"I've found one of the murder weapons," Smith told them.
He nodded to the crossbow.
"And no," he added. "I haven't touched it. I'm going to take a look upstairs."

Pete Richards had beaten him to it. Webber's assistant was taking photographs in the bathroom.
"What have you found?" Smith asked him.
"It looks like blood," Pete pointed to the sink. "I just wanted to get a few pics before we collected some samples."
"Is it alright if I have a look in the bedrooms?" Smith said.
"Be my guest."

The first bedroom Smith came to was completely empty. There was absolutely nothing inside. The carpet looked clean, and the curtains were closed. The second room was obviously the main bedroom. A double bed stood against the wall opposite the window. The curtains were closed in here too. A single cupboard was the only other item of furniture apart from the bed. Smith opened it to find half a dozen coat hangers on a rail.
"You didn't live here," he decided.

A low humming sound caught Smith's ear as he approached the third bedroom and when he pushed the door open, he saw where it was coming from. A chest freezer stood in the corner. There was nothing else inside the room. Smith placed his hand on the handle and realised the freezer was locked. He went back out to the landing and found Pete Richards in the main bedroom.

"Do you have a crowbar?"

"I've got one in the car," Pete said.

"Could you go and get it please? There's a chest freezer in the spare room, but it's locked?"

"Who keeps a freezer in their spare room?" Pete wondered.

"That's exactly what I thought."

Pete went downstairs and returned shortly afterwards with a crowbar.

"Do you want to do the honours?" Smith asked him.

"My pleasure."

It took Pete two seconds to break the lock on the freezer. There was a loud crack as the crowbar did what it was designed to do. Smith opened the lid wide and recoiled when he saw what was contained within. Pete Richards was equally horrified.

"Fuck me."

Thirty minutes later the dismembered bodies of what appeared to be three human beings were spread out on the floor of the spare room. Freezer bags containing arms, legs, hands, feet and torsos were lined up in a row. The heads were the last things to be pulled from the cold of the freezer. Three perfectly preserved human heads now stared up at Smith as he gazed down at them.

The mystery of what had become of Levi Wright's mother and father had been solved, and Smith was convinced the third head belonged to the man who'd called the police to report his suspicions about what Levi Wright had done to them. DNA tests would later prove Smith right. The head on the far right was once attached to the neck of Len Boswell.

CHAPTER FORTY TWO

"That makes eight."

DI Smyth had added the names of Mr and Mrs Wright and Len Boswell to the list on the whiteboard in the small conference room. Grant Webber and his team were still busy at the house in Westfield Crescent. Smith had left the spare room when Billie Jones had begun piecing together the body parts. She did it methodically – reconstructing the different pieces like she was constructing some kind of macabre jigsaw puzzle. Smith had witnessed some terrible things in the course of his career, but this was just too much. He'd been glad to get back outside into the fresh air.

"He still has one to go," he reminded the team.

"Kerry is still busy looking into any properties he may have access to," DI Smyth said.

"It was obvious he didn't live in the house in Westfield Crescent," Smith said. "There was nothing inside that suggested he resided there. He must have another property somewhere."

"Do you think he's already carried out his last murder?" Whitton aired what everyone else on the team were thinking.

"He hasn't." Smith was convinced of this.

"It's possible that he has," Bridge said. "And we haven't found the body yet."

"He wants the bodies to be found," Smith said. "That's important to him. He wants us to see what he's done."

"I agree," DC Moore said. "All of the victims were found relatively soon after they were killed. He wants his handiwork noticed. If he'd killed his final victim, we'd have known about it by now."

"Why keep the bodies in a freezer?" Whitton wondered.

"And why didn't the officers who were called out about his parents check the chest freezer?" Smith said. "That's unforgivable in my book. The PC I spoke to in Leeds said they went to the house in Westfield Crescent. They were called out to investigate the neighbour's claims that Levi had killed his parents. Wy didn't they smell a rat when they saw a chest freezer in the spare room? Nobody keeps a freezer upstairs in a spare room."

"I'm sure there will be a full investigation," DI Smyth said. "And heads are probably going to roll, but that's not our concern. From a jurisdictional perspective the bodies found in the house in Tadcaster are Leeds's headache."

"I disagree, boss," Smith said. "He's ours. He's killed five people in York, and this is York's party."

"Tadcaster falls under the remit of Leeds," DI Smyth pointed out.

"He's under investigation in York. I am not letting Leeds take over."

"Leeds are going to say otherwise."

"I don't give a damn what Leeds thinks," Smith said. "This one is ours."

Whitton slammed her fist down on the table.

"Territorial pissing isn't going to get us anywhere. We have a sick bastard to catch. A sick bastard who doesn't give a fuck who's in charge of catching him."

Everyone inside the room turned to look in her direction. Whitton's outburst was out of character, and it was unexpected.

"OK," DI Smyth was the first to find his voice. "We now know we're looking at the right man. Levi Wright."

He tapped the whiteboard where he'd written the name.

"Who is the man, and why has he suddenly decided to set off on a killing spree? It's a massive leap from an assault charge. Something changed in his life and caused him to start formulating a plan. You do not simply wake up one morning and decide you feel like murdering a whole load of people. What motivated him here? Where is the motive?"

"Now you're talking my language, boss," Smith said. "You're dead right – something changed in his life that affected him. Something caused him to crack, and we need to find out more about him to begin to understand what made him do this."

"I want someone to speak to his boss at the art gallery," DI Smyth said.
"We spoke briefly yesterday," Bridge said. "His name is Albert Frogg."
"Get hold of him now. Find out if the gallery was aware of Levi's criminal record and see if you can get any information about any friends he talked about. We also need to look into his time in prison."
"It was non-eventful," Smith said. "The prison officer me and Chalmers spoke to said he kept himself to himself, and he didn't associate with any of the other inmates at Full Sutton."

"According to the records," DC Moore said. "He doesn't have any siblings. He's an only child."
"And his parents are dead," Smith said. "By his own hand. He doesn't have any family, and he won't have any friends. That's how he's managed to plan these murders so well. Being a loner has its benefits."

Bridge took out his phone and opened his browser. He Googled the art gallery and scrolled down until he'd reached the *contact details* section. He was in luck – Albert Frogg's mobile number was listed on the page. He saved the number and pressed call.

Albert answered after a few rings and Bridge put the phone on speaker.
"Mr Frogg," he said. "My name is DS Bridge. We spoke briefly at the art gallery yesterday."
"Did you get what you needed from the CCTV?" Albert asked.
"That's not why I'm calling. I need to ask you a few questions about one of your employees – Levi Wright."
"He calls himself Lee now."

"I see. Were you aware that Mr Wright has a criminal record?"

"Of course," Albert said.

"And that didn't concern you when Levi applied for the job?"

"Why would it concern me? The York Art Trust is an equal opportunities organisation. We all make mistakes, and Lee has proven to be an asset to the gallery. What's this regarding?"

"Levi's name has come up in an ongoing investigation," Bridge said. "Is he employed full time by the trust?"

"That's right. He works here full time."

"Are you at the gallery now?" Bridge said. "I know it's Sunday, but you open weekends, don't you?"

"We're open Wednesday to Sunday."

"Is Levi there now by any chance?"

"He phoned in sick," Albert said.

"Do you happen to have an address for him?" Bridge said. "We're having difficulty locating him. His address must be on file at the gallery."

"I'll have to ask someone to take a look on the system."

"If you could do that now I'd appreciate it."

"Why are you investigating Lee?" Albert said.

"I'm afraid I can't tell you that. How long has he worked at the gallery?"

"Nine months or so."

"Does he ever talk about his friends?" Bridge said.

"Lee and I are not particularly close in a personal capacity."

"Does he socialise with any of the other people who work at the gallery?"

"I don't believe he does. Look, I'm rather busy at the moment. Could you please explain what this is all about? I have a lot to do."

"No problem," Bridge said. "If you could get that address for me it would be a great help. You can message it to the number I called you on. This is urgent."

"I'll do it for you now," Albert said.

He sent the details half an hour later and for everyone on the team it was the longest thirty minutes of their lives. The information contained in the message was also not what any of them wanted to hear. The address the art gallery had on file for Levi Wright was number 8 Westfield Crescent.

CHAPTER FORTY THREE

After the disappointment with the address the team were feeling despondent. None of them had any idea where to look next. The serial killer Smith had dubbed *The Loner* was out there somewhere and he was going to kill someone very soon. DC King had drawn a blank looking into any other properties Levi Wright may have access to. The only house listed in his name was the one in Tadcaster.

"He could be renting a place," DC Moore suggested. "He might have rented a house because he knew we'd be able to find the one on Westfield Crescent."

"It's very possible," Smith agreed. "He knows it wouldn't take us long to track him down through the Deeds Office, so he rents a place, and hides out there while he's busy on his killing spree."

"Won't his name be on the utility bills?" DC King said. "We might be able to find him that way."

"Not all tenants pay their bills directly to the service providers," Bridge said. "It's quite possible he has a pre-paid electricity meter and the account is in the landlord's name."

"How are we supposed to find him?" DC Moore said.

"I really don't know, Harry," Smith said.

"Do we know if he owns a car?" DC King said.

"He drives a black Ford Focus," Smith remembered. "His neighbour told me he has a Ford Focus. It'll be easy enough to get the registration number."

"I want that information five minutes ago," DI Smyth said. "And I want a BOLO issued. We need every pair of eyes keeping an eye out for that car. I think it's safe to assume he's still in the city somewhere."

"He's still in York," Smith said. "He's planned all of his murders here, and he's carried them all out here."

"The Ford Focus is quite a popular make of car," DC Moore said. "There are loads of them on the roads."

"Once we have the registration number we'll find it," Bridge said.

"Unless he's using false plates," Smith said.

"Why do you always have to be so negative?"

"it's not negativity," Smith argued. "I'm stating a fact. This is the most cunning killer any of us have had the pleasure of dealing with. He's got away with eight murders because he's extremely good at it. I very much doubt he would have overlooked the possibility that we'll try to locate his vehicle. He will not have made a rookie mistake like that."

"Get onto it anyway," DI Smyth said. "Every killer has to slip up somewhere along the line."

"This one won't," Smith insisted.

"You're not helping."

The room fell silent for a moment.

Smith was the first to speak.

"We need to think differently with this one."

"Go on," DI Smyth said.

"As far as I can see we've exhausted all avenues, and that's because we've investigated this the way we always do. *The Loner* knows every aspect of how a murder investigation is carried out. He knows what we focus on, and that's why he's put measures in place so as not to be caught out."

"The message he sent me was taunting us," Bridge said. "He thinks he's cleverer than us."

"I don't think that was his intention," Smith disagreed. "I didn't get the feeling that the message was written out of arrogance – *I'm almost done. Then I'll go*. That strikes me more as a statement of fact. He's almost finished and that will be the end of it. There's nothing else to read into it.

They weren't the words of a cocksure criminal – he was simply telling us how it's going to be."

"Often arrogance leads to a sense of invincibility," DC King said. "And if you look back through the history of serial killers that's when they make mistakes. I think Smith's right – he was telling us that he's nearly finished. There was nothing else to read into his words. He's not a serial killer desperate to be caught."

"Why do you think he killed his parents?" Bridge said.

"And why chop them up and keep them in a freezer all this time?" Whitton said. "Surely, he would have plenty of opportunity to dispose of their bodies in the past year. Why keep them close to him?"

"I think it suggests some form of regret," Smith suggested. "Perhaps killing them was necessary, but he wanted them close by."

"Dismembering your mum and dad implies a seriously deranged mind at work," DC Moore said.

"It was necessary," Smith said once more. "He wouldn't have been able to fit them into the freezer otherwise. He does what a situation necessitates."

"Why keep the neighbour?" DC Moore said. "What purpose did that serve?"

"Who knows? Only he will be able to explain that."

"We're wasting time on irrelevant theories and speculation when we should be putting all our efforts into finding him," DI Smyth said. "He's out there somewhere, and I want him found."

"Did Forensics find anything else in the house in Westfield Crescent?" Whitton asked.

"Nothing to suggest where he might be hiding out," DI Smyth said. "There were a stack of utility bills in a drawer in the kitchen, but all of them were for the house in Tadcaster. Webber didn't find any electronic devices. If we had a laptop or a phone, we might have got lucky, but there was hardly anything in the house, and none of it pointed to where he might be hiding out now."

"The body parts in the freezer are really freaking me out," DC King said. "I can't stop thinking about it. That must have taken some doing. I wonder what he used to cut them up."

"You are seriously not right in the head," DC Moore said.

"That must have taken a lot of effort," DC King carried on. "Not many people would be able to carry out a task like that."

"You sound just like Smith," DC Moore said. "You sound like you're becoming a fan of this sicko."

"I just find it fascinating what a human being is capable of when they're pushed far enough."

"His parents were the catalyst," Smith said out of the blue. "That's when this started. Something happened between them that resulted in them ending up in pieces in the freezer. That's when *The Loner* started planning all of this."

"What about the neighbour?" DC Moore said. "Where does he fit into the picture?"

"Collateral damage, Harry," Smith said. "Len Boswell isn't worth discussing. Something happened between Levi Wright and his parents that caused him to snap. He killed them and a plan started to form inside his head. Mr and Mrs Wright were the catalyst for all of this."

CHAPTER FORTY FOUR

The ticking of the clock was the only sound inside the room and it was getting louder with every second that passed. The minute hand had completed two full rotations of the old clock dial and darkness had descended on the city outside, but still they hadn't come for him. *The Loner* wondered if he had overestimated their competence. He thought he'd given them more than enough to be able to find him. The mobile phone was on the carpet where he'd thrown it earlier and it was switched on. That alone ought to be enough to pinpoint his location.

The car was parked in plain view outside in the street. Surely, they would be looking for it by now. The number plates on the Ford Focus would come up as flagged. The waiting was causing his mind to wander. Images and words were forming inside his head, and he couldn't stop them. He couldn't afford to get distracted by these things right now, but the memories wouldn't budge.

He recalled the night when he'd been forced to kill his parents. It wasn't what he would have wished for, but they'd left him with no option. He'd only spent a short period of time caged in Full Sutton, but he still found it difficult to readjust to life outside the prison walls. He became agitated when the terms of his license ended, and he was free to do as he pleased. The restrictions were reassuring – they offered him a semblance of order, and when the conditions of his parole were lifted it came as quite a shock. It was a week after this that everything changed.

"Father God," his mother said. "I come before you in Jesus's name." She took hold of Levi's hair and forced him to his knees.
"Pray, sinner."
"It's hellfire and damnation for you, boy," his father told him. "Eternal fire and excruciating pain."

"Father God." Levi had the words imprinted on his memory. "Thank you that You have a solution for everything, including my wild emotions."
The slap from his mother almost knocked him over. His cheek burned hot, and tears started to flow from his eyes.

"Father God," he sobbed. "I need your help in Jesus's name. I ask that you would please unite my heart to fear Your name. Take away my old shattered heart, and give me a new heart – Your heart. Let your heart beat in my chest, Father."

The second slap was much harder, and it sent him flying across the room. He hit his head on the table and a trickle of blood rolled down his cheek. His temple throbbed and his thoughts began to blur. A red mist descended over his eyes, and he knew what was about to happen. He could sense his parents' eyes on him, and he bowed his head.

"Sinner," his mother said. "Seed of Satan."
Levi raised his head and stared into the eyes of the woman who had given him life. She recoiled when she watched the emerald green darken. His lips curled up into a grim smile and his mother made the sign of the cross with her forefingers. Levi got to his feet and picked up the heavy stone statue of Christ on the sideboard.

"Devil's spawn," his father managed before Levi swung it at his head. His mother screamed and tried to escape out of the door. Levi got there first. He placed his hand on her neck and squeezed hard. The mist inside his head was gone now and he could see more clearly than he had in years. The woman who'd given birth to him gasped for air and stopped moving.

Levi's father was crawling away on his hands and knees. Blood was gushing from a deep wound on the side of his head.
"I'm sorry, Father," Levi said.
He brought the statue down again and again. When he was finished there wasn't much left of the back of his father's head.

Levi returned to his knees and continued with his prayer.

"Lord, your Word says that You Yourself will disciple and teach the children. Lord, the children need this. *They* can't fix this."

He stopped there and gazed upon the lifeless forms of his parents.

"*They* chose to release me to You. *They* chose to lift me up to You. Father please take me off their hands. I am Yours."

Levi had modified the prayer somewhat, but it seemed to have the desired effect, nevertheless. Calm descended throughout his body and his breathing slowed.

The clock ticked on, and Levi returned to the present. Impatience was settling in and that made him nervous. Why hadn't they come for him yet? He glanced at the phone on the floor and thought for a moment before he picked it up and swiped the screen. He fumbled with the settings until he found out how to withhold his number and dialled a number he'd stored in his memory bank months ago.

* * *

"How are you feeling?"

Smith was sitting at the end of Lucy's bed. Darren had picked her up from the hospital that morning and by all accounts, the teenage boy had waited on her hand and foot all day. He was now fast asleep on the sofa in the living room. Smith and Whitton had left him there, much to the chagrin of the dogs.

"I'm not in so much pain anymore," Lucy said.

She sat up further in the bed.

"What did the doctors say?" Smith asked.

"I don't think you want to know."

"Tell me the bits you think I can handle."

"I have to take things easy," Lucy said. "Avoid any unnecessary stress. I've got an English assignment that needs to be in tomorrow, and it's not finished."

"Don't worry about that," Smith told her. "That is definitely unnecessary stress. School's out for you for the foreseeable future. It's likely the schools will close by the end of the week anyway. The PM has addressed the nation again and the lockdown measures will be in place as early as Thursday. School is the least of your worries."

"Where's Darren?" Lucy said.

"Passed out on the sofa," Smith said. "Theakston and Fred are seriously pissed off."

Lucy laughed and winced. "Please don't make me laugh."

"Sorry. Is there anything you need? Are you in any pain?"

Lucy shook her head. "They gave me some painkillers. I'm scared, Dad."

"You don't have to be. We're not going to let anything happen to you. I promised your dad that, and I'm going to keep that promise."

"I thought I'd lost the baby. I really thought he was gone."

Smith shuffled up further on the bed and placed his hand on her shoulder.

"Don't think like that. You've had a scare, but the baby is going to be just fine. In a few months we'll have a screaming little human in the house. He's going to drive us all nuts, but we're all going to love him more than anything has ever been loved before. That's my promise to you."

"I love you, Dad."

Smith was knocked for a six. He really wasn't expecting this. He couldn't recall a time where Lucy had told him that.

"I love you too," he said. "It's late. Get some rest and sleep as long as you like. No school for a while."

"I happen to like school."

Smith smiled and kissed her on the forehead. "Goodnight."

"How is she?" Whitton asked when Smith came into the kitchen.

"She's a bit shaken up," he said. "But she'll be right."

"Do you want some coffee?"

"I'm going to have a beer. Can I get you one?"

"Sod it," Whitton said. "Why not. It's been a shitty day."

Smith took two beers out of the fridge and handed one to Whitton. "Shitty doesn't even begin to describe it."

Whitton took a long swig. "Are we going to catch this one?"

Smith sighed deeply. "I really don't know. He's the best we've ever seen, and I haven't managed to figure him out yet."

They were prevented from discussing it further by the sound of Smith's ringtone – *Oliver's Army*. It was DI Smyth.

"Boss," Smith answered it.

He drained the rest of his beer in one go.

"We've got a positive lead," DI Smyth said. "A call just came in from an anonymous caller in Clifton. He reported some suspicious behaviour at a property next door to him."

"Anonymous callers are hardly reliable, boss," Smith reminded him.

"Baldwin took the call," DI Smyth said. "And she sensed that this one was legit."

"Baldwin's sixth sense is rarely wrong. What did the neighbour have to report?"

"A man coming and going from the house at all hours. He claims the man alters his appearance from time to time, and this is the clincher for me. Baldwin had the presence of mind to ask if his neighbour owned a car and he answered in the affirmative. There's a black Ford Focus parked outside right now."

CHAPTER FORTY FIVE

It wasn't really necessary for Smith to attend the scene at the house on Burton Lane in Clifton, but if *The Loner* was inside, he wanted to be a part of it. He wanted to meet the man who had outsmarted him every step of the way. It had never happened before, and Smith had developed a morbid curiosity for him. He realised it probably wasn't healthy to think like this, but he had to stand face to face with the most outstanding serial killer any of them had ever encountered. He needed to look him in the eyes and take in every inch of him.

Whitton had stayed home with Lucy and Laura. Darren Lewis hadn't even stirred when Smith had left the house. It had been a draining twenty-four-hours for the teenager and Smith reckoned he would probably sleep the sleep of the dead tonight.

"Is that the car?" Smith asked DI Smyth.
He pointed to a shiny black Ford.
"The plates match," DI Smyth said. "It's the car belonging to Levi Wright. We've got him, Smith."
"Just like that."
Smith took out his cigarettes and lit one.
"Sometimes tip-offs are all it takes," DI Smyth said.
"Hmm," Smith said. "What's the plan?"
"Same as before."
"Armed unit?" Smith guessed.

64 Burton Lane was a semi-detached property with three bedrooms. The light was on upstairs, and all the curtains in the house were closed.
"We've got every available body standing by," DI Smyth said. "The armed unit are in position at the back of the house, and we have officers in place further down the road. If Levi Wright is in there, he's got two choices. He

can either come quietly, or he can leave in a body bag."

"That's not an option, boss," Smith said. "I want to know why he did this."

"If he gives any indication that he might turn violent the armed team have been given orders to take him down."

"I want to speak to him before that happens."

"You don't get a say in the matter," DI Smyth said. "Personally, I couldn't give a damn whether they take him dead or alive. If it saves just one life, it's all one to me."

"I need to know why?" Smith said.

"And you'll probably get the opportunity to ask him, but I am not taking any chances."

Smith finished his cigarette and lit another.

"Something doesn't feel right."

"It never does with you," DI Smyth said.

"Why phone in without giving your name?" Smith wondered. "Why would you do that?"

"A lot of people don't want to get involved."

"Have uniform spoken to the neighbours?" Smith asked. "The only people who can really see the comings and goings of number 64 are the ones opposite and the houses on either side."

"This isn't a hoax, Smith," DI Smyth said. "The car is registered to Levi Wright. What more do you need?"

"I just think it's suspicious that he's left his car outside in plain view. That's a stupid mistake to make."

"Everyone makes mistakes," DI Smyth said. "Even psychotic serial killers."

"No," Smith said. "Something else is going on here. The house has a garage, so why not park it in there?"

The lights inside number 64 came on one by one and Smith knew that could only mean one thing. The armed unit were finished searching the property. He and DI Smyth both kept their eyes focused on the front door.

"What do you think?" Smith asked.

"Either he's given himself up without a fight," DI Smyth said. "Or he's not home. I didn't hear any gunshots."

A few more lights were switched on in the nearby houses. Some of the neighbours had realised that something was happening in the quiet street. The door to a house three doors down opened and Smith watched as one of the uniformed officers ran over to tell the resident to go back inside. Curtains twitched on either side of the road but there was no activity at number 64.

"What are they doing in there?" Smith said. "They should have come out by now."

His phone beeped in his pocket, but he ignored it.

The headlights of a car appeared further up the road and the vehicle approached slowly.

"I don't like this," Smith said. "Why hasn't the road been sealed off?"

"It was supposed to have been blocked," DI Smyth said and took out his phone.

He walked away from Smith, with the phone held to his ear.

Nothing had changed in the house they suspected *The Loner* had been hiding out in. There was no movement behind the curtains, and nobody emerged from the front door. The headlights of the car were turned off as it parked behind Whitton's car and Smith realised it was Grant Webber. That's why the car had been allowed to pass through the cordon.

Webber got out and made his way over to Smith.

"What have we got?"

"Something iffy," Smith said.

He told the Head of Forensics about the anonymous call and nodded to the black Ford Focus.

"I smell something off too," Webber agreed. "I've attended the scenes of five of this monster's work, not to mention the grisly find in the freezer, and unless he deliberately wants to be caught there is no way he would leave a car registered in his name in such an obvious place."

"I think he's up to something," Smith said.

"Perhaps he really does want to get caught," Webber suggested. "It could be as simple as that."

"If that's the case it means there's another dead body out there somewhere. And nothing about this scenario strikes me as being simple. You want to get caught you walk into the nearest police station. You don't make an anonymous call and risk getting your head blown off."

"Some murderers have done precisely that," Webber reminded Smith. "There have been cases where a killer with nothing more to lose purposefully sets out to get killed."

"That shit only happens in America," Smith said. "No, I'm smelling a big, fat stinking rat right now."

DI Smyth returned. He nodded to Webber and turned to Smith.

"They've got him."

"Where the hell is he then?"

"They took him out the back," DI Smyth said. "It's protocol in high profile cases like these. We don't want the press getting wind of it before we've had the chance to figure out what we're dealing with. He's been taken away in the armed unit's vehicle. We're not taking any chances."

"When can I speak to him?" Smith said.

"That can wait until tomorrow." He looked at his watch. "Or should I say today. It's past midnight."

"I want to speak to him now."

"Go home, Smith," DI Smyth said. "Get some rest – you'll get the chance to find out what you want to know tomorrow."

"This was far too easy. We need to ask him if he's finished what he started. We have to find out if there's another dead body out there somewhere. At least let me take a look inside the house."

"No chance." It was Webber. "The armed unit are great at what they do, but they don't give a damn about trampling over potential evidence. Nobody else is going in there until I'm finished."

"Tomorrow," DI Smyth insisted. "Go home. It's over. It's all over."

Smith didn't know why, but he didn't think it was over at all. A terrible sense of dread rushed through him, and he knew better than to ignore it. He knew for a fact that this was far from over.

CHAPTER FORTY SIX

Smith and Whitton were given a head's-up about what was waiting for them outside the station the next morning. According to Baldwin the press had been camped there for most of the night. Smith had expected nothing less. If the man in custody was in fact *The Loner* it was the story of the decade. The representatives of the fourth estate were not yet privy to what had been found in the freezer in Tadcaster but Smith knew it was only a matter of time before that information saw the light of day. This was big news, and every blog, press site and newspaper wanted a piece of it.

Smith and Whitton were bombarded with questions as soon as they got out of the car.

"Do you have a name for us?" a man Smith recognised asked.

He was a veteran reporter for the York Post. Smith ignored him.

"Why has it taken you so long to catch him?" another man demanded.

Smith debated whether to remind him that the most prolific serial killer the city had ever seen had been apprehended in less than a week but decided not to. Instead, he grinned at the man and carried on walking towards the entrance of the station.

They managed to get inside without being questioned further. PC Simon Miller had been posted outside to prevent the press from gaining access. Smith needed a strong coffee inside him before he could formulate a plan for the day, so he headed straight to the canteen. The rest of the team were already there. Smith got the coffee from the machine and joined them.

"It didn't take the vultures long to sniff out a story."

"Are you really surprised?" Bridge said. "Journalism moves at ten times the speed it used to. Do we know if it's really him?"

"It's him," DI Smyth said. "Webber found more than enough to prove beyond a shadow of a doubt that it's our man."

"Did he find the phone?" Smith asked. "Did he find a mobile phone?"

"I don't know the details, but it's possible."

"There will be evidence on that phone that it was *The Loner* who made the anonymous phone call."

"Who cares?" DC Moore said. "We've got him. That's all that matters."

"Why did he make that call?" Smith said. "He wanted us to find him. Why is that?"

"There will be plenty of opportunity to ask him during the course of the day," DI Smyth said. "He's not going anywhere."

"What else did Webber find?" Smith said.

"A hunting knife with a serrated blade," DI Smyth said. "Among other things. It's not going to take long to match that knife to at least two of the murders. Webber also found bloodied clothing and a white stick of the kind used by blind people. No doubt more evidence will pile up, but the Forensics team has a mammoth task ahead of them, as do we. I want to start building a case against Levi Wright."

"Has he said anything?" Smith asked.

"I believe he's been nothing but cooperative since he was booked in."

"Has he asked for a solicitor?" Whitton said.

"No."

"He's planning something," Smith said.

"He's locked in one of the holding cells," DI Smyth said. "He is being observed around the clock. He is no position to plan anything."

"Don't underestimate him, boss," Smith said. "The bastard is up to something."

"We got a lucky break. Why won't you just accept that sometimes that's all it takes? Right, we have a lot of work still to do."

"Who arrested him?" Smith asked.

"What does it matter?" DI Smyth said.

"I want to know what he said when he was arrested."

"It will have been one of the armed officers."

"I need to know what they made of his state of mind when he was apprehended."

"Why are you so obsessed with this?" DC Moore said.

"Because I find it hard to believe I'm the only one on this fucking team who thinks that something feels very wrong."

"He was caught," DC Moore said. "And he was arrested. You ought to be happy. You should be celebrating right now."

"I'll celebrate when I know what the hell is going on. The name of the arresting officer will be on the report. Excuse me while I go and have a chat with the duty sergeant."

Sergeant Fox nodded to Smith when he walked up.

"How has he been?" Smith asked him.

"I assume you're referring to Mr Wright," Sergeant Fox said. "He's been as good as gold. Quiet as a lamb. Will you be interviewing him this morning?"

"Something like that. Who was the arresting officer?"

"Inspector Newton," Sergeant Fox said without having to check.

"One of the armed unit?"

"He's a good bloke. Why are you asking?"

"I want to know how he was when he was arrested. Were you on duty when he was brought in?"

"I was. I've been here all night. I was just about to knock off and go home to grab some sleep as it happens."

"How did he seem when he was booked in?" Smith said.

"Like he didn't have a care in the world. It's likely he's going to go to prison for the rest of his life, but if he's aware of this he didn't show it."

"Interesting. I'll let you get on home then."

"I still have to wait for Mike to come and take over. He's running late."

Smith decided to take a chance.

"Can I have a quick word with Mr Wright?"

"Is this going to come back and bite me on the arse?" Sergeant Fox said. "Because I'm not far away from retirement and I'd quite like to leave here with my pension intact."

"This is all on me," Smith promised.

"Five minutes. Holding cell 4."

"Thanks," Smith said. "I appreciate it."

Levi Wright was standing facing the wall inside the cell when Smith got there. He turned around immediately.

"Good morning, Detective Smith."

Smith took a moment to study him. He looked to be around thirty and he was slightly taller than Smith. His green eyes really were striking, and there was something in his gaze that Smith found extremely unsettling. There was serenity in the emerald eyes. A calmness that Smith hadn't expected.

"You'll have to excuse me for not shaking your hand," Levi looked down at his own hands.

They'd been bound in front of him with a thick plastic cable tie.

"They thought it necessary."

"It's because you're a sick psychopath," Smith told him.

"When am I going to be charged?"

"That will depend on how long it takes to build a case for the CPS. Where is the final victim?"

"I don't know."

"What do you mean, you don't know?" Smith said. "Where is the last one on your list? Where is number six?"

"There is no number six yet - that one is yet to happen."

"Then I believe you've failed. You fucked up, Levi."

"Could I have something to drink please?" Levi asked.

This wasn't the reaction Smith was expecting.

"In a minute. There's something I need to ask you first."

Levi's eyes darkened slightly. His gaze never left Smith's.

"The answer to your question is simple, Detective Smith," he said after a few seconds. "It's because you were taking far too long. I expected more from you, but I clearly overestimated your talents."

"You made that anonymous call, didn't you?" Smith said.

"Perhaps there's still hope for you yet. Consider it an act of God. He will always be there to guide you. Could I have something to drink now?"

CHAPTER FORTY SEVEN

Smith's suspicions had been confirmed but he was far from happy about it. From the brief conversation with *The Loner* it was very clear he was the one in charge. Even confined to a cell with his hands shackled, Levi Wright was still calling the shots and Smith didn't know how to interpret it. He decided to take it to the DI to see if he had any ideas on why Levi had done this.

"Are you out of your mind?" DI Smyth said. "You know full well that nothing he told you can be used as evidence. What were you thinking?"

"He didn't say anything relevant to the investigation," Smith lied. "He admitted to making the anonymous phone call, but his call history will confirm that anyway. I'm extremely concerned about this one, boss. He's planning something."

"Change the record. He's locked up in a police station. The balance of power has shifted in our favour."

"I don't think it has, boss. He told me he has yet to carry out the final murder, and I believed him."

"And you didn't think *that* was relevant to the investigation?"

"OK," Smith said. "Maybe that bit was, but he has something up his sleeve."

"Are you suggesting he could be planning an escape?"

"I don't know, but he's planning something, and we need to be extra vigilant. We need to take precautions when we interview him."

"And we will. Look, I appreciate you bringing your concerns to me, but you have nothing to worry about. He's a smooth operator. He has been one step ahead of us throughout but now that's all changed. It's bound to rattle him a bit, and he's compensating for that by coming across as cocksure. Nothing is going to happen here."

"When are we planning on interrogating him?" Smith asked.

"Soon," DI Smyth said. "He doesn't want the services of a legal representative, so that ought to speed things up a bit."

"How much have we fed to the wolves outside?"

"The bare minimum. PC Walker has compiled a press release, and it seems to be standard fare from what I can gather. We have a suspect in custody. Blah, blah, blah. They don't know who he is, but no doubt that will change during the course of the day. I presume you want to be involved in the interview."

"You know me, boss," Smith said. "I take it as it comes."

"Of course you do. I'll be there with you, but we are not going in there unprepared. Make yourself useful and get stuck in with the rest of the team. You may be the best detective I've ever met but it doesn't mean you're exempt from the grunt work."

"I'm not scared of getting my hands dirty," Smith said. "I'll just go out and smoke a quick cigarette before I make a start."

Smith had lost count of how many times he'd bumped into DCI Chalmers outside in the car park. Today was another one of those times. Chalmers was leaning against the wall of the station smoking a cigarette.

"Morning, boss," Smith said.

He took out his cigarettes and lit one.

"I heard you cracked the case," Chalmers said.

"I can't take any credit for it. A so-called anonymous tip-off came in and *The Loner* was caught at a house in Clifton."

"What do you mean, *so-called*?"

"It was him who made the call," Smith said. "The bastard phoned in to tell us where he was."

"Be very careful," Chalmers warned. "He's up to something."

"Thank God someone is on the same page as me. I told the DI as much, but he's so wrapped up with having the man in custody, he's not interested. I don't know what Levi Wright is planning, but he's planning something."

"Did you see Boris's speech?" Chalmers changed the subject.

"I did," Smith said. "It looks like the country will be locked down before the end of the week."

"The Super is planning another emergency briefing. I just thought I'd give you some warning."

"Thanks," Smith said. "I don't know what else he can bore the pants off us with though."

"Same old, same old. We're living in strange times."

Chalmers stubbed out his cigarette and stretched his arms.

"I'd better get back. Keep a close eye on your loner."

"I intend to," Smith told him.

He still couldn't figure out what Levi Wright had up his sleeve. He'd killed eight people without anybody suspecting a thing, so why was he so keen to give himself up now? It didn't make any sense. There was nothing stopping him from taking his final victim and disappearing forever. Nothing they'd managed to find out about him had got them anywhere near the man, and he was only apprehended when he volunteered his whereabouts. He was planning something, of that there was no doubt, and the more Smith thought about it the more he came to realise that that *something* had to involve being in police custody.

Was he planning on escaping? Smith didn't know. Prisoners escaping from custody happened, but it was extremely rare. The beep of his mobile phone interrupted his thoughts. He took out the phone and saw that it was Whitton. There were two messages. The first one was enquiring whether he was planning on doing any work today. Smith replied with a thumbs up. The second message made him groan when he read it. Whitton was telling him that Darren Lewis's parents had invited them round for a meal to discuss

Darren moving in with them. It was the last thing he needed right now. He didn't reply to this message – he would discuss it with Whitton face to face.

DI Smyth came outside just as Smith was extinguishing his cigarette.

"I was on my way back in," he said.

"We've got a situation," DI Smyth said.

"I'm listening."

"Levi Wright wants to tell us everything," DI Smyth said. "He's ready to explain everything to us."

"But..." Smith said.

"But," DI Smyth humoured him. "There are terms and conditions attached."

"Fuck him," Smith said. "He doesn't get to dictate the terms. We've got him whether he talks or not."

"Don't you want to know what made him do this?"

"Of course I do," Smith said. "But he cannot be led to think he's calling the shots. I'll get the truth out of him eventually."

"Aren't you going to ask what his terms are?"

"Go on."

"He wants to tell his story," DI Smyth said. "All of it. But he wants it broadcast live. He wants his confession transmitted live for the entire country to see. And he's refusing to speak to anybody but you."

CHAPTER FORTY EIGHT

"Surely this is against some kind of regulations," Smith said.

He was discussing Levi Wright's bizarre request in DI Smyth's office.

"It could swing any potential jury," he added. "If they hear his story on National TV bias will come into play."

"He's thought of that," DI Smyth said. "Unfortunately. He plans to plead guilty to all charges, so there will be no trial."

"I've never heard anything so ridiculous in my life. We can't do this."

"Apparently we can," DI Smyth said. "There is nothing that stipulates that a police interview cannot be broadcast. I've spoken to someone at the CPS and if Mr Wright is prepared to guarantee his guilty plea the broadcast can go ahead."

"I'm not doing it," Smith said. "Like I said, we've got enough to nail the bastard. He can keep his mouth shut forever for all I care."

"I know you don't mean that. You want to know his story more than any of us."

"Top brass will never go for it." Smith was clutching at straws now.

"Top brass have already okayed it."

"You're referring to Uncle Jeremy."

"I am," DI Smyth said. "And it's Superintendent Smyth to you. You know what the Super is like. He loves publicity, and this is publicity of the best kind. It makes him look good. His department has succeeded in bringing the most prolific serial killer the city has ever seen to justice."

"I'll think about it," Smith said.

"It's not up for debate, Smith. It's happening."

"When is this debacle taking place?"

"Tomorrow evening," DI Smyth said. "You need time to prepare. It's important that you're made aware of what's expected of you. There are dos and don'ts to consider. The whole city will be tuning into this, and after that, the entire nation. This thing is going to go viral, and it's important that you understand what's expected of you."

"I'm pretty used to interrogations by now," Smith said.

"That's what worries me. This one will be completely different to any interview you've ever been a part of."

"I'm really surprised the people with the pips have agreed."

"Chief Constable Cartwright expressed his concerns," DI Smyth said. "But Levi will speak to nobody but you, so the CC had no choice but to go along with it."

Smith was finding it hard to digest what the DI had just told him. He didn't know what *The Loner* had planned but he was certain there was a hidden agenda somewhere. What did Levi Wright have up his sleeve this time?

He voiced his concerns to DI Smyth.

"What's he up to, boss?"

"He wants to tell his story," DI Smyth said. "And he wants an audience when he does."

"Why?" Smith wondered. "And where does the sixth victim come into the equation? He was adamant that he will kill his final victim when I spoke to him. Perhaps he's planning on murdering me on National TV."

"Don't be so ridiculous. The interview will be conducted with tight security measures in place. He will be restrained and there will be officers on standby should he try anything."

"He has a hidden agenda," Smith insisted. "There's another reason he wants the interview televised."

"He's a religious man. He wants to confess, and he wants to do that in front of the whole country, it's as simple as that. The press liaison officer will talk you through how to conduct yourself, and he'll set up the broadcast. You're going to be famous."

"I don't want to be famous," Smith said.

"You're doing this. Who knows, there may be a promotion in it for you if you play your cards right."

"Never going to happen, boss," Smith said. "I need a moment to get my head around this."

"You'll be fine."

Smith left the office and went to look for Whitton. He found her by the front desk. She was talking to Baldwin and Bridge. Smith told them about Levi Wright's unusual request.

"You're kidding?" Whitton said.

"I wish I was," Smith said. "He wants to confess in front of the whole country, and he'll only speak to me."

"Bloody hell," Bridge said. "You lucky bastard."

"I don't want to do it," Smith told him. "But I don't have a choice in the matter."

"Can I have a word?" Whitton said.

"Shoot," Smith said. "I need a smoke. We can talk outside."

They went out to the car park. Smith lit a cigarette and took a long drag.

"Is this about Darren's parents?" he asked.

"They've got a point," Whitton said. "There are things we need to discuss."

"Can't we do that over the phone?"

"Our daughter is expecting their grandchild, Jason," Whitton said. "And we hardly know them."

"I don't want to get to know them."

"We're connected whether you like it or not. They've invited us round for a meal and I think that's very civil of them."

"Do I have a choice?" Smith said. "Because I'm getting a bit pissed off being forced to do stuff I really don't want to do."

"It's called being an adult. It'll be fine. We'll go over there and talk about how things are going to work when Darren moves in."

"You know who Darren's dad is, don't you?" Smith said.

"Of course I know who he is," Whitton said. "Frank Lewis is a petty criminal who happens to have a son who loves our daughter deeply."

"Don't you think it'll be a bit awkward?" Smith said. "Considering what we do for a living."

"Frank knows what we do, and according to Darren his dad has put that life behind him. We need to do this, Jason."

"You're right," Smith said. "As usual. I suppose it can't be as bad as having to interview a psychopath on National television."

CHAPTER FORTY NINE

Levi Wright shot up in bed so violently, something clicked in his neck. His breathing was rapid, and his forehead was covered in perspiration. He'd experienced visions and they weren't supposed to have materialised. He'd buried the memories deep somewhere at the back of his mind and he meant for them to stay buried.

He'd dreamed of the day that Len Boswell appeared in his life. The stern-faced man had moved in next door one summer and everything had changed after that day. Len and Levi's parents couldn't have been more different, but they'd become good friends, nevertheless. Len was devoutly religious, and he converted Levi's mother and father in a matter of weeks. Mr and Mrs Wright would pray morning, noon and night. Everything Levi did came under scrutiny, and he would be damned to hell on a daily basis for the mildest transgressions.

Another memory Levi had revisited in his sleep was of Christmas Day when he was twenty-three. He'd met a woman, and he told his parents about her. Len happened to be there at the time and the questions came thick and fast. Who was she? Who were her parents? Which religion did she practice? That was the one that cost Levi dearly. His new girlfriend didn't believe in God, and Levi had decided that he didn't either. Len Boswell had suggested a cleanse. Levi needed to purify himself. It was going to hurt but when it was over Levi would thank them for it. For twenty days and nights he was locked in a room and given nothing but water. He lost three stone and when he was finally given something to eat, he found it impossible to keep anything down.

He prayed with his parents and Len all the time after that.

Levi rubbed his neck and got off the bed. He wondered why the memories had returned. Perhaps they were back because of the upcoming live broadcast of his story. Maybe it was time for him to think about what made him the way he was today.

He was prevented from dwelling on it further by the sound of footsteps in the corridor outside. It sounded like there was more than one person. The steps got closer, and two men appeared outside the cell. One of them was Sergeant Mike Burns. He'd introduced himself the night before when he arrived to relieve Sergeant Fox as duty sergeant. Levi didn't know who the other man was. He was a short man with nervous eyes.

"Mr Wright," Sergeant Burns said. "This is Nigel Underwood. He's a crown advocate for the Crown Prosecution Services."

"Crown advocate," Levi repeated. "I'm honoured."

"I have some documents I need you to sign," Nigel said.

There was a tremor in his voice when he spoke.

He slid a file through the bars of the cell. "If you like, we can leave you in peace to peruse the documents."

"I'll sign whatever you want me to sign," Levi said. "What's in the file?"

"It would be better if you'd read the documents," Sergeant Burns told him. "That way there can be no confusion later on."

"As you wish."

Levi crouched down and picked up the file. His hands were still bound together, and it was tricky to open it. He managed eventually, and he flicked through the contents.

"Where do I sign?" he said when he'd scanned the pages.

"If you could initial every page," Nigel said. "And sign and date the final sheet. I trust everything is in order."

Levi shrugged his shoulders. "Could I have a pen please?"

Nigel took one from his pocket and slotted it through the bars. It landed on the floor of the cell with a quiet rattle. Levi picked it up and looked up at the crown advocate. His gaze was intense. Nigel Underwood took a step back.

"I don't bite," Levi said, his eyes never leaving the man from the CPS.

When he was finished, he handed the file back.

"Just drop it on the floor," Sergeant Burns instructed. "Pen too, then stand at the back of the cell."

"Why are you treating me like a monster?" Levi said. "I'm not Hannibal Lecter."

"You're worse," Sergeant Burns said. "Hannibal Lecter didn't chop up his parents and keep them in a freezer for over a year."

"No," Levi sighed. "They were killed by Nazi panzer fire."

"Stand at the back of the cell."

Levi did as he was ordered. Sergeant Burns picked up the file and the pen and handed both to Nigel Underwood.

"That's that then," the crown advocate said. "You will plead guilty to all charges and save the taxpayer the expense of a lengthy trial. Good day, Mr Wright."

Nigel couldn't get away fast enough. He walked away from the cell, leaving Sergeant Burns alone with Levi Wright.

"You might think you're the one in charge," the duty sergeant said. "But you're very wrong."

"I have no idea what you're talking about," Levi said.

"Let me make things clearer for you then. You're the one locked up. You're the one with his hands tied together. Get used to those bars, son because that's going to be what you'll be looking at for the rest of your life."

"Are you finished?"

"You're going to get your five minutes of fame," Sergeant Burns said. "You'll get to tell your sick, twisted story to thousands of people, but when it's over you're going to be the most despised man in the city. People are going to want you hung, drawn and quartered."

Levi smiled at him. "We'll see. Could you leave me in peace now? I'd quite like to pray."

"Your God isn't going to help you now."

"Please," Levi said. "A little privacy if you don't mind. I'll pray for your soul – I get the feeling that you need all the help you can get."

CHAPTER FIFTY

Smith had never been so relieved to walk out of the station at the end of the day. It had been a draining eight hours, spent in meeting after meeting getting ready for the upcoming televised interview with Levi Wright. Neil Walker had talked him through what was going to happen. The press liaison officer had given him tips on how to handle the immense pressure he would be under, and the young PC had impressed Smith when he'd asked him what it was he wanted from the interview. He'd stressed that that was the most important thing. It was imperative that Smith was in control. Smith had replied that all he wanted was to be able to understand why Levi Wright had done what he did. He wanted his motive.

He'd had to endure a tedious hour with Superintendent Smyth. It came as no surprise when the public-school idiot had talked about the image of York Police and how best to project that image in a positive way. Smith had smiled and nodded his head at the appropriate times, and he'd promised the Superintendent that he would do his best to make York CID look good. He'd drawn the line when Superintendent Smyth had suggested he wear a face mask during the interview. That was pushing things a bit too far.

Chalmers had given him what was probably the best piece of advice when he suggested that the best course of action was simply to listen. If Levi Wright wanted to bare his soul to the nation, let him. Let him confess his sins. Chalmers had warned Smith to be careful though. If at any time the tone of the interview suggested Levi was garnering sympathy from the public Smith was to steer it in another direction. It was very possible he would turn this into something that it wasn't, and it was important that the people tuning in didn't start to feel sorry for him. Smith was to make sure the citizens of York understood completely what it was Levi had done. He'd brutally murdered eight people, and they weren't to forget that.

Whitton was waiting for Smith outside in the car park.

"How are you doing?" she asked.

"I'm knackered," he said. "I didn't sign up for this shit."

"Why do you think he wants to do this?"

"Fame and fortune? Glory? I have no idea. I can't figure out why he wants to empty his soul to the entire country. He's not doing himself any favours. I'll give him three months in Full Sutton. He's killed innocent people, and that tends to be frowned upon by even the most hardened criminal. He'll be dead before the summer."

Whitton pressed the key fob and the doors to her car unlocked. They got in and she pulled away from the car park.

"At least you've got the meal with Darren's parents to take your mind off things," she said.

Smith groaned. "Damn, I'd forgotten all about that. I didn't think this day could get any worse."

"I want you to promise me you'll behave yourself."

"What's that supposed to mean?" Smith said.

"I know you," Whitton said and slowed down as the lights up ahead changed to amber. "Your mouth works before your brain sometimes. Darren's mum and dad are going to be an ever-present part of our lives from now on – accept it."

"If you insist."

"I mean it, Jason. This is important to Lucy."

"What time is this thing?" Smith said.

"Six."

Smith looked at the clock on the dashboard. That was in an hour.

"Enough time to get a few beers in me before we go then," he decided.

"Do we have life insurance?" Smith asked out of the blue when they were halfway home.

"No," Whitton said. "You said it was a waste of money. Why do you ask?"
"I've got a horrible feeling about this live broadcast," Smith said. "Levi Wright has something planned."
"He's not going to do anything on live television," Whitton said. "He'll be cuffed, and security will be tighter than ever."
"Why will he only speak to me? That's bugging me."
"Why should it bug you? He wants the highest profile detective along with him for the ride, and that happens to be you."
"As simple as that?"
"As simple as that," Whitton confirmed. "He is not planning on killing you live on air. Can you wear something respectable for this meal?"
Smith started to laugh. It came from nowhere, and he had no control over it. Whitton took her eyes off the road for a second and turned to look at him.

"Sorry," Smith said when he'd managed to control the fits of laughter. "You want me to wear something respectable for a meal with a criminal and his criminal sons? Mrs Lewis must feel a bit left out. She's the only one in the family that hasn't been arrested."
"I just want you to make an effort," Whitton said.
"Don't worry," Smith said and chuckled again. "I promise not to wear an orange jump suit."
"I'm serious, Jason."
"So am I."
He paused for a while and added: "Do I have any shirts with arrows on them?"
It was Whitton's turn to laugh now. "I really don't know why I married you."
"It's because I'm a high-profile detective," Smith said. "That's why they pay me the big bucks. I promise I'll be on my best behaviour this evening."

Darren Lewis had already fed the dogs when Smith and Whitton arrived home. Smith was impressed, even though it was clear Darren had fed

Theakston far too much when he had to help the chubby Bull Terrier up onto the sofa after watching him take a run up and fail miserably three times in a row.

He kissed the dog on the nose. "You're going a diet, my boy."

Fred joined his friend and settled down next to him. The grotesque Pug was soon grunting like a warthog in unison with Theakston's snores.

    Smith left them to it. After a quick shower he took a beer out of the fridge, downed it in one go and opened up another one. The beer buzz hit him straight away and he felt instantly more relaxed.

"You're not going to get drunk before you go, are you?"

It was Lucy. The sixteen-year-old was standing in the doorway to the kitchen.

"It's been a shitty day, Lucy," Smith told her.

"Alcohol is not the solution to everything," she told him.

"I beg to differ. Beer is precisely that. Beer solves all life's problems."

CHAPTER FIFTY ONE

Levi Wright was refusing to eat. He hadn't had anything for forty-eight hours and his stomach was letting him know about it. The acids were gurgling, and the burn was mildly uncomfortable, but Levi was taking the pain. He recalled his twenty days of isolation, and he knew that soon he would begin to hallucinate. He would see things that only existed inside his head. The friendly old duty sergeant had pleaded with him to eat just a little, but the tray remained where it was on the floor of the cell – the food untouched.

Tomorrow evening Levi would get to tell his tale. He would stand in front of thousands of people and invite them into the deepest recesses of his mind. He would revisit the caves and canyons of his subconscious and everyone who tuned into the live broadcast would be welcome to come along for the ride.

He would stand before God too. The on-off relationship he'd had with the Lord had been more *off* in recent years, but now He was back in Levi's life with a vengeance. He was going to bear witness to the ultimate sacrifice in His son's name. It wasn't going to be easy, but sacrifice wasn't supposed to be. The final mark of Christ would finish this, and that's all that mattered.

"You need to eat something." Sergeant Fox said.
"No," Levi said. "No, I don't."
"You've got a big day tomorrow. You need to keep your strength up."
"Do I disgust you?" Levi asked.
"Excuse me?"
"Do you find me abhorrent?"
"My job is to make sure you're treated according to the guidelines set out in law," Sergeant Fox said. "I'm not here to judge. That luxury is way beyond my pay grade. You'll get your day in court, and that's when you'll be judged."

"Do you believe in God?"

The question caught Sergeant Fox off guard. He paused for a moment before replying.

"I believe in good and evil," he said. "I would think that comes with the territory in this job."

"Am I evil?" Levi said.

"That brings us back to the topic of judgement."

"You must have an opinion of me."

"I believe you need help," Sergeant Fox said. "It's not my place to say where that help is to be had. Eat something. You'll feel better for it."

"You're a good man," Levi said. "But sometimes good men have to suffer. Jesus was a good man, and he suffered for all of us."

"I have to get back to work."

"I'm sorry," Levi said. "I really am sorry you had to be dragged into this."

"It's my job. It's my job to…"

"No!" Levi screamed.

Sergeant Fox took a step back.

"I'm sorry," Levi said calmly. "I am truly sorry."

Sergeant Fox turned to leave. As he did so he caught a brief glimpse of the eyes of the caged man. Two fierce blue orbs burned brightly in their sockets.

*　*　*

"Come in, come in."

Jenny Lewis was a small woman with short black hair. She had the same blue eyes as Darren, and when she smiled her lip curled up slightly like his did. The family likeness was very apparent.

She stepped aside and let them in. Lucy made a beeline straight for her and they hugged like they'd done it dozens of times before.

"How are you, love?" Jenny asked. "No more nasty frights."

"She's been taking it easy," Darren said.

Smith noticed that he didn't embrace his mother.

"Darren has been looking after me well," Lucy said.

"Glad to hear it," Jenny said and caught Smith's eye. "You must be Mr Smith."

"Jason, please," Smith found himself saying. "Mr Smith makes me sound like a boring old man."

"You are a boring old man sometimes." It was Laura.

"And who might you be?" Jenny asked her.

"Laura. I'm seven."

"You have very pretty eyes, Laura."

"She gets those from her mother," Smith said.

"Hi, Jenny," Whitton said.

"Hello, love. Come through. Frank and Gary are out on a job right now, but they promised to be back in time for tea. God, that sounded terrible, didn't it?"

"Mum," Gary said.

He looked like he wanted to make himself invisible right there.

"They're doing a service on one of the neighbour's cars," Jenny explained. "Make yourself comfortable in the living room. Can I offer you something to drink? I imagine you'd like a beer."

She looked at Smith.

"That would be great," Smith said.

"Make that two please," Whitton added.

"I'll give you a hand," Lucy offered.

"You shouldn't be exerting yourself," Darren said.

"I'm going to fetch a few drinks," Lucy said. "I'm not about to lug a beer barrel up from the cellar."

Jenny laughed. It was a hearty, genuine laugh.

"You've got your work cut out with this one, love," Jenny said to Darren. "Let's go and see to those drinks."

"Can I come too?" Laura said.

"Course you can," Jenny said.

Smith, Whitton and Darren sat in silence. The teenager looked especially uncomfortable.

"Sorry about my mum," he said.

"Don't ever apologise for your mother," Whitton told him.

"She seems like a real character," Smith admitted. "And she's obviously very fond of Lucy."

Darren chuckled. "I think she prefers Lucy to me sometimes."

"She's raised two boys," Whitton explained. "It's only natural."

The sound of the front door slamming could be heard, and loud laughter followed.

Darren sighed deeply. "My dad and my brother are back. Let the fun begin."

CHAPTER FIFTY TWO

The food was served, and Smith was pleasantly surprised. Jenny had placed something that resembled a huge version of one of Marge's steak and ale pies on the table. Large plates of potatoes and vegetables accompanied it.
"This looks amazing," Whitton said.
"It's a favourite of my Frank's," Jenny said. "Steak and Guinness pie. My mother was Irish, you see, and I inherited the recipe."
Whitton cast a sly glance in Smith's direction, and he smiled.
Frank Lewis noticed. "Is there some kind of private joke you're keeping to yourselves?"
"Frank," Jenny raised her voice. "That's enough."
"Sorry," Whitton said. "Frank is right. That was a bit rude. It's just that my husband has been eating nothing but steak and ale pies since he arrived in York twenty years ago. He's not very adventurous."
"He knows what he likes," Jenny said. "There's nowt wrong with that. I'll dish up, shall I?"

Gary Lewis finished first, but Smith wasn't far behind him. The pie wasn't as good as Marge's, but it was close.
"That was delicious," he said.
"It's all in the sauce," Jenny said. "Help yourself to seconds."
"Thanks," Smith said. "But I'm stuffed."
Frank got up abruptly. "I'll sort us out with a couple more beers, then I think it's time we got down to business."

He returned to the table five minutes later. The smell of smoke that came back with him suggested he'd gone out for a quick cigarette. He handed Smith a beer and sat back down.
"I hear you want our Darren to move into your place."

"We've discussed it," Whitton said. "And it looks like the lockdown is coming into effect by the end of the week. People are not going to be allowed out and it'll mean Darren and Lucy will never see each other."

"We don't know how long it's going to go on for," Smith carried on. "It could be weeks, or it could drag on for months, but we think it would be better for Darren and Lucy to be together."

"And you're OK with this?" Frank looked him directly in the eye when he said it.

"It was actually Jason's idea," Whitton told him.

Frank nodded. "Did this discussion of yours maybe consider Lucy moving in here? Or are we not good enough for you?"

"We don't think anything of the sort." It was Smith. "We've grown to really like Darren – he's a great kid, and it's clear he has Lucy's best interests at heart. Lucy is the one we need to prioritise. Lucy and the baby. She's settled at our place, and that's the only reason we reckon she'll be better off staying there."

"He's right, love," Jenny said. "Uprooting the poor lass now isn't going to be good for her or the baby."

Frank stared at her.

"It's our grandchild we're discussing here," Jenny added.

"You're the boss," Frank said.

The look she shot her husband told Smith he wasn't joking.

"Right then," Frank said. "That's that sorted."

"Can I go now?" Gary said.

Darren's older brother hadn't spoken a word during the meal.

"Can I have a quick word before you do?" Smith said.

Gary nodded but his eyes were full of suspicion.

"It's nothing to do with the police," Smith assured him. "I've been having some problems with my car, and I was hoping you would take a look at it."

"Good luck with that," Whitton joined in. "That car needs putting out of its misery."

"What's wrong with it?" Gary asked.

"It doesn't work." Whitton got in first.

"It's getting on a bit," Smith said. "And it just needs a bit of attention. I'd be grateful if you could help. I'll pay you what you usually charge. I'm not asking this as a favour."

"I'll come round and take a look," Gary said. "It probably just needs a service."

"It needs a lot more than that," Whitton said.

Gary got up from the table and left without asking permission this time.

Jenny brought dessert and the atmosphere around the table was more relaxed. Smith wondered whether to bring up the subject of the complaint that was lodged after Darren was arrested but Frank beat him to it.

"The woman I spoke to at the complaints department seems to think we might have a case with our Darren's arrest."

"Are you saying the IOPC have got involved?" Whitton said.

Frank looked at her as though she was speaking French.

"It's the Independent Office for Police Conduct," Smith translated.

"I'm surprised it's gone that far," Whitton said. "Usually, a complaint is handled internally. Especially a minor one like this."

"The woman at wherever you said she's from reckons it's because the copper who arrested our Darren refused to back down and admit he was wrong. We would have settled for a simple apology, but he was having none of it."

Smith thought for a moment about the implications of this. If it had been taken over by the IOPC it was serious and the consequences could be far-reaching.

"Can I ask if my name was mentioned at all?" he said. "When you made the complaint did you mention me?"

Frank shook his head. "Gary said you thought Darren had a good case, but I know how you lot operate. If it came out that you'd suggested filing a complaint against one of your own, it wouldn't do you any favours. I bullshitted a bit and said I'd got some legal advice from a friend. Your name won't come up."

"Thank you," Smith said. "I appreciate it."

He was relieved. He didn't care to dwell on the consequences of having his name come up in an IOPC enquiry. It would be a headache he really could do without. He didn't know then that the implications of what he had suggested were to be far worse than he could ever imagine. The repercussions of this were going to affect him for a very long time.

CHAPTER FIFTY THREE

Smith was experiencing mixed emotions. He was apprehensive about the pending live broadcast of Levi Wright's confession, and he was also concerned about what would happen afterwards. *The Loner's* request was unprecedented, and Smith knew there had to be an ulterior motive behind it. He'd been unable to sleep and he'd thought about little else in the darkness of the bedroom, but he still hadn't been able to come up with a reasonable explanation why a serial killer would want to bear his soul on National television.

Smith was also feeling relieved. The meal with Darren Lewis's parents hadn't been as bad as he'd feared. The food was delicious and, after a few teething problems with Darren's father the evening had run very smoothly. Frank Lewis had agreed to let Darren move in and he'd also had the presence of mind not to involve Smith in the complaint against PC Griffin. Smith would be eternally grateful to him for that.

"Are you ready?" Whitton asked and rattled her car keys.
"As ready as I'll ever be," Smith said. "Where are the rest of the Smith clan?"
"Where do you think? It's half-seven – they don't have to go to school, so they're where any self-respecting kid would be on a Tuesday morning."
"Lucky bastards," Smith said. "I could do with a few more hours in bed myself."
"Did you sleep at all last night?"
"On and off," Smith lied. "Let's get this show on the road, shall we?"

They arrived at the station five minutes later. They passed only two cars on the way. It took them half the time it usually did to get to work but the absence of life on the streets was rather eerie. Smith didn't like it one little bit. He told Whitton he needed to smoke a cigarette before he faced the day, and she went inside the station without him. A small blue car drove up and parked a few metres away from him. Smith watched as a short man got out. It was PC Griffin. The piggy-eyed PC spotted Smith and walked straight up to him. Smith exhaled a cloud of smoke in his direction.

"Your plan backfired, Smith," PC Griffin said.
"You can't win them all," Smith said. "What plan are you referring to?"
"The complaint made by the kid who knocked up your daughter. That's what I'm referring to. It's been thrown out. York Police are not taking it further."
He doesn't know, Smith thought. *He doesn't know it's been handed over to the IOPC.*
He decided not to tell him this. He would leave it as a nice surprise.
"You have a good day," he said instead.
PC Griffin didn't have a retort to this. He marched inside the station.

DI Smyth was waiting by the front desk when Smith went in.
"Morning, boss," he said.
"Are you ready?" DI Smyth said.
"Am I ready for the pantomime of the decade? Not really. How's the prisoner bearing up?"
"He's refusing to eat. He hasn't touched a scrap of food since he was brought in."
"Good," Smith said. "That ought to make him easier to handle."
"You're not still hung up on that. He's not going to try anything. It will be impossible for him to try anything while he's locked up in here."
"I suppose having a couple of snipers on hand during the broadcast is too much to ask."
"You suppose correctly," DI Smyth said. "Although it might make for interesting entertainment."

"I'm up to speed on how the live shitshow is going to happen," Smith said. "I'd quite like to get stuck into some proper police work in the meantime."

"Good," DI Smyth said. "Because we need to prepare ourselves in case the live confession goes tits-up. It's possible he may use the limelight to deny everything."

"I thought he'd signed some kind of guarantee with the CPS."

"He's killed eight people," DI Smyth said. "He's not going to care about breaking a contract. We need to build a watertight case against him in the meantime."

"I can live with that."

* * *

Seven hours later Smith decided he'd done everything he was going to do today. The team had worked tirelessly to tie up loose ends and get all the necessary paperwork in order. It was a tedious way to spend the day but, unfortunately it was a necessary part of the job. When four o'clock came around, Smith reckoned they'd put together a package of evidence that the CPS would be happy with. He didn't believe Levi Wright would use the broadcast to tell the public he was innocent – he wanted to confess, but they had to consider every eventuality.

Smith found Whitton in the canteen. She was sitting at a table with Baldwin.

"Are you coming home to freshen up before the broadcast?" Whitton asked him.

"I'm not needed back here until six," Smith told her. "The live thing starts at seven and PC Walker just wants to go through a few things again before we go live."

"Are you nervous?" Baldwin said.

"I'm dreading it. I hate this kind of thing. Chalmers suggested I sit back and let him talk for most of it, and I'm inclined to agree with him."

"I'm off home," Baldwin stood up. "I'll tune into the broadcast and cheer you on."

"Thanks, Baldwin," Smith said and turned to Whitton. "I bumped into PC Griffin this morning. The dickhead thinks the complaint against him has been thrown out."

"That's not what Darren's dad told us."

"I don't think he knows yet," Smith said. "I don't think Griffin has been informed. You know how secretive the complaints people are."

"Perhaps he's apologised. Frank said that's all they wanted from him."

"I very much doubt that. People like PC Griffin think they're above apologising."

"Let's go home," Whitton said. "I'll make us a bite to eat, and you can grab a shower before you have to come back here."

"Give me five minutes," Smith said. "I've just got a couple of things I need to do first."

He got up and left the canteen. Whitton didn't even bother to ask where he was going.

    He found PC Griffin in the locker room. He was getting changed, ready to go home for the day.

"Stop what you're doing," Smith said.

"My shift has finished," PC Griffin said.

"I'm telling you that it hasn't. Every available officer is expected to work overtime this evening until they're informed otherwise."

"You can't force me to work overtime," PC Griffin said and started to remove his tie.

"No," Smith said. "It's your choice, but if you don't show your willingness to muck in at a time like this, it won't do your future career prospects any favours. In a few hours' time the most proficient serial killer any of us has ever seen will be standing in front of the TV cameras to tell his story. It is an unprecedented occasion, and you really do not want to go home right now."

PC Griffin appeared to be mulling this over. He stopped fiddling with his tie and his piggy eyes narrowed.

"OK," he said. "Where am I needed?"

"I knew you'd come around eventually," Smith said. "I've already spoken to the duty sergeant, and I've got a job for you that you're going to thank me for one day. Report to Sergeant Burns and he'll tell you what's expected of you."

CHAPTER FIFTY FOUR

After a brief from PC Neil Walker where the press liaison officer had refreshed his memory about what to expect, Smith was as ready as he would ever be. He'd been assured that it would be as much like an ordinary interview as it was possible to make it. The only people inside the room where the interrogation was to take place would be Smith and Levi Wright, and the only real difference was the level of technology at play. A total of eleven high-tech cameras had been set up inside the room, nine of which would be focused on the man Smith had dubbed *The Loner*. Sound checks had been carried out during the course of the day and everything was set. Levi would be brought in, accompanied by no less than four armed officers. His hands would be bound in front of him and, before the feed went live his legs were to be shackled to the metal chair bolted to the floor. The camera angles were as such that the people watching wouldn't be privy to this.

"He's waiting for you," DI Smyth said.

It was five minutes before seven.

"How is he?" Smith asked.

"Remarkably calm. He still hasn't eaten anything, and Sergeant Burns told me he's very weak because of it. He's not going anywhere, Smith. Relax - you can do this."

A man with a mole on his cheek walked up to them.

"I just need to do a final check on the sound."

He examined the microphone attached to Smith's shirt collar.

"All good. Could you just say a few words for me."

"What do you want me to say?" Smith said.

"Anything that comes to mind."

"I need my fucking head examining for agreeing to this," Smith said.

The man grinned. "That'll do."

He held up a mystery device and swiped the screen.

"Could you say that once more please."

Smith did. He emphasised the *F* word this time.

"You're good to go," the technician said. "Break a leg."

Smith went inside the interview room and took a seat opposite Levi Wright. *The Loner*'s gaze was focused on something above Smith's head. His eyes were green. PC Walker's words still rang fresh in Smith's head. This was definitely not an ordinary interview situation. This was as far from any interview Smith had ever conducted as it was possible to get. Nothing that was said within the four walls of this room would be admissible as evidence. Anything Levi said was for entertainment value alone. He could admit to having killed the Pope and they wouldn't be able to use it against him.

It was very warm inside the room and Smith was already feeling uncomfortable. Levi Wright was the one shackled and incapacitated, but it was Smith who felt the more defenceless. Levi had free rein in here, but everything Smith said would be under scrutiny, ready to be picked apart at a later date. He needed to be extremely careful how he conducted himself.

"One minute before we're live," a voice said from a speaker somewhere inside the room.

Smith looked across at the man about to confess to the murders of eight people. He wondered what else he was going to tell the people tuning in. What else did he want to get off his chest?

Levi made eye contact and Smith held it. He'd promised himself he wasn't going to be intimidated. *The Loner* was a monster, but he was still just a man – he was flesh and blood, nothing more.

"Don't fuck this up."

Smith flinched. He hadn't even noticed Levi's lips move. It was also the first time he'd heard him swear.

"Thirty seconds," the voice told them.

"You're going to be taken from here soon," Smith said. "And you'll be transferred to a place much worse than the hell you believe in."

Levi nodded.

"The people in that place will have watched this," Smith carried on. "Some of them will fall in love with you, but most of them won't. You'll be put in a cage where nobody can get to you, but one day a mistake will be made and that's when they'll attack. You won't even see it coming."

"And we're on in ten."

It was almost time. Smith took a few deep breaths, careful not to make Levi aware of his agitation.

The countdown had begun. The voice reached number 4 in the countdown, and the room fell silent. Smith had been instructed to keep watching the red light in the corner of the room. When it turned green it was all-go – it was lights, camera, action.

CHAPTER FIFTY FIVE

"Could you please state your name for the record," Smith said.

"Go to camera 4," one of the team said.

His name was Bert, and he was the chief visual operator. He was part of a team controlling the broadcast from a van outside in the car park.

"I want a bit more volume on Smith," he added.

"Levi Aaron Wright."

"He's got a voice made for the movies," Donna Love said.

"Zoom in on his face," Bert directed.

The screen in front of them showed the footage exactly as it would be broadcast to the world. A live stream had been set up, and anyone who had logged in could watch what was happening for free.

"What's happening?" Bert asked.

It looked like the screen had frozen. The close-up of Levi Wright's face wasn't moving.

"It's like he knows exactly which camera is on him," Donna said. "That's really creepy."

"Levi Aaron Wright," Smith repeated after a few seconds. "You are not under caution. We're way passed that stage, and anything you say today cannot be used against you in a court of law. What is it you want to tell the world? Do you want them to hear how you murdered five people in a matter of days? Do you want them to understand what made you kill them? Are you looking for absolution – forgiveness from their family and friends, because if that's why you're here, I can save you the trouble. It's not going to happen. Or are you here to tell the audience what you did to your parents? Do you want them to know how you killed them and chopped them into small enough pieces so you could fit them inside a chest freezer? You kept your mum and dad in a freezer for over a year. You subjected your neighbour to the same treatment. I'm sure the people watching are wide awake now. I reckon you have their full attention now, Levi. The floor's yours."

* * *

"What the hell is he playing at?" Bert said. "He was instructed to lead the way and then keep his mouth shut for most of the interview."

"Look at Levi's face," Donna said. "Look at his eyes."

Bert did and what he saw was an expression of mild amusement on the face of the man sitting opposite Smith.

"This wasn't part of the script," Bert said. "What a mess. What if he clams up completely?"

He didn't. If anything, Smith's words seemed to spur him on.

"I want to go back to when it all started," Levi said. "If I may."

He looked at Smith as though he was asking for his approval.

"It's your party," Smith said.

"I wasn't always this way. Mine was a happy childhood. I had two parents who loved me dearly."

And then you killed them, chopped them up and kept them in a freezer, Smith thought.

He didn't voice this thought.

"When I was twenty-three," Levi continued. "I lost my way. A man came into our lives and changed me. He changed all of us. His name was Len."

"Len Boswell?" Smith said.

"He moved in next door and introduced God into our lives. But it wasn't the god all of you know. It was a different god. God would not condone what I was subjected to in His name. When I got out of prison, my mother and father locked me up for almost three weeks. I was given nothing but water, and I was told I was evil so many times I eventually believed it. Len Boswell made me what I am today."

He's looking for sympathy, Smith thought.

Chalmers had warned him about this, and he knew he had to steer the narrative away from what might swing the public in Levi's favour.

"Why did you kill your parents?" he asked.

Levi closed his eyes and exhaled a long breath.

"Picture a wasp," he said. "A wasp will sting over and over again until it's squished underfoot. It will not stop. No man will put up with that forever. You would not let a wasp sting and sting and sting, would you?"

He observed Smith with his head tilted at an angle.

"This isn't about me," Smith said.

"It had to stop," Levi told him. "I'd been stung to the point where something had to give. I choked my mother to death, and I beat my father with a statue of Christ."

"Why did you chop up their bodies?" Smith said. "You kept them in a freezer for over a year. What made you do that?"

"Remorse."

Smith resisted the urge to roll his eyes at this. It was clear that Levi was putting on an act.

"Despite what they did to me," Levi said. "Despite the pain they inflicted, I still loved them, and I wanted to keep them close. I had to keep them nearby – I needed them."

"You killed Len Boswell," Smith said. "You chopped him up too and you kept him in the freezer with your mother and father. I don't understand why you did that. You didn't love *him*."

"It was what my mother would have wanted."

"When did you decide that you were going to kill six people?" Smith said. "What made you want to kill six people and carve the mark of Christ on the cross into their skin?"

"Sinners need to be punished," Levi said.

"You killed five innocent people, Levi," Smith said. "Five people who did nothing to you. These people didn't wrong you in any way. You didn't even know them. I don't understand how you can justify that."

"Sinners must atone for their transgressions. My mother spoke those words to me on a daily basis."

"Do you know what I think?" Smith said. "I think you're trying to justify your actions using the Bible as an excuse. You weren't passing judgement when you carried out your vile, twisted killing – you were acting on some perverted desire. You're sick, Levi – of that there is little doubt, but don't try and pretend you did this because of God or Jesus Christ or what you've read in the Bible."

"Sinners must atone," Levi said. "Don't you dare belittle my mother's words."

"You killed five innocent people."

A smile formed on Levi's face. He looked up at one of the cameras in the ceiling and the smile grew. His eyes darkened and then they changed colour. The emerald green had morphed to blue in an instant.

"All of them had sinned. And if you'll let me talk, I'll explain it to you."

The light in the corner of the room changed to red. Smith had been told about this. There would be a ten-minute break in recording to allow for advertisements in the live feed. The subscription to view the footage was free, but commercial rates were at a premium, and now the companies who'd paid that premium were being promoted on the site.

CHAPTER FIFTY SIX

"Please tell me you got a close-up of that."

Bert, the chief visual operator had worked on some controversial media before, but the subject matter of this footage was by far the most exciting of his career.

"We got it," Donna said. "This is good. This is seriously good. This shit is going to need a rating never considered before if it's going to be shown on TV. Did you see his eyes?"

"I've never seen anything like it. If Detective Smith ever considers a change of career, I'd hire him in a heartbeat. That bloke is a natural. He knows how to get just the right reaction at exactly the right time."

"The ratings are through the roof," Donna said. "We're getting more hits than Boris's lockdown speech."

* * *

"Is this what you wanted?" Levi said.

The light in the corner of the room remained red. Smith wondered what was being advertised on the site right now. He was also thinking about who might be watching. He was blissfully unaware that life was never going to be the same after today. He was going to be recognised everywhere he went.

"I think this is more about what you want," he said. "You think you're in charge, but you're mistaken. I can walk out of here any time I want, but you can't."

"You're not going to do that," Levi said. "You want to know more. You can't help it."

"You killed five innocent people, Levi."

"You'll see. You've been found wanting, Detective Smith. I'm not all evil. There is still decency in me, and I'm going to spare you the embarrassment of telling the world what you couldn't see. I killed five sinners, and I'm going to kill one more before the clock strikes midnight."

This time Smith did roll his eyes.

"You'll see," Levi said once more.

"We're back on in ten," the voice told them.

The light turned to green again and Smith took a deep breath.

"Melissa Grange," Levi said. "She was wanton. A hussy and a devourer of men. She needed to be stopped."

Smith was forced to listen as Levi listed his victims in order together with what he believed their sins to be. It made for painful listening. Jennifer Wells had cheated on her boyfriend. Karen Salway had once attended the same church as Levi, but she'd turned her back on God. Steven Lemon liked to view pornography, and Sally Dean suffered from greed because Levi had once witnessed her refusing to give a beggar a coin or two. All in all, their transgressions were slight, and Smith was starting to wonder whether Levi Wright was delusional. All five of his victims had crossed his path one way or another, but none of them deserved what had been done to them. On a positive note, Smith knew for a fact that the sympathy vote for *The Loner* was dwindling rapidly.

"So now you know," Levi said.

"You carved the mark of Christ into the skin of your victims," Smith said. "What was the point of that?"

"You wouldn't understand."

"Help me to understand."

"Jesus died for us," Levi said. "He died for you. When he was put on the cross, he suffered terribly. The wounds on his head, hands, wrist, feet, back and chest are important. They symbolise the ultimate sacrifice. The sinners I killed needed to be marked before they faced the judgment of God. I suffered along with them."

"How exactly did you do that?"

"I have the marks too. If I wasn't shackled like a pig I would show you."

"I'll take your word for it," Smith said.

"What else would you like to know?" Levi said.

"You recited the Loner's Prayer after you killed them," Smith said. "Can you explain that."

"It came from Saint Rita of Cascia. She was the patron saint of loners, and her prayer is very dear to me."

"Are you a loner, Levi?" Smith asked.

"Very much so. A loner has only himself to consider. A loner travels his path alone. It's a very peaceful existence."

Smith was feeling drained. The interview had been an exhausting one, and he had a sudden urge to get the hell away from the psychopath sitting opposite him. But there was still one question he needed to ask.

"Who is the final victim, Levi?" he said. "The public may not be aware of this but there were six names on your list. Who are you going to kill next?"

"I don't know."

"And I don't believe you," Smith said. "I'm just a bit concerned it might be me, because I once drove my car without insurance. Is that a worthy sin for you? I think we're done here. I'm starting to feel slightly ill."

He looked up at one of the cameras. "Could someone please get this piece of human waste out of here."

"You'll remember me, Detective Smith," Levi told him. "You'll remember me as the one that got away."

The light on the ceiling was still green. The footage was still being broadcast live.

"You're going to spend the rest of your life behind bars," Smith said. "And after tonight that life is going to be a very short one. Will someone please get this delusional idiot away from me."

"I'm walking out of here tonight," Levi said. "I'm going to walk out with blood on my hands."
The red light came on and the door to the room opened. Four officers came inside, one of them unlocked the shackles pinning Levi to the chair, and he was escorted out.

Smith left the room shortly afterwards. He made his way down the corridor and was stopped at the front desk by PC Black.
"I wouldn't go out there, Sarge. Press are everywhere."
"Thanks for the head's-up, Jim," Smith said. "But journalists don't faze me."
"You were great in there," PC Black said.
"Did you watch it?"
"I think the entire country tuned in, Sarge. He came across as a bit of a nut job, didn't he? I mean, killing people for stupid reasons like that."
"He's delusional," Smith said. "He needs help. He still reckons he's going to get out of here tonight. He said he's going to walk out with blood on his hands."
"As long as it's not my blood," PC Black said. "Are you really going out there?"

Smith nodded and went outside. The first camera flashes assaulted his vision when he'd only walked a few steps. There were more journalists than he'd ever seen before. Questions were fired at him from all directions, and he ignored every one of them. He took out his cigarettes and lit one as he walked. Some of the press contingency walked with him and more questions came. Smith opened Whitton's car and got inside. He knew she wouldn't be very happy about him smoking in the car, but he didn't care. He needed to get as far away from the station as possible. He turned the key in the ignition, engaged first gear and sped out of the car park.

CHAPTER FIFTY SEVEN

Whitton handed Smith a beer the moment he stepped inside the house.

"I thought you might need this," she said.

"Thanks," he said. "Did you watch it?"

"We all did."

Smith took a long swig of beer. "That's better. You didn't let Laura watch it, did you?"

"Of course not. It was just me, Lucy and Darren. Darren's brother phoned him straight afterwards and said he'd fix your car for free. You're a celeb now."

"I don't want to be a celebrity. I just want to put this case behind me and forget about it. The man is seriously deranged. I wouldn't be surprised if he's shipped off to a mental facility."

"He seemed convinced he was going to walk out of the station tonight," Whitton said. "It was like he really believed it."

Smith's phone started to ring in his pocket. He took it out and the screen told him it was someone not in his contacts list. He let it ring out.

"You're going to be inundated with calls for a while," Whitton said. "You know what the press are like. You did well tonight. I thought you were going to lose it for a moment, but you didn't let him get to you."

"I wanted to kill him with my bare hands."

"He's not worth it. Have you spoken to the DI?"

"Not yet."

Right on cue the phone started to ring again, and the ringtone told him exactly who it was.

"Boss," Smith answered it.

"You trod a fine line in there tonight," DI Smyth said.

"I got what I wanted. For what it's worth."

"Do you think he was telling the truth?"

"I reckon he was," Smith said. "Most of the time. I think he really believed the people he killed had sinned."

"Your comment about driving without insurance was a bit stupid. The press could latch onto that, and it could cause trouble at work."

"I think the press has more juicy stories to cover than a DS driving without insurance," Smith said.

"I sincerely hope so," DI Smyth said. "I'll let you get on with your evening. Enjoy your day off tomorrow."

"I wasn't aware I had a day off."

"You do now. You've earned it. Get some rest."

Smith knew that wasn't going to happen. He was too hyped up from the interview. He'd had no sleep in almost two days, but thoughts were flying around inside his head at breakneck speed, and he wasn't able to slow them down. He finished his beer and took another one out of the fridge.

Lucy came into the kitchen and hugged him tightly.

"What was that for?" Smith asked her.

"For being my dad the super cop," she said.

"I don't feel like a super cop."

"That interview was amazing. My friends have been messaging me non-stop about it. You have now officially reached the rank of *cool Dad*. You were so calm in there. I had to look away when his eyes changed colour, but you were sitting right opposite him and it didn't bother you at all."

"It bothered me," Smith admitted. "I just hid it well."

"You can't fool me, Dad. You're my hero."

"You're going to have to get used to that," Whitton said. "People are going to look at you differently from now on. You're always going to be the detective who interviewed *The Loner*."

Smith took a sip of beer. "Can we talk about something else? I think I've had about as much as I can take of Levi Wright."

* * *

"Jim," Sergeant Fox said. "I've got a job for you."
PC Black looked up from the desk at the duty sergeant.
"What is it, Sarge?"
"The bloke who was supposed to be babysitting Mr Wright has been relieved of his duties, and I need someone to take over."
"Why has PC Griffin been relieved?"
"Something to do with an IOPC investigation. He's been suspended."
"What did he do?"
"Who knows?" Sergeant Fox said. "Mr Wright isn't going anywhere, but he needs to be supervised. You know the drill – suicide risk and all that."
"I'll be right there," PC Black said. "I just need to let my wife know I'll be working late."

Levi Wright was asleep on the bed inside the holding cell when PC Black arrived. He was breathing deeply, and his chest was rising and falling. PC Black sat down on the chair outside the cell and took out his mobile phone. He opened up his library app and looked for something that would help him to stay awake. He chose a book he'd read before – *The Art of War*. He would read it in more detail this time.

An hour into the book, PC Black was interrupted when Levi coughed and when he turned to look at him, he realised *The Loner* was sitting up on the bed. He coughed again, louder this time.

"Could I have something to drink, please?" Levi asked. "It feels like I have a fur ball in my throat."

"I'll get you some water," PC Black said.
He got up and headed for the staff room. He found a plastic beaker in the sink, filled it with water and returned to the holding cell.

Levi was standing by the bars of the cell now. PC Black passed the beaker to him, and Levi took it in both hands. He turned around, lifted the beaker to his mouth and drank the water in one go.
He turned to face PC Black again. "Would it be too much trouble to have some more?"
"No problem," PC Black said.

He saw it too late. Levi leaned forward to pass the beaker back through the bars, but his hands were no longer bound with the cable ties. The beaker had also changed – a piece had been snapped off. Before PC Black had time to react, the jagged plastic slashed at his neck and he gasped. The attack was brutally accurate, and his carotids were severed in one clean go. PC Black put his hands to his neck and felt the warm blood as it gushed out. Levi Wright stood and watched as PC Black tried in vain to stem the flow. The experienced PC collapsed to his knees as the life blood ran out of him. He was dead in less a minute.

Levi reached through the bars and found the keyring attached to PC Black's belt. He unclipped it and retrieved the keys. He found the one that unlocked the cell, opened the door and dragged PC Black inside. He removed his clothes and set about doing the same to the dead police officer. The blood had stopped flowing now.

Before dressing PC Black in his own clothes, Levi leaned over and carved a wound an inch long in his chest with the sharp piece of the plastic beaker. "So humble..."
PC Black didn't hear any of the Loner's prayer, nor did he bear witness to the emerald eyes changing to blue as Levi Wright looked down at his corpse.

Levi put on PC Black's uniform and cupped up a handful of arterial blood. He smeared some on his nose and mouth and left the cell, making sure to lock the door behind him. He made his way to where he'd been checked in. The duty sergeant was looking at something on his mobile phone behind the desk. Levi bowed his head and put his hands to his face. Sergeant Fox looked up from his phone as he rushed past.

"Nosebleed, Sarge," Levi said. "I just need to pop to the bathroom."

Sergeant Fox nodded and turned his attention back to his phone.

CHAPTER FIFTY EIGHT

Smith had finally managed to drift off to sleep when he was woken by a wide-eyed Whitton. It took him a moment to realise this wasn't part of the dream he was having. The bright light inside the room was burning his eyes.
"He's escaped," Whitton told him.
Smith sat up in bed. "What?"
"Levi Wright has escaped."
Smith rubbed his eyes. "Could you repeat that?"
"He's escaped, Jason. Levi Wright has gone."
"How is that even possible?"
"The DI said he somehow managed to overpower the officer keeping an eye on him, and he opened the cell and dragged him inside. He put on the PCs uniform and pretended to be suffering from a nosebleed. Sergeant Fox watched him go."
"This isn't happening," Smith said. "This isn't fucking happening. He did it, didn't he? He said he was going to walk out with blood on his hands, and he did precisely that. Is the PC OK?"
"He's dead. The DI said his throat had been slashed."
"Fuck. What time is it?"
"Just after midnight," Whitton said.

    Smith and Whitton were dressed and out of the house ten minutes later. Drops of rain were falling and the temperature had dropped.
"It was my idea to get PC Griffin to babysit him," Smith said when they were almost at the station.
"It's not your fault," Whitton said.
"I suppose it could have been worse," Smith said. "PC Griffin was a dickhead anyway."

"He didn't deserve to die."

"I'm just saying it could have been someone who actually belonged in the job. This is the balls-up of all balls-ups. Why didn't the duty sergeant stop him? How could he just let him walk past? Levi Wright looks nothing like PC Griffin."

"I suppose we'll find out the details soon enough."

Bridge's Toyota and DC Moore's Subaru were parked in the car park when they arrived at the station. The DI had obviously brought in the whole team. An ambulance was also parked close to the entrance. Smith and Whitton went inside and were met by DI Smyth.

"What the fuck happened?" Smith asked him.

"It's not yet clear," DI Smyth said. "Sergeant Fox said PC Black rushed past with blood all over his face and nose. He said he had a nosebleed, and he was going to the bathroom."

Smith froze. "PC Black?"

"When he didn't come back for quite some time," DI Smyth said. "Sergeant Fox went to find him. He wasn't in the bathroom and when Sergeant Fox went to check the holding cells, he found him locked inside Levi Wright's cell. His throat had been sliced open. Looks like he used a piece from a plastic beaker."

"What was PC Black doing there? PC Griffin was supposed to have been given that job."

"He's been suspended pending the outcome of an IOPC investigation. He was relieved of his duties and PC Black took his place."

"I need some air," Smith said and went outside to the car park.

"What's up with him?" DI Smyth said. "We'll find him. Levi Wright can't have got far. We've got everyone out looking for him. We'll find him."

"It's not that, sir," Whitton said.

She told him about the complaint about PC Griffin, and she also mentioned the fact that Smith had recommended that Darren Lewis go ahead with the complaint.

"He's going to blame himself," she said. "If PC Griffin hadn't been suspended PC Black wouldn't have even been there. Smith really liked PC Black."

"There's no point in dwelling on it," DI Smyth said. "We have a dead PC and a psychopathic killer on the loose. I need Smith's head in the game right now. Where would he go? We need to put our heads together and figure out where he would go."

"He's not stupid enough to go back to the house in Clifton," Whitton said. "Or the place in Tadcaster where he kept his parents in the freezer. Perhaps he has another hideout. Did anyone else see him dressed as PC Black?"

"There was hardly anyone around. PC Miller was manning the front desk but he didn't leave that way. He must have gone out the back."

Smith came back in, and the smell of cigarette smoke came in with him. All the colour had drained from his face.

"This isn't your fault," DI Smyth said. "I need your focus to be on figuring out where Levi Wright would go now."

"It's my fault, boss," Smith said. "I was the one who persuaded Darren to lodge that complaint. PC Griffin wouldn't have been suspended if I hadn't done that and PC Black would still be alive."

"That's enough. You can feel as sorry for yourself as you like when we've got Levi Wright locked up again, but in the meantime, you're going to put it out of your mind. Where would he go? Where would your loner go now? Bridge and DC Moore are watching the footage of the interview again to see if there are any clues there, but you got closer to the man than any of us. Think – where do you believe he would run to?"

"I don't know," Smith said. "He didn't say anything in the live broadcast to give us a clue. He spoke mostly about his parents and his other victims."

"What about a church?" Whitton suggested. "Do we know what church he used to go to? He told you he killed Karen Salway because she turned her back on God. She went to the same church as him. Do we know what church it was?"

"No," Smith said. "And there are dozens of churches in York."

"It needs to be considered," DI Smyth said. "We have every available officer out looking for him. We have his house and the place he rented under surveillance, but it's still not enough."

"He planned this," Smith said. "He had this in mind the whole time."

"How could he possibly have planned it?" DI Smyth said. "How would he know PC Griffin would be replaced with PC Black? PC Griffin is almost a foot shorter than Jim Black. His uniform wouldn't have even fitted. There were far too many variables beyond his control for this to have been planned."

"He seized the opportunity," Smith said. "The details of the murder weren't mapped out beforehand but the murder itself was. He told me he was going to walk out with blood on his hands and that's exactly what he did. Heads are going to roll for this. We have a serial killer who told the entire nation he was going to escape from police custody, and we let him. There's a serious shitstorm heading our way."

"And that's why we need to find the man. How are we going to do that?"

Smith looked him in the eyes. "I think I might know someone who can help us."

"I'm all ears."

"I just need to make a quick phone call," Smith said and went back outside.

"I hate it when he does that," DI Smyth said.

"At least he didn't tell us he'll let us know when he's figured it out," Whitton said.

"There is that I suppose."

Smith returned a few minutes later.

"Well?" DI Smyth said.

"She's coming here," Smith told him.

"Who are you talking about?" Whitton said.

"The prettiest shrink in York. Dr Fiona Vennell. She watched the live broadcast, but she's agreed to come here to watch it with us. She's going to try and shrink the head of *The Loner*."

CHAPTER FIFTY NINE

"Could you please take a seat, sir," Jackie Lloyd told the policeman. "I'll get someone to come and take a look at you as soon as possible."
Jackie looked at the tall police officer. The blood on his lower face had dried. His mouth and nose was covered in it, and there was something vaguely familiar about the man. She found herself drawn to his green eyes. He'd come into the hospital and informed her he'd been injured while apprehending a suspect. Jackie hadn't worked at the hospital for very long, and that's why she didn't think it odd that a police constable would come to the hospital alone.

"Thank you," the officer said.

He walked away and took a seat in the waiting area. A few minutes passed and a short man wearing glasses approached him. He introduced himself as Vince Dewbury and he was a senior nurse.
"What happened to you?" he asked.
"Slight altercation with a drunk on the Hull Road. We seemed to have different opinions about whether I should arrest him or not. It appears he won the argument, and I ended up with this."
He pointed to the blood on his face.
"It's probably worse than it looks," he added.
"Let's get you seen to," Vince said. "Has the incident been reported? It needs to be logged."
"We can do that later. Is there a bathroom I can use? I think I'm going to be sick."
Vince helped him up.
He pointed to the corridor to the left of the reception desk. "Go down the corridor and you'll find the Gents on the right. I'll wait for you here."

He watched as the tall PC followed his directions. The front door of the hospital opened, and two men burst in. One of them had a deep gash in his forehead and his friend was holding him upright. It was clear they were intoxicated. Vince Dewbury's attention was caught by the men, and he wasn't aware that the *injured* PC had walked right past the Gents and turned left in the direction of the Pathology department.

* * *

Smith introduced Dr Vennell to the rest of the team, and they made their way to the small conference room. Bridge didn't even try to hide the fact that he liked what he saw. His eyes were glued to the pretty psychologist from the moment she came in. He might be in a serious relationship with Billie Jones, but old habits die hard.

DC Moore had set up the big screen in the room and connected it to a laptop. They were going to watch the footage of the interview with Levi Wright and Dr Vennell had promised to do her best to see if there was anything in it that might give them a clue as to where *The Loner* might be now.

They sat down and DC Moore brought up the file with the footage of the interview on it. Smith wasn't particularly keen to relive it so soon, but if there was any chance that the location of Levi Wright would be revealed somewhere in the undertones of the interview it had to be done.

"The interview isn't very long," DI Smyth said. "So I suggest we watch it in silence, then watch it again and comment on anything that might help us."

Dr Vennell agreed. She'd brought along a notepad, and she told them she would make notes throughout the interview.

"Would you like something to drink?" Bridge asked her. "The machine in the canteen does very reasonable coffee."

"Maybe when I'm finished," Dr Vennell told him. "Let's get started."

DC Moore started the footage. Even though Smith was present throughout it was rather surreal watching it from this perspective. He realised that the main focus was Levi himself and he was glad. The camera had zoomed in on his face. Dr Vennell wrote something on her notepad before he'd even started speaking.

They reached the halfway point and Dr Vennell asked DC Moore to pause the file.

"What did you talk about during the commercial break?" she asked Smith.

"He told me I'd been found wanting," Smith told her. "He said I'd missed the connection between the victims. He said I should have known he killed them because they'd sinned."

"Their transgressions hardly warranted a death sentence," Bridge said.

"What else did he tell you?" Dr Vennell said.

"He kept saying, *you'll see*," Smith said. "I think he was referring to his plan to escape."

"Interesting," Dr Vennell said. "Let's watch the rest."

DC Moore resumed the footage to the part where Levi outlined the reasons for killing his five victims. Their *sins* were revealed, and then he went on to speak about the rationale behind his prayer and the mutilation of the bodies. The footage reached its conclusion and DC Moore stopped the file.

"What are your initial thoughts?" DI Smyth asked Dr Vennell.

"It's clear he suffers from delusions of grandeur," she said. "He believes himself to be a higher being, worthy of doling out punishment to those he believes to have sinned. It's possible this stems from his treatment at the hands of his parents – especially his mother. He mentions her specifically more than once. I wouldn't be surprised if he had a much stronger bond with her than he did with his father."

"A lot of documented serial killers have grown up with a domineering

matriarch." It was Bridge. "It seems to be a common denominator in many of the psychopaths throughout the ages."
Dr Vennell nodded.

"Start it from the beginning," DI Smyth said.
They watched it again. Dr Vennell wrote notes the whole time.
"He's remarkably calm," she commented.
"He's a psychopath," DC Moore said.
"He believes he's in complete control," Smith said.
"I'm inclined to agree," Dr Vennell said. "His hands are bound, and he's shackled to a chair, but in his mind, he is still the one in charge."

A minute passed, and Dr Vennell stood up abruptly.
"Stop it there and go back a bit."
"What is it?" Smith said.
"He killed his parents and kept them in a freezer," Dr Vennell said. "Rewind it to when he tells us about that."
DC Moore did as he was asked.

"There," Dr Vennell said. "When you asked him why he chopped up his mother and father and kept them in the freezer he told you it was out of remorse, and he still loved them. He wanted to keep them close because he needed them. Then, shortly afterwards he said he did the same to the neighbour because it's what his mother would have wanted. He's still controlled by his mother, even though she's been dead for over a year. His mother is everything to him."
"How does that help us though?" Whitton said.
"I believe there's a strong possibility he'll go to her."
"She's dead," DC Moore said. "He chopped her into little pieces and shoved her in a freezer."
"And he kept her close," Smith said. "He needed her to be close to him. He's finished what he set out to do, but he hasn't quite finished."

"He needs to tell her," Dr Vennell said. "He needs to tell his mother what he's done."

"Am I the only one who thinks this is totally nuts?" DC Moore said.

"Mr Wright's brain isn't wired like most people's," Dr Vennell said. "He doesn't think like a normal, rational person."

"Where were the body parts taken?" Smith asked.

"They were shipped off to Pathology," DI Smyth said. "They needed to be tested to confirm they are who Levi claims they are."

"That's where he's gone," Smith said. "He's gone to the hospital to visit the pieces of his mother."

CHAPTER SIXTY

DI Smyth had wanted to mobilise the armed unit, but Smith had argued that it would take too long. They needed to get to the hospital now. It was possible Levi Wright's visit to the pieces of his mother would be brief. For once DI Smyth had backed down and let Smith have his way. They were standing outside the station. Smith was smoking a cigarette.

"I want Chalmers with us," he said. "The DCI's right hook is more effective than any armed team."

"It's almost two in the morning," DI Smyth reminded him.

"Chalmers won't care," Smith said.

He took out his phone and walked away.

DI Smyth took out his own phone. He needed to warn the staff at the hospital not to go anywhere near Levi Wright. Uniform had already been dispatched but they were to wait for further instructions before they went inside the hospital.

Smith came back and the grin on his face told DI Smyth that Chalmers would be with them on this one.

"He was a bit pissed off about being woken up," Smith said. "But he's going to meet us at the hospital."

"I've just spoken to someone there," DI Smyth said. "It looks like your psychologist friend was right on the money. A uniformed officer came in earlier covered in blood. He asked to use the bathroom, and nobody has been able to find him. He matches the description of Levi Wright."

"The bastard is still wearing PC Black's fucking uniform," Smith said.

"Calm down. We're going to get him. We're going to make damn sure he pays for what he's done."

Dr Vennell came outside and walked over to them.

"Your evaluation was right," Smith said. "He's at the hospital."

"Glad I could help," Dr Vennell said.

"I'm going to bring the car round," DI Smyth said.

"You've given us something we never would have figured out on our own," Smith said to Dr Vennell. "We won't forget this."

"I was just doing what I've been trained to do."

"Speaking of which," Smith said. "I suppose I ought to go and do what I was trained to do. Wish me luck."

"Good luck." Dr Vennell leaned across and kissed him on the lips.

Smith wasn't expecting it. He broke free and looked at her. She was gazing into his eyes.

"I think I'm a little bit in love with you, Detective Smith."

"Don't be," Smith warned. "It won't do you any favours."

DI Smyth drove up and Smith was glad. He got into the car without saying anything further to Dr Vennell.

The drive to the hospital passed in silence. Smith was still agonising over what had happened to PC Black. He didn't think he would be able to forgive himself for that. PC Black was a good officer. He was also a family man with a wife and two children. Those children were now going to have to grow up without a father. As they got closer to the hospital the guilt turned to fury and Smith let it. He was going to stop *The Loner* if it was the last thing he ever did, and he knew deep down that the rules had changed for this one. Everything he'd ever been taught – everything in the police rule book didn't apply right now. This was a case where necessary force equated to as much force as possible. They were going to take Levi Wright down and if his heart stopped beating in the process, so be it.

Chalmers had beaten them there. The DCI was standing next to his BMW smoking a cigarette in the car park at the hospital. Smith got out of DI Smyth's car and walked straight over to him.

"You've got a bloody nerve," Chalmers said.

"Good morning to you too, boss," Smith said. "Do you want to back out?"

"Not bloody likely. What do we know?"

"The DI spoke to someone at the hospital and he's here. He came in dressed in PC Black's uniform and pretended to be injured. They haven't been able to find him and that's because he's gone to visit his mother. Or should I say the pieces of his mother."

"Sick doesn't even begin to describe it," Chalmers said. "Do we know if he's armed?"

"If he's wearing the uniform, it's safe to assume he brought along the baton and the pepper spray, but I doubt we'll have to deal with anything worse than that."

"Let's go and get him then."

"Hold your horses," DI Smyth had joined them. "We need to secure the area first."

"We haven't got time to mess around with that," Smith argued. "We have to go in now. The DCI will agree with me."

"He's right," Chalmers said. "We go in now."

Chalmer's famous right hook wasn't the only reason why Smith had requested his assistance at the hospital. His rank would come in handy and the expression on DI Smyth's face told Smith he was well aware of this. He looked extremely annoyed.

"What's the plan of action then?" he said.

"We go in there and get the bastard," Smith said. "Just the two of us. When he killed PC Black this became something else altogether."

"Be careful," DI Smyth said.

"You know me, boss."

"That's what concerns me."

Smith and Chalmers went inside the hospital and headed straight for the department where Dr Kenny Bean worked. Smith was grateful that Dr Bean wasn't on duty right now. He and the peculiar pathologist had become close in the past few years, and he didn't want anything to happen to him.

A woman in a white coat intercepted them before they got to the Pathology department. She introduced herself as Dr Franklin and she told them exactly where the body parts were.

"Is anyone else in there?" Smith asked her.

"There's nobody working in Pathology right now."

"Did you see him go in?" Chalmers said. "He's wearing a police uniform."

"No," Dr Franklin said. "If he wanted to get inside the room he will have needed to break the window in the door. It's locked with a heavy-duty lock."

"That won't stop him," Smith said. "I need you to get everybody out. We have officers standing by outside, but I don't want anybody anywhere near this part of the hospital."

"Has this been authorised?"

"There's no time for that," Smith said. "I need you to trust me. We're going to do everything we can to prevent him from leaving, but if he does manage to get free, he will not hesitate to kill anyone who gets in his way. Could you do that for me please."

Dr Franklin nodded.

"We're going to need the key to the room," Chalmers said.

Dr Franklin took out a set of keys and showed him which one would open the lock on the door.

"Thank you," Smith said. "Nobody is to come anywhere near here. We'll give you a minute to organise something before we go in."

CHAPTER SIXTY ONE

Smith stopped in the corridor leading to the room where the doctor had told them the body parts were being stored. He looked at Chalmers and nodded his head. The glass in the top half of the door to the room had been smashed in. The sound of a low voice could be heard inside the room. They'd found *The Loner*.

Chalmers put a finger to his lips, and they stood and listened. Smith could only make out certain words, but he knew for a fact that Levi Wright was reciting the Loner's prayer. Levi was talking of such compassionate love for thy crucified Jesus. Chalmers indicated with a flick of a finger that they were to proceed towards the door. Smith was glad Chalmers had thought about the key to the lock. The gap where the pane of glass had been was barely wide enough to fit through and crawling through it would put them at a distinct disadvantage.

"What are we going to do?" Smith whispered.
"We open the door and go in," Chalmers whispered back. "Or did you have another plan?"
"Yours sounds good."

They crept towards the door and the words Levi Wright was speaking became clearer. His tone was gentle and his words, soothing. Smith thought it sounded like he was talking to his mother.

Chalmers located the keyhole and inserted the key. Levi carried on talking to the pieces of his dead mother. The key was turned and there was a quiet click. Levi stopped talking. Chalmers pushed open the door and he and Smith ran into the room.

Smith wasn't expecting what greeted them inside the room. Levi Wright was standing over one of the freezer compartments. He was naked apart from a pair of black boxer shorts. Scars covered his chest and legs. There were more scars on his arms. Some of them were old wounds, but a few were inflamed. These had been inflicted very recently.

"On your knees," Chalmers said. "Put your hands behind your head and get on your knees."

Smith did a quick survey of the room. This was where the bodies were stored before they were taken to be examined. There were no instruments Levi could use as a possible weapon.

He stood, stock still in front of them.

"On your knees," Chalmers told him again.

He stayed standing.

"It's over, Levi," Smith said.

Levi nodded and turned to face whatever it was inside the freezer compartment.

"Goodbye, mother."

"You've said your farewells," Chalmers said. "Now get down on your bloody knees before I get upset."

"You don't want to make him upset," Smith said.

"I'm truly alone now," Levi said.

He took a step towards Smith and looked into his eyes. Levi's eyes were changing.

Something was changing inside Smith too. Flashes of images came into his head. He saw the face of Steven Lemon's bedridden mother as she talked about her faith in God. Karen Salway's little Yorkshire Terrier was there in his mind's eye, as was Gary Lewis. Smith recalled Darren's brother's anguish because he hadn't been able to save Sally Dean in time. These were people to whom Levi Wright had caused tremendous pain, and Smith could feel something building up inside him.

PC Jim Black's cheerful face was all he could see now. He held onto it for as long as he could because he knew he would never see it again. Jim's wife would never see it, nor would his two children.

Smith felt his body tense up and his fists clenched without him realising it. Levi Wright was still staring, unblinking. His fierce blue eyes were at odds with the smile that had formed on his lips.

"I'm truly alone now. But God will pave the way for me."

The fury inside Smith was reaching boiling point. He took a step towards the nearly naked man in front of him. Levi's eyes never left his, and that's why he didn't see what was about to happen next. Smith let loose a punch with every ounce of rage he had inside him behind it. His fist connected with Levi's face – there was a loud crack as the bones in his nose were shattered, and he flew backwards into a metal filing cabinet. He hit his head hard and collapsed to the floor.

Then all hell broke loose. Officers in uniform swarmed into the room. The troops had arrived. DI Smyth came in behind them and stopped dead when he spotted Levi Wright's lifeless body.

"What happened?" he asked Smith.

"He banged his head," Chalmers got in first. "While he was resisting arrest."

DI Smyth walked over to get a closer look. Levi Wright was out cold. Blood was gushing from his nose.

DI Smyth looked at Smith. "Banged his head?"

"It's just like the boss said," Smith said. "I'm going outside for a smoke. I don't think I'm needed in here anymore."

"I'll come with you," Chalmers said. "Someone else can clean up that mess."

Smith took out his cigarettes and lit one. Chalmers followed suit.

Smith rubbed the knuckles on his hand. They were throbbing in time with his heartbeat.

Chalmers took a long drag of his cigarette. "Not bad. You've got a long way to go before you can match the famous Chalmers' right hook, but that wasn't bad at all. I didn't know you had it in you."
"Neither did I," Smith said. "Neither did I."

CHAPTER SIXTY TWO

Four months later

Smith had never seen Darren Lewis look as exhausted as he looked now. Lucy's waters had broken sixteen hours ago, and they'd rushed her to hospital. The events of *The Loner* investigation were still fresh in Smith's head, but he tried not to dwell on them too much. It had been the most mentally exhausting case of his career and it had taken its toll on him for a while.

Following the live interview with Levi Wright Smith's life had changed dramatically. People recognised him on the street, and some of them had even asked for his autograph. He was invited to partake in interviews on television by numerous broadcasting companies and he'd declined every offer.

Levi Wright had been evaluated and sent to a secure psychiatric facility. Smith had predicted as much. It was highly likely he would never get out. He hadn't spoken a single word since he was captured.

The lockdown had kept crime to a minimum and life at work had been extremely quiet. Smith sometimes felt like he was in some kind of limbo, and he secretly wished for another juicy case to get his teeth into. He didn't relay this wish to anybody else. The restrictions were going to be eased soon, so perhaps Smith would get what he wanted sooner than he thought.

Life in the Smith household had been filled with tension at times. Two teenagers and a seven-year-old, cooped up twenty-four-seven was a recipe for disaster and Lucy, Darren and Laura had clashed heads many times. Theakston and Fred had loved every minute of it. The chubby Bull Terrier and the hideous Pug had had the company of humans all day and night.

PC Black's funeral had been a sombre affair. The memorial for *The Loner's* final victim was one Smith would never forget. He still blamed himself for PC Black's death and he reckoned he always would. PC Griffin had been reinstated after a full investigation by the IOPC. The board of conduct had ruled that he'd made a rookie error, but he'd pleaded inexperience and they'd given him the benefit of the doubt when he promised he wouldn't make a similar blunder again. Darren Lewis received a half-hearted apology, and the matter was dropped. Smith knew instinctively that he needed to keep a close eye on the piggy-eyed newbie. PC Griffin wasn't likely to forgive and forget easily.

Darren looked at Smith and then he looked at Whitton. They were sitting in the corridor outside the room Lucy had been taken to in the early hours of the morning. Laura was sitting next to them.

"Well?" Whitton said.

Darren adjusted the face mask he was wearing. "It's a boy."

The smile on his face was something Smith would never forget. His mouth was covered but the smile was all in his eyes. Darren Lewis was the happiest boy on the planet right now.

Laura was the first to talk. "I want to meet him."

"You will, sweetheart," Whitton said.

"I want to meet him now."

"How's Lucy?" Smith asked.

"She's fine," Darren said. "She's knackered but she's OK."

"What about the baby?" Whitton said.

"He's doing fine. The doctor said he's perfectly healthy."

"Can we go in and see them?" Smith said.

"I want to see the baby," Laura said.

"I'll go and find out," Darren said.

A smile had formed on Smith's face too. It wouldn't budge.

"Well, Granny," he said to Whitton. "How does it feel?"

"I don't know," she said. "I really don't know. How do you feel, Granddad?"

"It feels great to have another bloke in the family. I don't feel so outnumbered now."

"I'm going to help look after him," Laura said. "Can I help look after him?"

"I'm sure Lucy and Darren would like that," Whitton told her.

The doctor told them they could have five minutes with Lucy. She'd gone through quite an ordeal, and she needed to rest. She was sitting up on the bed with the minute's-old new addition to the Smith clan in her arms when they went in. Smith took a look at the bundle she was holding, and goosebumps started to crawl up his arms. His top lip started to quiver, and he couldn't stop it.

He pulled up a couple of chairs and he and Whitton sat next to the bed. Laura was standing next to them, staring at the baby. For once she was lost for words.

"How are you feeling?" Whitton asked Lucy.

"I'm definitely not doing that again," she said.

Smith laughed even though he could feel a tear forming in the corner of his eye.

"Do you want to hold him?" Lucy asked him.

"I wouldn't want to break him," Smith said.

"Don't be silly. He's strong. He weighs nine pounds."

"God," Whitton said. "Laura was only seven and it felt like I'd popped out a bowling ball."

Lucy held the baby closer so they could get a better look at him. His eyes were closed, and his scalp was covered in fine black hair.

"You can hold him, Dad," she said to Smith.

He took the baby from her and held him close to his chest. He was heavier than he expected him to be.

"I wanted to name him after my dad," Lucy said. "But I thought it would be cruel to call him Nigel so we're going to call him Andrew. It was my dad's middle name."

"Dr Brown would have liked that," Whitton said.

"Andy Smith," Darren said. "If that doesn't sound like the name of a footy player I don't know what does."

"Dad," Lucy said. "Meet Andrew Jason Smith."

The goosebumps spread quickly and now both lips were trembling. Smith quickly handed the baby back to his mother.

"What's wrong?" Lucy asked.

Smith looked at her. The tears were flowing freely now, but he was still smiling.

"What's wrong, Dad?"

"Nothing," Smith sobbed. "Absolutely nothing."

"Why are you crying?"

"Andrew's granddad is crying because right now he's the happiest man in the world," Whitton explained.

Tears were forming in her eyes too now.

Lucy kissed the baby on the top of the head.

"Your *cool Dad* status is going to take a bit of a knock once this gets out," she said to Smith.

"I don't care," he said. "Everything I care about is right here in this room, and I couldn't give a fuck about anything else."

THE END

Printed in Great Britain
by Amazon